Books by Tom Hoffman

The Eleventh Ring

The Thirteenth Monk

The Seventh Medallion

Orville Mouse and the Puzzle of the Clockwork Glowbirds

Orville Mouse and the Puzzle of the Shattered Abacus

The Eleventh Ring

by Tom Hoffman

Copyright © 2015 by Tom Hoffman

All rights reserved.

Cover design by Tom Hoffman Graphic Design
Anchorage, Alaska

No part of this book may be reproduced in any form or by any electronic or mechanical means including information storage and retrieval systems, without permission in writing from the author. The only exception is by a reviewer, who may quote short excerpts in a review.

This book is a work of fiction. Names, characters, places, and incidents either are products of the author's imagination or are used fictitiously. Any resemblance to actual persons, living or dead, events, or locales is entirely coincidental.

Tom Hoffman
Visit my website at thoffmanak.wordpress.com
Printed in the United States of America

First Printing: January 2016

ISBN-13: 978-0-9971952-0-0

With lots of love
for Molly, Alex, Sophie, and Oliver

A very special thanks to my wonderful editors
Debbie, Alex, Beth, and Karen
for their invaluable assistance
and excellent advice.

Table of Contents

PART ONE

PART TWO

"Bartholomew, the universe is old beyond our comprehension. Many civilizations and species have come and gone before us. We are not the first to be here, and others will follow us long after we are gone."

– Bruno Rabbit

"All chaos is order misunderstood."

–Alexander Pope

Bartholomew the Adventurer
Trilogy • Book One

The Eleventh Ring

PART ONE

Chapter 1

The Visitor

Bartholomew Rabbit was lost in the world of dreams. His room was all shadows, save for the light of a clouded moon filtering in through the faded curtains.

There was a blink of light at the foot of his bed, then rippling air, then a figure wearing a dark green cloak, a flowing hood concealing its features. The figure held motionless, staring silently at the slumbering rabbit.

A pale blue beam of light shot out from its paw, creating a soft glow around Bartholomew's head.

"He speaks with her in his dreams but forgets their words."

The visitor's gaze moved about the room.

"There are no photographs of her to be seen."

The cloaked figure stood for long moments in the echoing stillness of the room. A pink cloud emerged from beneath its hood and drifted across the bed. It gently enveloped Bartholomew and was drawn into him.

Bartholomew turned restlessly in his sleep, a frown appearing on his face.

"You must find it. It is yours and you must find it."
A blink of light and the visitor was gone.

Chapter 2

The Cavern of Silence

Bartholomew Rabbit absently stroked his soft furry chin. “Perhaps it rolled under the sofa. I could have been laying there reading a book and unwittingly knocked it to the floor, where it bounced off the table leg and rolled straight under the sofa.”

“Sir, you’ve searched there three times already, and found nothing. Why don’t you describe the missing object to me, and I will help you look for it?”

“Hmm, well, let’s see, it’s extremely valuable of course, and small enough to roll under a piece of furniture. Since it can roll, its shape is obviously more spherical than boxy in nature, and it’s probably a darker color, one that blends in well with other dark colors. No need to fret, Parfello. With both of us looking now, I’m certain it will turn up shortly.”

For six days Bartholomew had been endlessly scouring the house for a missing object. He couldn’t name it or even clearly describe it, and yet during his searches he often seemed on the verge of hysteria. This was not like him, and his servant Parfello had been doggedly trying to determine the cause of this very concerning behavior.

Parfello closed his eyes and stood motionless. To all the world it looked as though he had fallen asleep, but the truth would prove to be far more interesting than that. When he opened his eyes again he saw Bartholomew lying on the floor, his head buried beneath the couch.

"Parfello, would you please open the curtains? It's quite dark under here, and this dust is dreadful. You might want to consider cleaning under the furniture on a daily basis. You do realize how important it is that I find it, don't you? It belongs to me. I've had it for ages, and I don't believe I can go on without it. I do wish I could remember who gave it to me."

"I am well aware how important it is, sir. You have mentioned that several times today. And yesterday also, if I am not mistaken. I will schedule a thorough daily cleaning under all the furniture, starting tomorrow morning."

"And don't forget to wax."

"Very good, sir."

This brief conversation had confirmed to Parfello the course of action he must take. He waited until after dinner when Bartholomew was finishing a large glass of white wine.

"Sir, I completely understand your deep concern over this missing item. I would be equally vexed if I had such a valuable item disappear, especially one so dear to me. I have given it much thought, and may have a solution. There is a rather extraordinary place I know called the Cavern of Silence. It is said that any question you ask there will be answered if you wait patiently for the reply. It occurred to me you could travel to this mystical site and ask the cavern to describe your lost treasure."

Bartholomew looked doubtfully at Parfello.

"Not to be rude, but that sounds a little silly. A mystical cavern that answers questions?" He swirled his wine. "On the other paw, I simply must find it before..." Bartholomew frowned, leaving his sentence unfinished. He waggled his head, then nodded. "Pack my bags, Parfello. I will visit your magical cavern. It would seem I have no other options open to me."

"Very good, sir."

When Bartholomew rose the next morning he found Parfello had packed two handsome leather satchels for his trip. He eyed the pair of gleaming handcrafted bags.

"Parfello, I'm sorry to say this will not do. I need a pack containing only the essentials. Something an adventurer would carry with him."

"An adventurer, sir?"

"Indeed. As I lay in bed last night I realized I have always liked the idea of becoming an adventurer. I believe such a life would suit me well. So, I have decided to treat this outing to your Cavern of Silence as my first adventure, and consequently will need an adventurer's pack. Perhaps a canvas sack with a heavy strap on it, but something with some age to it. A perfectly crisp new bag would give it away that this was my first adventure. That would not do."

"Indeed not, sir. Perhaps the gardener might have such a pack in the tool shed. I will search for an old canvas pack with a heavy strap on it which resembles something an experienced adventurer might carry with him on one of his exploits."

A short while later Parfello returned with an old wrinkled canvas sack covered with dirt, stains, dried leaves and cobwebs. He held it gingerly with one paw.

"Will this be adequate, sir?"

Bartholomew studiously eyed the bag.

"Perfect. You have hit the bull's eye. Put all my gear into the pack and I shall be ready to depart on my first adventure."

"Your gear, sir?"

"Do you know nothing about adventuring? The sum of everything in my pack is called my gear. Simply take everything out of the two valises and put it in the pack. Voila, it has become my gear."

"Very good, sir. I shall prepare your adventuring gear."

"Excellent. Just having this pack is making me feel quite adventurous."

An hour later Bartholomew closed the front door behind him and was on his way. He carefully studied the map Parfello had given him, heading north towards the Cavern of Silence. Along the way he ran into any number of rabbits out for a stroll, and occasionally they would strike up a conversation with him.

"Good day to you, sir."

"And to you, my friend."

"A lovely day for a stroll, is it not?"

"Ah, a stroll. If only life were that simple. I am on an adventure, not just ambling about for a breath of fresh air."

"An adventure? That sounds quite lovely."

"I would hardly use the word lovely to describe adventuring. Adventures can be quite perilous you know, especially when one is searching for a priceless lost object and lives may very well be at stake. Who knows what dastardly forces may try to thwart my every effort."

"Oh my, do be careful sir."

"Thank you, I fully intend to. That is part and parcel of being an adventurer. I am quite familiar with all manner of dangers."

In the evenings Bartholomew would set up his small camp and cook dinner over a fire. It was not something he was accustomed to, but he quite enjoyed the novelty of it and after several nights became rather skilled at it.

It was on the fourth day that he came face to face with the rabid wolf. He was walking through a dark forest, absently listening to the soft crunchy noises the pine cones made under his feet, when his ears perked up at the sound of a low growl.

"Good heavens, I believe my stomach is telling me it's time for lunch."

As he looked around for a place to prepare his meal he spotted the wolf. It stood about thirty feet behind him and was both enormous and terrifying. Its teeth were bared and covered with white foam, its red eyes narrow and threatening. With a low growl it crept towards Bartholomew.

Bartholomew responded in the manner of a true intrepid adventurer. He gave a loud yelp, dropped his pack, and scampered up the nearest tree. Soon he was high above the wolf. It wasn't until several hours later that he was able to descend from his lofty perch. He gathered up his pack and was on his way again. As he strolled along, he pondered his reaction to the wolf.

"I did successfully avoid being eaten by the beast, but the manner in which I avoided him was quite unsuitable for a rugged adventurer. I believe I shall begin carrying a stout walking stick to use as a weapon of defense in case the need arises again."

Farther along the forest path he found a long, heavy stick.

"Ah, this will do quite nicely. No more scurrying up trees for me."

Bartholomew reached the entrance to the Cavern of Silence late the next afternoon. After he had set up camp, he opened his adventuring pack and removed a long climbing rope Parfello had thoughtfully provided. He lashed one end of the rope to a nearby tree and tossed the other end down into the dark cavern. He peered into the abyss below.

"This looks rather perilous indeed, but it is something which must be done." Saying those words made Bartholomew feel quite like a brave adventurer.

Gripping the rope firmly, he lowered himself into the Cavern of Silence. His eyes soon became accustomed to the darkness and he could see a rocky ledge jutting out directly below him. When his feet touched the ground he released his grip on the rope. His eyes swept the cavern, but he saw nothing out of the ordinary. A few narrow beams of light shone down from the opening above, illuminating a jagged wall on the far side of the cavern. He wasn't sure what he had expected from a mystical cavern that would reveal the answers to all questions, but this was not it. This was far worse than he had imagined. It was darker, damper and more foreboding. Could this dismal place truly answer his question?

Sitting on the ledge, he took a deep breath and began to speak.

"I am missing something, but have no idea what it is. To be quite truthful, the loss of this item is causing a severe ache inside me. For the life of me, I cannot think what this phantom item might be, but I know it holds great importance for me. I can't even say for certain that an actual item is missing. It's all quite confusing and at times I feel as if I shall go mad if I don't find it. As though my own life may be at stake." It was somewhat awkward baring his soul to a cavern, but he pressed on.

"Cavern of Silence, please describe to me this missing object."

He waited. He listened. There was no answer. He asked again. And again.

Hours passed. Day turned to night. Night turned to day. Supplies were running low, and he knew he could not spend much more time in the cavern.

"Cavern, I don't know if I am a fool on a fool's errand, but if you are truly there, please describe to me the missing object. I am asking for nothing other than this."

A bumblebee flew by. A leaf fluttered down from far above.

His eyes drooped. His head nodded, his long ears falling limply across his face. He was drifting between asleep and awake when the Cavern of Silence finally answered.

"You must find your Great Gem."

Bartholomew's eyes popped open. He sat up straight, listening intently for the voice. He was alone in a black void of silence. There was only the voice of the Cavern.

"Who said that!? Great Gem? What is the Great Gem?"

"It is what you are missing and what you must find.

Go now and seek guidance from the Tree of Eyes."

"Wait! You must tell me more about this Great Gem and where to find the Tree of Eyes."

The Cavern of Silence did not speak again. Its answers had only led to more questions.

Bartholomew's journey home was quite uneventful. When he arrived he described his trip in great detail to Parfello, although in that version he had soundly defeated the rabid wolf with his heavy walking stick. Their conversation continued long into the evening.

"Parfello, the Cavern of Silence told me to seek guidance from something called the Tree of Eyes. Have you ever heard of such a creature? Do you know where I can find it?"

"This is beyond anything I am familiar with. All I know is words spoken by the Cavern of Silence are to be considered absolute truth. You must do as it says and find the Tree of Eyes."

The search for the elusive tree began in Bartholomew's library. He spent countless hours reading scores of volumes, including *The Ancient Book of Maps and The Book of Mysterious and Forgotten Places.* He even attempted to read a dusty old Latin tome about the nature of trees which was so bewildering it brought on an excruciating headache.

Twice a week he accompanied Parfello on shopping trips into Lepus Hollow, and while he was there Bartholomew made it a point to question any visiting merchants and travelers he happened to see. He heard any number of strange and marvelous tales, but none concerning the Tree of Eyes. The hunt for this enigmatic tree continued, day after day, week after week.

It was a curious intervention of fate which brought an end to his search. Bartholomew was attempting to decipher some ancient hieroglyphs when he was struck by another splitting headache. Blindly reaching out for his bottle of *Madame Beffy's Headache Tonic*, he knocked over a vase filled with glass marbles. They fell to the floor with a great clatter. As he watched them bouncing and skittering across the stone tiles, he had an unexpected thought. The wild, chaotic path of the marbles was not really chaotic at all. Each marble was precisely following the known laws of physical motion. He was not witnessing chaos, but order and perfection. Each marble was exactly where it should be at every moment in time.

He was surprised by this thought. It was completely unlike him to think of such things, but he was not displeased. In fact, he felt rather proud of this grand idea.

Despite his headache, he got down on his knees to gather up the marbles. Reaching under the sofa he pulled out five marbles, a mummified carrot, and a tattered old book titled *Dr. Mazlow's Guide to Unusual Trees*. Bartholomew had never seen the book before.

The marbles forgotten, he returned to his chair and began to read. It was a personal journal written by the naturalist Dr. Mazlow, recounting one of his expeditions and the wide variety of unique trees he had discovered.

Halfway through the book Bartholomew silently mouthed the word 'eureka'. He had found his answer on page thirty-three in the carefully drawn sketch of a tree covered with eyes. The caption below the drawing read, 'The Tree of Eyes is universally disliked by the few rabbits who have met it'. There was also a map detailing the tree's location. Bartholomew studied the peculiar drawing with growing trepidation. "What am I getting into? A tree covered with eyes? When I think about it, this is quite a disturbing creature." He put the book down and leaned back in his chair.

"The mystical Cavern of Silence told me to seek guidance from the Tree of Eyes, and after no small effort I have found it. Why then do I hesitate? This is exactly the marvelous adventure I have been looking for. I could sit safely in this chair forever, but where would that get me? I have chosen to become an adventurer, and what is it that adventurers do? They chase after disturbing creatures like the Tree of Eyes."

It took Bartholomew several days to ready everything he would need for his journey to the Tree of Eyes. This would be a far lengthier adventure than his short trip to the Cavern of Silence, and demanded a great deal more preparation. He filled his pack with all the necessities; stout walking boots, a sturdy coat to ward off the cold, extra clothes, dried food, matches, a saw, a sleeping bag, rope, and most importantly, *Dr. Mazlow's Guide to Unusual Trees.*

Parfello stood by the doorway the next morning. "Please be careful and have a safe trip, sir. I am certain you will find what you are looking for."

"Thank you, Parfello. I would not be setting out on this adventure without your advice regarding the Cavern of Silence. You have started a chain of events which I feel will have a very happy ending. I have no idea how I know this, but I believe it to be true."

Stepping out the front door, Bartholomew was filled with a great exhilaration. He was beginning his first true adventure.

The journey was long and arduous, the worst leg of it being an unexpected frigid mountain pass absent from Dr. Mazlow's map. Even with all his gear, Bartholomew nearly froze to death traversing the jagged, icy trail. It was a dreadful experience, and he would avoid the pass in all future travels. The one positive outcome was he now had a thrilling adventure story to tell at dinner parties. It had also given him a deep sense of his own mortality.

Safely on the other side of the mountain range, Bartholomew surveyed the broad green valley below. The Tree of Eyes was down there somewhere. He opened Dr. Mazlow's journal and studied the drawing of the Tree of Eyes. Probably no more than a dozen rabbits had ever heard of this tree, and fewer had seen it. He wondered what Dr. Mazlow meant by 'universally disliked'. He hadn't used words like 'despised', 'deadly', 'poisonous', 'ferocious', 'bloodthirsty', or 'evil', but simply 'disliked'. It was a curious choice of words to use in describing a tree. Returning the tattered journal to his pack, he set out for the valley below.

He stopped twice to make camp, something he quite enjoyed now. He slept soundly, the chirping birds lulling him to sleep at night, and the warm sun waking him at dawn. He was beginning to feel like a real adventurer.

Chapter 3

The Tree of Eyes

The afternoon of his third day in the valley found Bartholomew swatting at clouds of annoying insects as he pushed through the dense foliage, eventually emerging into a broad clearing. In the center of the clearing lay a small lake, and standing on the edge of the lake was a single tree. It was not exceptionally large, but it was covered with eyes.

Bartholomew froze as if he'd discovered a poisonous viper under his pillow. He was also strangely mesmerized, unable to remove his gaze from the tree. A thousand eyes blinked, moving about in all directions. Bartholomew's legs were trembling.

After several minutes his anxiety began to subside. The Tree of Eyes had taken no notice of him. He remembered Dr. Mazlow's description – the Tree of Eyes was simply 'universally disliked'. That didn't sound especially threatening – not like a deadly venomous spider or a ferocious rabid wolf. He cautiously stepped several feet closer to the tree. Could it talk? Was that even possible? How could a tree guide him to a missing Great Gem that he had never owned? He laughed nervously to himself. "Few rabbits have seen what I am seeing at this moment. We shall find out shortly who is the more fortunate."

He studied the tree carefully and decided to treat it as he would a stranger on the street. He would be cordial, polite, and sincere. He would be more than respectful, full of kindness and concern. He walked towards the Tree of Eyes, keeping his motions smooth and steady, his manner exuding the utmost confidence. Some of the eyes turned their gaze toward him. His mouth became strangely dry.

"A very good day to you, Most Wondrous Tree of Eyes," he said, "I am searching for The Great Gem and I seek your profound guidance in this crucial matter. Your services have come highly recommended to me by way of the Cavern of Silence, a very old and dear friend of mine." Maybe that had been too much, especially the part about the Cavern of Silence being an old and dear friend. He watched closely as all the eyes turned in his direction.

He heard a delicate and whispery voice. "I am sorry, my child, I am old and frail, and could not hear your words. It pains me to say there are times when I cannot hear even the sound of my own leaves rustling in the gentle spring breeze."

"Good Lord," thought Bartholomew, "it talks!"

He repeated the question in a loud and clear voice. "I am searching for The Great Gem and I seek your profound guidance in this crucial matter."

"Ahh. All is clear now, where once all was clouded. Great Jam. You are searching for Great Jam. You must gather some of the local raspberries and make your own Great Jam, my child. They are succulent and delicious, especially those which grow by the lake."

"GREAT GEM, I AM SEARCHING FOR THE GREAT GEM. I AM NOT SEARCHING FOR GREAT JAM."

There was a snickering noise and some of the eyes began to quiver.

"DID YOU WANT SOME GREAT TOAST TO GO ALONG WITH THAT GREAT JAM?"

The eyes began shaking violently with horrendously loud shrieking laughter. The branches lashed about wildly, tears flowing freely from the eyes. After several minutes the laughter died down, ending with a few small snickers and some annoying giggles.

"Whew, that was a good one. Great Jam." Some of the eyes began laughing again.

Bartholomew stood speechless in front of the tree. He now clearly understood Dr. Mazlow's choice of the words 'universally disliked'. This would require a little more thought than he had anticipated. The eyes were no longer looking at him. They moved about in a random fashion, focusing on nothing and on everything.

With his new understanding of the Tree of Eyes, Bartholomew decided to take a different tack altogether. He would disarm the tree with humor, something it obviously enjoyed. He shuddered involuntarily at the thought of hearing its maniacal shrieking laughter again. He took a deep breath. "I am in control here, not this ridiculous tree. I will simply imagine I am walking into a pub and have spotted an old friend. An old friend who happens to be covered with leaves and has a thousand eyes. He shuddered again. "I can do it, I am an adventurer, and I completely understand my opponent." He chuckled to himself, "This will be as easy as eating a slice of Great Toast covered with Great Jam."

He approached casually this time, with a pleasant, carefree attitude. "Ahh, lovely day, isn't it? Ha, that reminds me of a rather amusing story I heard the other day. It seems two oak trees walked into a pub, one of them with a monkey sitting on–"

"LEAVE NOW OR BE DESTROYED IN A HORRIFIC FLAMING INFERNO OF ETERNAL DOOM!!"

The very ground Bartholomew stood on shook violently from the sheer volume of the monumentally loud blinding explosion of sound. He could hear nothing except a dreadful hollow ringing in his ears. He felt nauseous, terrified, and not sure he could remain standing much longer. He sank to his knees, crawling away from the Tree. Once he was a safe distance away, he collapsed and closed his eyes. He did not move until the ringing had stopped.

Finally he could hear again. He lay motionless, listening to the voices from the Tree of Eyes.

"Magnificent, truly magnificent. Unprecedented in Tree of Eyes history."

"You are to be congratulated on that astonishing display. You have a rare gift indeed."

"Do you really think so? It was just my standard Giant Dragon voice but with far greater volume, slightly lower pitch, and a more strident tone. I admit I have been practicing, but I never thought it was anything special."

Other eyes chimed in.

"It was more than magnificent. It was powerful, thundering, and terrifying!"

"I think it scared me more than it scared that rabbit!"

There were wild bursts of raucous laughter.

"It scared me so badly I almost jumped off the tree myself!"

Loud snorting and guffawing.

"Did you see that rabbit? Good heavens, I think he may have... you know... eeew."

Shrieks of laughter followed.

Bartholomew had heard enough. He had never felt anger such as this. His eyes narrowed to two small slits. He rose up and brushed the leaves and grass off his fur. He would not be made a fool of again. This is a tree, nothing more. Well, besides all the eyes and the fact that it could talk. He stepped over to his pack, opened it and removed a large saw he used for firewood. His eyes were ice, his heart carved from solid stone. He was Bartholomew the Adventurer, and this battle of wits would end here and now. He walked slowly and deliberately towards the tree. "Oh my, I have run dreadfully low on firewood. Whatever shall I do?"

The voices from the Tree of Eyes stopped. The only sound was the crunching of dry leaves under Bartholomew's feet. "You will pay for your boorish and insolent behavior. You will tell me where to find the Great Gem or suffer the most dire of consequences." Bartholomew raised the saw so all the eyes could clearly see it.

"Is that my sweet little honey bunny? Is that my dearest little Bartholomew?"

Bartholomew stopped. His paws went limp. The saw dropped to the ground.

"Mom?"

"Oh, my Barthy Bunny, how I've missed you. Whatever are you doing in this big scary woods all alone? Don't you worry, mommy is here now to take care of you. Did you bring your warm coat and mittens?"

Bartholomew was stunned beyond reason. His mother had died years ago. His thoughts were jumbled and confused. Was this really her, somehow speaking through the Tree of Eyes? How could it know her voice? It had to be her. Didn't it?

"I... I... I'm looking for something called the Great Gem. I'm supposed to find it. The Cavern of Silence said I should."

"Oh, my sweet little bunny, mommy will help you find your shiny new Great Gem. Mommy is a grown up and she knows just what little bunnies should do. They should look in the Swamp of Lost Things. That's where all the lost things in the whole world go, and that's where you'll find your big sparkly special jewel. That old swamp is all wet and soggy though, so don't forget to pack a big pair of bouncy galoshes to keep those two little wiggly feet of yours dry."

A long branch from the Tree of Eyes reached out, gently resting on Bartholomew's shoulder, its leaves softly caressing his ears. Bartholomew was filled with a comfort and warmth he had not felt since he was a bunny. He wanted his mom to hold him. He was so tired. He wanted her to hold him in her arms and softly sing to him while he slept.

"Oh, dearest little snuggle bunny, it's not time for sleepy-land yet. We have a long way to walk tonight. The Cavern of Silence will be so happy when you find the special Great Gem that belongs only to you and nobody else. Come along, little bunny, mommy will show you the way to the Swamp of Lost Things."

Chapter 4

The Swamp of Lost Things

Bartholomew lay in the warm summer sand. He could hear the laughter of young bunnies as they frolicked about, serenaded by the low rhythmic roaring of the breaking surf. He was drifting, drifting, his paws gently massaging the warm... muck. Muck?

His eyes opened. He found himself lying in the thick, oozing mud at the edge of the foul smelling Swamp of Lost Things. He tried to remember how he had gotten there, but had only a hazy memory of walking for hours through a dark, bleak forest, his mother's voice guiding his every turn.

What sort of creature could call up the voice of his departed mother? In his heart he knew he had not been speaking with his mother, that the Tree of Eyes had been tricking him somehow. He hoped he would never set eyes on this creature again. "Eyes...ughh." He shuddered.

Opening his pack, he removed a small pencil and Dr.

Mazlow's tattered journal. He read the caption beneath the sketch again. 'The Tree of Eyes is universally disliked by the few rabbits who have met it.' In small letters he added, 'Especially Bartholomew the Adventurer'.

The putrid smells of the swamp pulled him back to the moment. He rose and stood at its edge, without the slightest idea of where he should go. After some thought, he decided he would use logic to determine his next move, something he imagined a rugged adventurer might do.

"The Cavern of Silence told me to seek guidance from the Tree of Eyes, which I did. In its own very disturbing way, the tree did give me the guidance I asked for. It said, "Little bunnies should look in the Swamp of Lost Things." Did it send me here to avoid being converted into a stack of firewood? I don't think so. It could have easily choked me into oblivion with its branches after it began using my mother's voice. It didn't hurt me, instead it filled me with a sense of comfort, warmth and safety. For better or worse, I will follow its advice and enter the Swamp of Lost Things."

Bartholomew stepped tentatively into the thick oozing muck of the swamp. He sank down to his ankle, then pulled his foot out with an unappealing *glurp* noise and took another step forward. He did it again. And again. He kept doing that for almost half a day.

Everything about the swamp was dreadful; the heat, the humidity, the putrid bubbling gas belching up from beneath the water, the buzzing insects, and the horrid slippery things that often bumped up against his legs. He really did *not* want to know what they were.

The only good thing about the swamp was the little

islands dotting the landscape. Each was a miniature oasis with room for a campfire, and flat ground where he could sleep in comfort if he covered his face to keep the mosquitos away. A few of the islands had small fruit trees which he used to supplement his food supply.

The islands were a blessing, but they didn't tell him where to go. The Tree of Eyes had said, 'Little bunnies should look in the Swamp of Lost Things'. But where exactly should little bunnies look? His only option was to move deeper into the swamp.

On the morning of the fourth day he woke and saw a narrow plume of smoke rising from a far-off island. This could be good news or bad news, depending on who or what was sitting by the fire. It was a risk, but it would help immensely if he could talk to someone who was familiar with the area. He ate his breakfast, packed his gear, and headed towards the distant island.

Several hours later he had a much clearer view of the island. It appeared to be covered with green grass, but he could now see there was no campfire. What he had taken for smoke was really steam rising up from the island's perimeter. Perhaps it was a natural hot spring? He had read about them – water was heated to great temperatures deep beneath the ground, then rose to the surface, releasing clouds of steam. The closer he got to the island the hotter the water became. Finally it was almost unbearable, and with three great leaps he landed on the island.

He had been mistaken on two counts. There was no fire and there was no green grass. The island was covered with hundreds of thousands of spherical green stones, each about the size of a small marble. He picked one up and examined it. It was quite beautiful. It was not a uniform color, but composed of many different shades of green plus some lovely blue and pink highlights. It had an oily, iridescent look to it, and as he rolled it around in his paw the colors swirled and changed their hue. He had never seen anything like it before. He picked up a dozen or so of the green stones and put them in his pack. It could be a rare gemstone, perhaps something of value. He would have them examined by an expert when he returned home. He noted in Dr. Mazlow's journal the precise location of the island, naming it *Greenstone Island.*

As he made his way deeper into the swamp, Bartholomew found his pace gradually slowing. His determination and strength were fading more rapidly than he would have expected, and he didn't know why. His food supply was running low, and slogging through the putrid quagmire was exhausting, but there was some other force at work here. He pushed on through the swamp for what seemed like an eternity. Even time seemed to be slowing down, and the days grew to be endless.

The scorching heat of the sun mercilessly beat down on him as he trudged onward. His eyes burned from the blazing sun's glare and brought on another of his ferocious pounding headaches. He could see nothing but the vile stagnant swamp in every direction. The incessant buzzing flies and mosquitos grew bolder as his strength diminished. It felt as though his very life force was being drained out of him by the swamp.

"Why did I even come here? What is the purpose of all this? Some cruel cosmic invention so the universe can witness my suffering? The Cavern of Silence, Tree of Eyes – are they even real, or are they some perverse distortion of something I once read? Am I only lying in a sick bed having a fevered hallucination?"

He gathered his strength, trying to focus his jumbled thoughts. If he turned around now he would not survive the journey back to the edge of the swamp. And if he went forward? He had no idea, no idea at all. His mind slipped. He felt hollow inside, as though his body was a brittle paper shell. There was nothing left of him. He was losing himself to the swamp. Bartholomew the Adventurer fell to his knees and began to weep. Tears rolled down his long furry nose and splashed into the dark swamp water. Deep sobs poured out of him. "I am lost forever. I am lost in the Swamp of Lost Things."

His eyes blurry with tears, he blindly stood up and tried to take a step forward. Something bit his leg. It was one of the slippery things he didn't want to know about. He yelped loudly and fell forward. As he reached out to stop the fall his arm plunged deep into the foul muck. His paw pressed against something smooth and hard. The instant Bartholomew touched it he knew it was something wonderful. He grasped it firmly, and with the strength he had left pulled it up from the unyielding goop. It was a Golden Sword in a purple velvet sheath. Bartholomew stared at it with wide eyes. There was not a speck of mud or a single drop of water on it. It shone brilliantly in the setting sun.

"What manner of object is this? It is surely no accident that in my darkest moment I would find such a treasure as this. This sword appeared as if by magic and has filled me with a strength and hope previously unknown to me."

He rose up, the sword in one paw. He was himself again. He was Bartholomew the Adventurer, and nothing would stop him from finding his Great Gem.

Searching out a nearby island, he settled in for the night. A large fruit tree provided his dinner. He scrutinized the Golden Sword for any clues to its origin. It was beautifully crafted with curious characters deeply engraved into the blade. They were vaguely similar to the ancient Lapinoric hieroglyphs, but he could make no sense of them. A large blue gemstone, possibly a sapphire, was mounted on the hilt. It was exquisite and obviously had great value. Where had the sword come from? What was its purpose? He knew nothing about swords or fighting. He was an adventurer, not a warrior. He looked closely at the large blue gemstone. Could this be the Great Gem? His hope surged until he heard the Cavern of Silence speak.

"No, Bartholomew, it is not the Great Gem, but you are getting closer. There are many forces at work here. Above all else, do not lose hope again."

Bartholomew froze. How could he hear the Cavern of Silence deep in the swamp? Had some creature followed him from the cavern? He looked around, his eyes scanning the small island. There was nothing. He was alone.

Bartholomew put the sword down, trying to calm himself. As the evening sun sank below the horizon, he curled up under the fruit tree and closed his eyes. He woke up during the night to a brilliant moon shining down from a starry sky. The moon's reflection off the surface of the swamp was unexpectedly beautiful. His gaze traveled across the glimmering water and he noticed a small flickering light in the distance. There was no doubt it was either a campfire or a lantern. With his paw he drew an arrow in the sand pointing towards the light.

In the morning Bartholomew awoke, quickly remembering the light he had seen the night before. He found the arrow in the sand and looked out across the swamp. In perfect alignment with the shaft of the arrow was a distant island, larger than any of the islands he had seen so far. He stared at it pensively. He was not one to get feelings about things, but he was having a very bad feeling about this island. He didn't want to go there, but felt there was a reason why he had to go. These new feelings he was getting were confusing.

He ate breakfast and packed his gear. He picked up the Golden Sword, holding it in one paw. Whenever he held the sword his fear diminished.

"The Cavern of Silence told me I am nearer to finding the Great Gem, and I have a strong feeling going to this dreadful island will bring me closer to it still. But the question remains, what is the Great Gem and why must I find it?"

He stepped into the swamp and headed towards the island where he had seen the flickering light. It took him most of the day to reach it. What he had thought from a distance to be a steep hill turned out to be an oddly shaped wooden house. It stood two stories tall and was cobbled together with many different sizes and shapes of boards. Some of the boards were painted and some were not. On the roof was a wooden platform with a sailing ship's telescope mounted on one of the railing posts. A rickety catwalk crossed over to the roof of a second building about twenty feet away. At the end of the catwalk a brass bell hung from a rusty iron stand. He wondered what they used the telescope for. Who were they watching? What was the purpose of the bell?

The whole structure looked as if it would fall over if he gave it one solid kick. The yard was covered with refuse; bottles, tin cans, papers, old clothes, and scraps of wood and metal. There was a crudely painted red sign with white lettering above the front door. It read:

THE SKEEZLE BROTHERS

Lost Treasures

Inquire Within

Bartholomew gripped the Golden Sword tightly and knocked on the door.

"Enter!"

He opened the door and peered in. The inside resembled the outside. It was built from a mishmash of old boards and scraps of metal. There was a long wooden counter on one side of the room and dozens of shelves and cabinets on the opposite side. The shelves were filled with a huge assortment of seemingly random objects. At the far end of the room was a wide green metal door. There was a heavy wooden beam across the door, with each end resting in a sturdy metal bracket. Whatever was behind the door would not be able to get out. The sight of this barred door did nothing to diminish Bartholomew's bad feeling about the island.

Behind the counter were two very peculiar looking creatures. They looked like large wild rats dressed in brightly colored troubadour's clothing. One wore a long yellow cap with a silver crescent moon medallion dangling from the end of it. The other creature was clothed in a similar fashion, but was sporting a purple cap. Bartholomew knew instantly what they were, and could not hide the jolt of overwhelming fear that shot through him. They were Grymmorian shadows, the source of countless terrifying nightmares when he was a bunny.

"You may rest easy, my friend. We are shadows, but there is no cause to be afraid." They looked at each other with large toothy grins. Bartholomew's paws went cold.

"I.. uh... that is to say...I'm searching for something which has become lost to me."

"Then you have come to the right place, my friend. To be quite honest, we have been expecting you. Bobo saw you only yesterday through our telescope. You were sleeping on a distant island. Most visitors to the swamp eventually find their way here, some coming in just to pass the time, and some to browse through our fine assortment of lost treasures. Some guests, however, are looking for something a little more specific." He raised one eyebrow and gave Bartholomew a knowing look.

"Who exactly are you?"

"As the sign clearly says, we are the Skeezle Brothers and we deal in lost treasures. I am Ozzie and this is my brother Bobo."

"You're Grymmorian shadows?"

"That is quite true. As you can plainly see we were born shadow folk, but we arrived in the swamp when we very young and know nothing of their customs, and have none of their... unusual tendencies." They looked at each other and laughed in a strangely high pitched manner. Their laugh reminded Bartholomew of the Tree of Eyes. He did not like this place. He did not trust the

Skeezle Brothers and he wanted to leave right now.

The Cavern of Silence spoke once more. "The greatest gifts in life often come wrapped in very strange packages."

Bartholomew covered his ears with his paws. Where was that voice coming from? Why was it telling him this? He should trust the Skeezle Brothers? That underneath their clearly malevolent exterior they were good and gentle creatures? This could not be true, and yet... he had come to trust the Cavern of Silence more than he trusted his own feelings.

"So my friend, what exactly is it you have lost?" Ozzie gave Bartholomew a sickly smile which was really more of a grimace than a smile. An identical smile appeared on Bobo's face. Bobo kept glancing down at the Golden Sword. Bartholomew's legs were feeling shaky.

"I am looking for my Great Gem. The Cavern of Silence and the Tree of Eyes sent me here."

"Ahh, yes, the Cavern of Silence and the Tree of Eyes." Ozzie tried to sound as if he were quite familiar with those names, but his nervous darting eyes said otherwise. "Well, if THEY sent you here, then this is where you should be. Since you have lost a Great Gem, what better place to look than in our safe and secure Gem Room behind the green door. We have dozens and dozens of stunningly beautiful lost gems back there. I'm sure you will find yours in no time at all." The grimace smile appeared again.

"Feel free to browse through our gems at your leisure. I do have one small request, however. Because of the large number of priceless gems, no weapons are allowed in the Gem Room. You may be assured this rule applies to everyone. Once you have paid in full for your Great Gem, your sword will be promptly returned to you."

Very reluctantly Bartholomew handed the Golden Sword to Bobo.

With their gleeful grins barely disguised, Bobo and Ozzie removed the large beam from the green door and swung it open. It was dimly lit inside and Bartholomew could make out only indistinct gray shapes. Bobo pushed him forward into the room, saying, "Please take a seat and I will be in momentarily to light all the candles and unlock the gem cases."

Bartholomew walked to the center of the gloomy room. He heard the green door slam shut behind him and the sound of Ozzie and Bobo throwing the massive wooden beam back onto the heavy metal brackets.

"Did you find your Great Gem yet??" There were shrieks of laughter from outside the green door. Bartholomew began to feel queasy. He sat down on the floor, putting his head between his paws.

Chapter 5

Oliver T. Rabbit

"I assume you are here to rescue me?"

Bartholomew's head jerked around towards the voice. His eyes were now accustomed to the dim light, and he could make out the figure of a plump rabbit sitting in a chair on the far side of the room.

"Rescue you?"

"Indeed, sir. Since it is painfully obvious you don't recognize me, I shall make my own introduction. I am Oliver T. Rabbit, Certified Representative of the Excelsior Electro-Vacuumator Corporation and currently the Director of Research and Material Acquisitions. I cannot simply loll about this place with so many pressing scientific matters demanding my attention. I ask you again, sir, what is your plan? How exactly are you going to rescue me?"

He was interrupted by a rapid pounding on the green door. "What's taking so long in there? Can't decide which stunningly beautiful gem is yours?" More high pitched squeals of laughter. "We'll be leaving now and won't be back for a number of days. We have just acquired a priceless golden sword and shall be selling it at considerable profit to a wealthy gentleman who lives on the other side of the swamp. If you get hungry, perhaps you could cook up a little rabbit stew." The shrieks of laughter seemed to go on forever, but finally Bartholomew heard the front door slam shut and there was silence once again.

"The Golden Sword has served its purpose." It was the Cavern of Silence.

What was its purpose? To get him locked up in this horrid place with a pompous and overbearing rabbit? Memories from the swamp unexpectedly flooded his thoughts. Memories of the sword giving him hope and strength in the moments when he had fallen to his knees in the putrid muck. Had the Cavern of Silence sent him these memories to remind him of the sword's true purpose? When he thought about it, the sword had also gotten the Skeezle Brothers out of the house. Maybe that was its purpose. Maybe it was all three things. A new thought popped into his head.

"Oliver T. Rabbit, did you hear that voice? The one that said something about a Golden Sword serving its purpose?"

Oliver T. Rabbit looked confused. "Do you mean the Skeezle brothers? They said they were leaving to sell a golden sword. That voice?"

Oliver T. Rabbit had not heard Cavern's voice. Only Bartholomew could hear it. He couldn't decide if that was good or bad.

"I suppose it was just my imagination. I find all of this quite disconcerting. I'm afraid I'm not here to rescue you, Oliver T. Rabbit. I am a prisoner as much as you."

"Drat. That is a bit of bad luck. Well, perhaps all is not lost. Do you have anything to eat in that pack of yours?"

Bartholomew sighed. Why on earth had the Cavern of Silence put him in the same room with a rabbit like this? This was feeling less and less like a thrilling adventure.

Bartholomew shared the last of his bread and cheese with Oliver T. Rabbit. He tried as best he could to make pleasant conversation.

"What brought you to this dreadful swamp and into the clutches of the Skeezle brothers?"

Oliver T. Rabbit's response was guarded. "As I mentioned, I am the Director of Research and Material Acquisitions at the Excelsior Corporation. They sent me into the swamp to follow up on some rumors we had heard about... ah... some product related materials. You know, keep the old production lines rolling and that sort of thing. I happened upon the Skeezle's shop, just as you did. They claimed they had what I was looking for, and in my blind eagerness I fell into their trap. Do you happen to have anything else to eat? It's been three days since I've had even a bite. They gave me water, but other than that I've had nothing."

Bartholomew wasn't sure what he had left in the pack. He dumped its contents onto the table.

"Let's see.... I think have an orange here somewhere. Yes, here it–"

"What is that?? What is that right there??"

"An orange?"

"No, that!! Those green stones!"

"I found them in the swamp."

"You found them? You found them? In the swamp?

You found them in the swamp??"

"Yes, I just said that. I found them on an island in the swamp. The entire island was covered with them."

Oliver T. Rabbit began huffing and gasping for air, his paws shaking. Bartholomew was afraid he was having a heart attack.

"Are you all right? You don't look well at all."

"Yes, yes, I am quite well, thank you. More than well. You have no idea what you have found. This is what I have been looking for. Three months searching this hideous mosquito infested morass, and I find it in this dismal little shack."

"What is it? Are they valuable?"

"Indeed, sir. Their value is beyond what you can possibly imagine, but not for the reasons you are probably thinking. These are not pretty baubles to be mounted on the rings of wealthy rabbits. You have found nothing less than a gigantic vein of duplonium." He looked at Bartholomew as though he expected him to fall over in a faint.

"Duplonium?"

"Good heavens, rabbit, do you know nothing of the natural elements? Duplonium is an inconceivably rare and utterly unique element. Its value lies in the nature of its reaction with water."

"Oh, that would explain the steam. The whole island was surrounded by boiling water and steam."

"Yes, yes, of course it would be. If you put a small piece of duplonium in a beaker of water, the water will quickly boil away without diminishing the mass of the duplonium in the least. Add more water and you get more steam. You could do this for hundreds of years with the same small piece of duplonium."

"And this makes it valuable for... making coffee and tea?"

Oliver T. Rabbit looked at Bartholomew as though he had three eyes and a dancing blue lizard on his head. He began to sputter.

"It makes it valuable because of steam power, you blithering buffoon! If you put duplonium in a closed system where the steam cannot escape, you can power an electrical generator for hundreds of years! It is a source of unlimited power. Unlimited. Can you grasp that simple concept??"

Bartholomew felt as though he should be insulted by Oliver T. Rabbit's tirade, but he felt nothing of the sort. He liked Oliver T. Rabbit's zeal and enthusiasm. It was good to see someone so passionate about something. He had a very good feeling about Oliver T. Rabbit, a rather surprising outcome of their meeting.

"I have a map. I will make a copy of it for you. The duplonium is yours for the taking."

For once in his life Oliver T. Rabbit, Certified Representative of the Excelsior Electro-Vacuumator Corporation was speechless. He looked as though he was having a difficult time processing Bartholomew's words, but then reached into his pocket and pulled out a checkbook.

"Your name is Bartholomew Rabbit?"

"Yes?"

Oliver T. Rabbit scribbled out a check and placed it on the table in front of Bartholomew. "This finder's fee is courtesy of the Excelsior Electro-Vacuumator Corporation. You, my friend, are a very, very, very wealthy rabbit."

Bartholomew looked down at the check. So many

zeros. He would not have to work another day in his life.

"Good heavens. Is this real?"

"It is real and you are quite welcome, my friend. And please, from this day forth call me Oliver. I am in your debt until the end of my days. Now, let us get out of this dreadful place."

Oliver's eyes searched the piles of old parts and pieces of broken machinery scattered about the room. He began rummaging through the mounds of refuse, looking for something.

"Ah, this will do nicely." He picked up a section of narrow copper tubing about two feet long.

He sat down at the table, setting the copper pipe in front of him. "Duplonium, if you please." He held out his paw. Bartholomew handed him one of the round balls of duplonium. Oliver took out a silver pen knife and opened it, carefully cutting off a piece of duplonium the size of a robin's eye. The duplonium was not a brittle gemstone, but was more like a dense clay. He rolled the piece of duplonium around between his paws until it took on a spherical shape.

"Now good sir, if you will kindly hide behind that large crate and cover your ears, I shall unlock the green door." He gave a great laugh.

Bartholomew had no idea what Oliver was planning, but he hid behind the crate and covered his ears. Oliver joined him there with the copper tube and the tiny sphere of duplonium.

"I shall now demonstrate a rather dynamic secondary property of duplonium."

He placed the duplonium sphere inside the copper pipe and put the end of the pipe in his mouth. Resting the pipe on top of the crate left his paws free to cover his ears. His cheeks puffed out for a moment, then he blew with all his might into the tube. The duplonium shot across the room like a tiny meteor. There was a thundering explosion and the massive green door simply vanished. It had been projected forward at an inconceivable velocity. It shot through the front room of the house, blasted through the front door, and splashed into the swamp over a half mile away.

Bartholomew stared at Oliver with a completely dumbfounded expression on his face.

Oliver nodded. "Exactly as I suspected. The direction of the blast is relative to the velocity and momentum of the duplonium projectile."

"Suppose you had been wrong?"

"I am never wrong, sir. I am a man of science."

They rose up from behind the crate and walked through the massive hole where the green door had stood only moments before. Bartholomew had to admit he was glad Ozzie and Bobo hadn't been there. They were unscrupulous scalawags, but they were living creatures. All things change, and maybe one day they would change for the better. As he walked past the long wooden counter he eyed the lost treasures they had accumulated over their years of thievery, and noticed a pair of dark glasses sitting in a silver box.

"Ahh, these will do nicely to prevent those dreadful headaches brought on by the swamp's blazing sun." He laughed to Oliver, "This seems to be a fair trade – a pair of dark glasses for a colossally valuable Golden Sword." He felt for the check in his pocket. He would not miss the Golden Sword at all.

They filled their packs with food from a small

storeroom – payment due from the Skeezle brothers for holding them captive. Bartholomew squinted as they walked into the bright sunlight. As much as he disliked the swamp, it felt wonderful to be free again.

Stopping at the edge of the island, Bartholomew handed Oliver a map showing the location of the duplonium vein. They shook paws warmly. "Thank you again, Oliver, for the most generous check. A lesser rabbit would not have disclosed the true value of the duplonium. I appreciate your kindness and honesty."

"You have done me and the Excelsior Electro-Vacuumator Corporation a great service, Bartholomew. You deserve every penny of your finder's fee. And I also thank you for sharing the last of your food with me. I don't believe many other rabbits would have been as generous as you. Here is my card. You may call on me at any time. I am in your debt always. Perhaps I shall send you a few scientific texts regarding the nature of our natural elements." He laughed loudly, clapping Bartholomew on the shoulder.

Bartholomew grinned. "I would like that. I insist you come and visit whenever you get the chance."

Oliver gave a quick wave and turned east towards Greenstone Island. Bartholomew donned his new dark glasses and headed south, deeper into the Swamp of Lost Things. He was on his own again.

Chapter 6

The Most Beautiful Island

With ample food and his new awareness of the local pitfalls and perils, Bartholomew found his passage through the swamp to be far less taxing. There were times when he forgot about the swamp completely and let his thoughts wander off on their own. Often times they circled around the Great Gem, trying to gain insight into its true nature.

"It is still such a puzzle. I know it is far more than just an exquisite sparkling gemstone. The universe is guiding me towards it, and a mere bauble would not be worthy of this effort. It must be something the universe cares about, but what could interest the universe?"

At that point his thoughts usually moved on to something else, as he had no idea the answer to that question.

The scenery remained much the same as he slogged farther into the swamp. There were more islands, more muck, more buzzing insects, more noxious fumes bubbling up from beneath the water, and more slippery things swimming past him. He decided to call them Eeps, the sound he involuntarily made when one of them bumped against his leg. He had not been bitten a second time, and for that he was sincerely grateful.

Four days had passed since his escape from the Skeezles, and in those four days the universe had offered him no guidance. He was beginning to feel a vague uneasiness, but remembered what the Cavern of Silence had said. “Above all else, do not lose hope again.” He trudged on.

As darkness began to fall he found an island covered with trees and set up camp. He looked up at the brilliant stars. It was such a grand universe and he felt so very small in comparison.

He built his campfire and soon had a fine dinner cooking. When he had finished eating he cleaned up, doused the fire with water, and curled up for the night. Moments later he was asleep.

In the morning he rose and packed his gear. In the light of day he realized the island was larger than it had appeared in the dim evening light. Slinging his pack onto his shoulder, he headed through the dense foliage to the other side of the island. It didn’t take long to get there, and it didn’t take long for him to spot the rectangle.

The dark vertical rectangle stood about a quarter of a mile away. It was eight or ten feet tall, its geometric shape standing in stark comparison to the organic nature of the swamp.

The details of the object gradually revealed themselves as he moved closer. It seemed to be made of wood, and there was something shiny glinting in the sunlight near its center.

Finally he stood before it. It was a simple wooden door with a brass door knob. A simple wooden door which happened to be mysteriously floating by itself several inches above the swamp. There were no markings, no letters, and no carvings on the door itself, but in the center of the brass door knob there was a single engraved symbol.

He took off his dark glasses to get a clearer look at the door knob. The door vanished. He stared blankly at the empty space where the door had been, doubting his own senses. "Good heavens, have I gone mad? There was a door there. I saw it with my own eyes." He stepped back, unconsciously angling himself for a better view, then put on his dark glasses to reduce the glare off the surface of the water. The wooden door reappeared.

The truth had revealed itself. "Without these glasses the door is invisible." He took them off and examined the frames and lenses. There were no markings on either. They looked entirely ordinary to him, but it was only when he looked through them that he could see the door. He wondered where the Skeezles had gotten them. From some unfortunate captive? Buried in the swamp? There was simply no telling where they had come from.

He tried to piece together the chain of events which had brought these extraordinary glasses into his possession. "The Cavern of Silence told me to seek out the Tree of Eyes, which led to the headache that caused me to knock over the vase of marbles. The falling marbles led me to Dr. Mazlow's journal. The journal led me to the Tree of Eyes, and the Tree of Eyes to the

Swamp of Lost Things and the Skeezles, where I found the glasses which have allowed me to see this miraculous door. All the events in my life are tied together by invisible strings."

It was overwhelming, and a feeling inside him grew – a palpable, almost physical connection to everything, as if the entire universe was somehow inside him, or his physical body was composed of all the stars and planets and galaxies. He had never before experienced such a sensation. It was a feeling of absolute bliss. When it had passed, he thought, "Perhaps such a feeling as that is something the universe might care about."

Bartholomew turned his attention back to the mysterious door, kneeling down to examine the knob. In the center of the knob was the engraved image of a single eye, which unfortunately revealed nothing to him. He stood up, sliding his paw slowly across the rough surface of the door. If he turned the knob and opened it, what would he see? If he could enter, could he return? If he came back, would he be the same?

"You are close now." It was the voice of the Cavern of Silence.

Bartholomew twisted the knob and pulled the door open. There was no explosion of light, no choir of angels, no shrieking demons. There was only a long, empty hallway lined with doors. Bartholomew counted them. There were six doors on each side, and one door at the far end of the hallway. The side doors were dark, but the door at the end of the hall had light shining through the gap beneath it. Taking a deep breath, Bartholomew stepped up into the hallway.

He tested the knob on the first door, but it resisted any attempt to open it. The second door did the same, as did the other side doors. He walked to the door at the end of the hall. Gripping the knob, he quickly turned it, and with a soft click the door opened. Bartholomew was nearly blinded by the bright light which flooded into the hallway. It took almost a half minute for his eyes to adjust to the brilliant glare.

When they did, he saw in front of him a stunningly beautiful island surrounded by a blue-green sea which sparkled like diamonds drifting through sunlight. The motion of the waves was hypnotic, and it was several minutes before he could turn his gaze back to the island. There was a soft carpet of thick green grass covering the island, highlighted by patches of brilliantly colored flowers. Hundreds of tall graceful trees swayed gently in the warm breeze coming off the shimmering sea.

Bartholomew stepped into the cool, soothing water, the sand firm beneath his feet. The scent from the blooming flowers was delicious. He wanted to stay here forever.

He saw a single white wooden chair sitting under a magnificent old tree. What was this place? Was he dreaming? In truth, it made no difference to him whether he was or not. This place was real to him now, and that was all that mattered.

He moved through the sparkling water to the sandy shore. Stepping into the soft green grass, he made his way up the gentle slopes of the island. The island appeared circular, perhaps a mile across in any direction. Small streams of crystal clear water from an unknown source ran down to the sea, with ornately carved wooden bridges spanning their width. The flowers were indescribably beautiful – the colors seemed to glow. He sat down in the white wooden chair and breathed in the scent of the island.

A movement in the sky caught his attention. He looked up to see a profoundly beautiful creature. It was a large bird and its feathers seemed to be all colors at once. Long graceful streamers trailed behind it, the creature moving so slowly that it appeared to be floating rather than flying. As he watched the floating streamer bird, Bartholomew had the surprising realization he had no idea how long he had been watching it. He had no idea how long he had been on the island. Had he been here a day? A month? A year? He could no longer sense the passing of time. It didn't feel like an eternity, which was an infinite amount of time, but it was as if time did not exist at all. When he returned home he tried to describe the sensation to Parfello, but he simply could not.

During his stay on the island Bartholomew spoke frequently with the Cavern of Silence about anything he happened to think of. He was learning a great deal from Cavern. Bartholomew's awareness, and the questions he asked, deepened with each conversation.

Bartholomew had forgotten about the Great Gem. He slept, he woke, he ate berries and fruit from the trees, and he talked with the Cavern of Silence.

Bartholomew called his new home The Most Beautiful Island, and he gave names to all the different areas he discovered. His favorite spot he called The Garden With No End. The flowers there continuously changed their shapes and colors, endlessly shifting from one exquisite form to another. It was a living kaleidoscope, and as he watched it he was often unsure whether he was sleeping or awake. It was here in The

Garden With No End that he had his idea.

"Cavern, I've been thinking about you a lot. You are everywhere I go, but only I can hear you. You're a part of me, aren't you? A deep and hidden part of me which was always there, but a part I never listened to – a self within a self."

The moment this thought occurred to him, a glowing white gem appeared in his paw. It filled him with a warmth and a joy which was quite foreign to him. He had found his Great Gem. He knew every living creature had one, and he knew it was every creature's destiny to find it.

The Cavern of Silence answered Bartholomew's question.

"Everything you have said is true. I am a self within you, but I am not bound by time and space as you are. Your search for the Great Gem is now over. Your clear awareness of me has brought an end to that adventure, but in finding it you have opened the door to a far greater adventure. For better or worse, this is a door which cannot be closed again."

Bartholomew had no idea how long he remained on the Most Beautiful Island after he found his Great Gem. He only remembered the Cavern of Silence saying, "The island has served its purpose for now. It is time for you to return home. Parfello will be wondering what has become of you."

Bartholomew was distraught at the thought of leaving the island. "I can't go. This is my home now. It is unthinkable I should leave this paradise and return to that ghastly swamp. I would stay here forever."

"Bartholomew, this is your first visit to the island, but it will not be your last. It is time to go."

Bartholomew filled his pack with fruits and berries and strolled around the island one last time. He walked down to the shore and through the shimmering sea to the wooden door. Without looking back he opened the door and stepped through. He could smell the noxious fumes of the swamp before he was halfway to the other end of the hallway.

His journey home was relatively uneventful. He skirted around the Skeezle brothers' house, but did walk past Greenstone Island. It was covered with rabbits and massive steam powered excavating machines. Oliver's trip home must have been a safe one. He smiled, wondering what kind of reception Oliver received when he gave news of the duplonium discovery. Bartholomew felt in his pocket for the check from Oliver. It was odd, his finding the Great Gem was changing him in ways he would not have suspected. When he thought about how wealthy he was, it didn't seem to matter.

It didn't take him as long to return home as it had taken for him to reach the Most Beautiful Island. This time he knew the way and knew what areas to bypass. He avoided the frigid mountain pass which had almost cost him his life, using instead a narrow valley several miles to the west which cut through the mountain range. There were difficulties crossing one of the rivers, but it was still far safer than the pass had been.

One evening as he sat in front of a blazing campfire, he found himself recalling the events of his recent adventure. He would liked to have seen the look on the Skeezle brothers' faces when they returned and saw the damage the duplonium had caused. He laughed out loud every time he thought about it. What in the world would they think had happened?

Once he reached the far side of the valley, it was only a four day jaunt to his home. On the last day of his travels, as he swung his pack up to his shoulder, he grinned and said to no one in particular, "Perhaps you have heard of me. I am Bartholomew the Adventurer."

His reunion with Parfello was both joyous and surprising. Swinging open the gate to his old stone home, he noticed something odd. Everything looked different somehow. He couldn't quite put his paw on it, but there was something. "Cavern, it's all different. The trees, the flowers, my home... it all looks..."

"Perfect?"

"Yes, that's it exactly. It's perfect. Every part of it is perfect. How can that be? How could it have changed like that?"

"Your home has not changed, Bartholomew. It is you who has changed. Finding the Great Gem and your experiences on the Most Beautiful Island have changed the way you see the world. You are beginning to view it as it truly is, not just as you think it is. It will take time for you to become fully aware of just how profound these changes truly are."

Turning towards his house, Bartholomew saw Parfello's startled face in the window. He dashed down the path, reaching the front steps just as Parfello flung the door open.

"Master Bartholomew, you have returned! You were gone for such a long time I feared you may have been lost."

"I found my way home, old friend. It was an adventure to remember, and I shall tell you about it in great detail. But first, you must see this. I found the mysterious something I was missing. It is called the Great Gem."

Bartholomew opened his paw and showed Parfello the beautiful glowing white gem. Parfello's mouth opened wide. "Oh my, that is a most remarkable gem indeed." Then he smiled and whispered, "It looks almost like this one, doesn't it?" He opened his own paw to reveal an almost identical glowing white gem.

Bartholomew stepped back and looked at Parfello in amazement. "But... you... you knew all along what I was missing?"

"I had a feeling. I spoke to my own inner voice who confirmed my suspicions. It was only then that I told you about the Cavern of Silence. If you haven't already guessed, the cavern you visited was a very ordinary cavern. It was simply a place of silence and reverie where you could quiet the outside world and listen to your own secret voice."

"I'm still confused. I have seen your paws a thousand times but never noticed your Great Gem before. How is that possible?"

"Ah, that is one of the mysteries of the Great Gem. Until you have found your own, you can see no others. It's all rather ironic if you think about it. You went through this entire adventure to find something you could have found while sitting in your own living room."

Bartholomew smiled. "Quite true, but I think in this case my search for the Great Gem has changed me almost as much as finding it has. I have become a true adventurer, but an adventurer who is glad to be home."

Bartholomew the Adventurer
Trilogy • Book One

The Eleventh Ring

PART TWO

Chapter 1

A Voice in the Night

Bartholomew was adrift on an ocean of silence. The name leaped like a fish into the night air, hung for a moment, then plunged back into the depths. The name jolted him awake, his eyes searching the shadows of his room for any movement. Finding only stillness, he lay his head back down on the pillow. The voice he had heard was unfamiliar to him, but the name it had spoken was not. He let himself go, let himself drift back into the silence. Sleep carried him away, but not before he had murmured the name.

"Clara."

The next morning Bartholomew arrived later than usual for breakfast. Parfello greeted him as he always did.

"Good morning, Master Bartholomew, I trust you slept well?"

"Pancakes will be fine, thank you."

Parfello glanced over at Bartholomew. The last time he had seen him this distracted was in the days before his trip to the Cavern of Silence.

Bartholomew had a faraway look as he sat gazing out the kitchen window. This morning he had asked the Cavern of Silence about Clara, but there had been no reply, which was unusual. He had the singular sensation that something important was beginning, and it had started when he heard Clara's name in the night.

Parfello went to town for groceries, leaving Bartholomew alone with his thoughts. His gaze remained unbroken until a quick movement near the front fence jarred him from his reverie. He spied a shadowy figure walking towards the gate, pushing a large wooden crate on a cart in front of them.

"Blast! Another salesrabbit!"

Bartholomew dropped to the floor, silverware clattering down around him. He crawled across the kitchen towards the window. Once he was safely concealed under a table he relaxed.

"These are the most persistent salesrabbits I have ever had the pleasure of not meeting." For the last week a series of door to door peddlers had been knocking on Bartholomew's door. He wondered if his newfound wealth had anything to do with it. So far he had successfully avoided them by hiding under tables and behind couches, waiting patiently until they left. He sat quietly, listening to the approaching footsteps.

He chuckled to himself. "Victory is mine, my peddling friend."

His smile vanished when he heard the Cavern of Silence speak.

"Every atom, every molecule, and every bouncing marble is exactly where it should be at every moment in time."

Bartholomew had a sinking feeling he knew what

the Cavern of Silence was telling him.

"Are you saying the salesrabbit is where he should be and I need to answer the door?"

"I am merely reminding you that the most valuable gifts in life often arrive in strange packages. Do not reject what life puts before you."

Bartholomew crawled slowly out from under the table and stood up.

"Very well. Perhaps he is here to give me a free tin of chocolate creams."

The Cavern of Silence made no reply.

Bartholomew waited for the inevitable knock on the front door. When it came he took a deep breath and swung the door open.

"How wonderful to see you, my old friend! I have missed your company indeed."

"Great heavens! Oliver T. Rabbit, as I live and breathe. What in the world are you doing here? Whatever the reason, I am more than happy to see you. Please come in."

Oliver pushed the heavy cart through the doorway. He grabbed Bartholomew's paw and shook it until Bartholomew thought his bones would rattle.

"How is my very wealthy friend Bartholomew doing? You found what you were looking for? You made your way safely back from that dreadful swamp, I see."

"Indeed I did. You must stay and visit for at least several days. I shall tell you about the rest of my adventure and you in turn must tell me about yours."

"I would love to stay. Consider it done. But aren't you curious to know what I have in this mysterious crate?" He laughed loudly, raising one eyebrow in an overly dramatic fashion. "Have a seat my friend, and I will unveil it as only a Certified Representative of the Excelsior Electro-Vacuumator Corporation can do."

Bartholomew seated himself in a chair facing Oliver. He had a feeling he was in for quite a show. Oliver took a deep bow and began.

"Good sir, allow me to introduce the newest scientific marvel of this generation. I present to you a mechanical cleaning system based on the astonishing scientific principle of negative air pressure, powered by the fantastically rare and unthinkably energetic element known as duplonium. In combination with the modern miracle of steam power, this amazing element produces endless quantities of the very same forces found in Zeus's own lightning bolts. I am of course referring to nothing less than pure electrical energy."

He paused, winking at Bartholomew, then went on. "This, my friend, is the extraordinary, revolutionary Model Mark III Prototype Excelsior Electro-Vacuumator. You will find nothing else remotely like it in the world today."

Oliver dramatically flipped down the sides of the crate to reveal a large and complex two-wheeled mechanical contraption covered with dials, tubes, and colored levers.

"Please remain seated while I demonstrate the astonishing cleaning abilities of this fantastic machine." He placed his paw on a red lever.

With the word "prototype" echoing in his ears, Bartholomew remembered what the duplonium had done to the Skeezle's house.

"Wait!!"

Oliver did not even hesitate. He flipped the red lever.

The sound was unthinkably loud. Later, Bartholomew would describe it as the mating of a hurricane with a trumpeting bull elephant. Bartholomew again shouted at Oliver to stop, but his voice was drowned out by the earsplitting roar of the vacuumator. He leaned forward, extending his arm towards the red lever, but before he could shut off the vacuumator the room abruptly became silent. He could see clouds of dust billowing out from the vacuumator, but he could hear nothing until the Cavern of Silence spoke.

"The most valuable gifts in life often arrive in very strange packages."

He pulled his paw back and the screaming roar of the Mark III Electro-Vaccumator returned.

Bartholomew watched as Oliver dashed about the room, dragging the long hose from the vacuumator behind him. He jabbed the end of the hose here and there as dust flew about in every direction.

"Why is Cavern asking me to endure this noisy and terrifying display? Suppose the duplonium explodes?" In the end, Bartholomew's trust in the Cavern of Silence outweighed his own fears, and so he watched and waited patiently for Oliver to finish his exceedingly exuberant demonstration.

Finally it was over. Oliver reeled in the vacuumator hose, leaned over and flipped the red lever. Blissful silence filled the room.

"Oliver, that was marvelous, especially the part where the duplonium did not explode and convert my house to a pile of flaming splinters."

Oliver roared with laughter and held up his paw. "One moment, sir. The demonstration is not yet complete."

With a great flourish he unlatched a large green canister from the Vacuumator and raised it into the air.

"The proof, good sir, is in the pudding." He flipped the canister over and dumped its contents onto the floor. When the cloud of dust had settled, Bartholomew saw a great pile of dirt, crumbs, buttons, dust, threads, pebbles, scraps of newspaper, and dried carrot slices.

Oliver continued. "This, dear friends, displays the astonishing suction power of the Mark III Electro-Vacuumator and the astonishing power of duplonium, a huge vein of which was recently discovered by that legendary adventurer, Bartholomew Rabbit." He took a deep bow.

Bartholomew clapped loudly and pointed to the dusty mound on the hallway floor. "Perhaps as an encore you could–" He stopped in mid-sentence. In the middle of the pile lay a small white irregular shaped piece of cardboard.

"Great heavens, you've found the missing puzzle piece! You have found my missing puzzle piece! You have no idea how long I have been looking for that." Bartholomew reached down and picked up the small cardboard piece. He turned to Oliver and laughed, "I am indeed impressed, sir. Please deliver a Mark III Prototype Vacuumator to my home at your earliest convenience."

"Done and done, sir. Please accept this Mark III Electro-Vacuumator as a token of sincere thanks from both myself and the Excelsior Corporation. It may reassure you to know this astonishingly powerful device is powered by a single piece of duplonium no larger than a pinhead, and would destroy only half of your lovely home should it explode." He roared with laughter at his joke, then reached out and shook Bartholomew's paw. "On a personal note, good sir, I am happy I could help you complete your jigsaw puzzle. An unsolved puzzle can be very difficult to live with indeed."

Oliver's voice was jovial, but Bartholomew was inexplicably filled with a feeling of deep sadness at his last words. He felt like crying. How curious. He had learned to pay close attention to feelings which came to him from the Cavern of Silence.

Parfello entered the room and Bartholomew graciously introduced Oliver.

"It is a great pleasure to meet you, Oliver. Bartholomew has spoken of you so often I feel we are already friends. I do hope you are enjoying your visit to our lovely town of Lepus Hollow."

"You reflect my own feelings, Parfello. Bartholomew mentioned you many times during our adventures in that veritable paradise known as the Swamp of Lost Things." He laughed loudly, then continued. "It may surprise you to know I am not entirely unfamiliar with Lepus Hollow. I lived quite near here for a time when I was a bunny. I have many fond memories from those days, but also some less happier ones. But that is life, is it not? If we have more happy memories than sad ones, I believe we are doing quite well in this uncertain world of ours."

Bartholomew and Parfello nodded in agreement. Neither questioned Oliver about his less than happy memories. Their conversation turned to the wonders of the new Mark III Vaccumator and the story of Oliver's triumphant return to the Excelsior Corporation. Then they mutually agreed that Oliver should retrieve his belongings from the inn where he was staying, and take up residence in Bartholomew's home.

Chapter 2

The Mystery of the Puzzling Eye

After Oliver had left for the inn, Bartholomew took his missing puzzle piece into the drawing room. In front of him stood an ornate mahogany table surrounded by plush chairs. On the table lay a jigsaw puzzle, a lovely pastoral scene with several sheep grazing in a meadow. One of the sheep had a missing eye. Bartholomew carefully inserted the lost puzzle piece. Voila, the sheep was whole, the puzzle complete. He felt as if an enormous weight had been lifted from his shoulders. It was a blissful feeling, as though the universe was somehow pleased by this. Why would the universe care about him finishing a jigsaw puzzle? There had to be more to it. There had to be something he was missing.

Was he somehow connected to Oliver? Oliver had played an important role in helping him find his Great Gem, and Oliver's arrival had now led him to the missing puzzle piece. Was the unknown force guiding him towards something? He removed the puzzle piece, studying it intently. An eye. A single eye. Of course! He had seen the identical image on the brass door knob in the Swamp of Lost Things. What could that mean? He tried to think.

"One single eye on the door knob and again on the puzzle piece. What meaning does a single eye hold for me?" Out of nowhere, out of everywhere, a bright red image appeared in his mind. He slapped his paw to his forehead. "It's from *The Complete Adventures of Renegade Rabbit, Private Eye*!"

Bartholomew moved quickly to his library. He hadn't thought of Renegade Rabbit since his school days. As a bunny he had read all the stories at least a dozen times. Renegade Rabbit, master of observation and deduction. There was no mystery he couldn't solve. Rolling the ladder to the far end of the library, he scampered up to the top shelf, sliding his paw along the dusty books until he came to a large red volume. Pulling it out from the shelf, he examined the cover. Beneath the title was a single eye embossed in gold leaf.

"Either I'm completely mad or I'm not. Renegade Rabbit, Private Eye, I will let you decide. Let's see if you can solve Bartholomew's Mystery of the Puzzling Eye."

Bartholomew flipped the book open. A small, stiff rectangular piece of paper fluttered down to the floor below. Bartholomew backed down the ladder, his eyes never leaving the tattered yellow rectangle. He leaned down and picked it up, quickly flipping it over. The world stopped.

It was a photograph of his dearest childhood friend, Clara Rabbit.

This was not what he had been expecting. Bartholomew sank down into a reading chair, his eyes brimming with tears. He repeated Clara's name over and over, his thoughts pulling him back to the school yard where they used to play. He could see himself and Clara running toward the swings, so young, and so filled with promise. He remembered the other bunnies teasing them, saying that he and Clara would one day marry. It had embarrassed him terribly, but he had never denied it, and neither had Clara. When he returned after the summer holiday for his final year of school, he learned that Clara and her family had moved away without notice. Nobody knew where they had gone. It was a mystery not even Renegade Rabbit could solve.

He had dreams of Clara for years after that, often having long conversations with her which were lost to him the moment he woke up. He put the photo of Clara in a silver frame and placed it on the hall table near the front door. He would see her when he left the house, and again when he returned. He had never had another friend like Clara.

Chapter 3

Oliver's Revelation

Oliver returned that evening with his belongings, but excused himself, saying he was tired from the long journey. Even the offer of a glass of Orvieto Pinot Grigio would not sway his decision to retire for the night.

Hours later, Bartholomew lay in bed staring at the ceiling, unable to sleep. He was certain his new adventure had started, but he had no idea where it was taking him. He was in the midst of it now, and Clara was a part of it. It had started with Clara's name being spoken in the night, then Oliver's arrival, and the missing puzzle piece which had led to Clara's photograph. He had so many questions. Was Clara alive? Where had she been all these years?

"I have to sleep. Thinking about this will gain me nothing. All I can do is wait for events to unfold." He listened to the rhythmic ticking of the clock and was finally carried from awake to asleep, set adrift again on the ocean of silence. When he woke up, however, he was standing in the shimmering blue waters surrounding The Most Beautiful Island.

He looked around him. His sudden presence on the island was astonishing, but at the same time felt completely natural. He dipped his paw in the cool water, splashing it on his face. He smelled the air and the scent of the flowers. A floating streamer bird sailed past him. This was as real as his first visit. He remembered the words Cavern had spoken almost three months ago.

"This is your first visit, but it will not be your last."

He walked to the shoreline and climbed the grassy slopes up to the island. Nothing had changed since his first visit. The flowers and trees were still beautiful beyond description. The white wooden chair was exactly where he had left it. As he walked across the island, he recalled the Garden With No End where he had discovered his Great Gem. He walked past a stand of flowering trees and found the pathway leading to the garden. Ducking beneath a low branch, he entered the Garden With No End. Standing in front of him was Clara.

Bartholomew couldn't move, couldn't speak, could barely think. Clara was older, but it was her. He would know her anywhere, at any age. He forgot how long he had been there. They gazed at each other for... a moment? A thousand years? Bartholomew didn't know. Clara spoke only five words.

"Bartholomew, you must help me."

Clara vanished and Bartholomew was again lying in his bed.

When he spoke with Oliver the next day, Bartholomew didn't mention his nocturnal visit to the island. Oliver was a man of science, but this was beyond science. It wasn't the first time he had withheld information from Oliver. When he described his adventure in the Swamp of Lost Things, he hadn't mentioned the Hallway of Doors and was purposefully vague about the Most Beautiful Island. He said he had stumbled upon a rather lovely island and stayed there for a while. The island had given him time to relax and reflect on his life, and he had decided to let his conscience guide his decisions more. He didn't mention the Tree of Eyes or the Cavern of Silence or his conversations with them. He hoped the time would come when he would be able to broach these topics with Oliver.

After a hearty breakfast Oliver stood up and said," Now we must get to the business of teaching you and Parfello the approved operating procedures for your new Mark III Electro-Vacuumator. As you know, this is a complex and powerful mechanical device. We have joked about a duplonium explosion, but in truth, if operated incorrectly the resultant effects could be quite catastrophic." He attempted to give them both a severe look, but it was so unlike Oliver that it almost made Bartholomew laugh. He nodded, trying to adopt an equally somber expression.

"If you will both follow me to the front hallway, we shall begin. There is no need to take notes, as everything I say can be found within this operating manual which I am holding." He held up a weighty volume for them to see. Bartholomew felt as though he was back in a school science class again, a feeling he did not particularly enjoy. He pulled out a chair and resolutely sat down, doing his best to appear interested.

"Before we begin, I will humbly admit that I played

a crucial part in the design of this marvelous machine. I am accordingly quite familiar with every aspect of its function. Now, as you know, the Vacuumator is powered by duplonium. The duplonium heats water, turning it to steam, which then drives an electrical generator. This system provides the energy needed to run the device. Now, this is very important – this small blue lever which I am pointing to must first be flipped to the ON position. NEVER try to start the device with..."

Oliver droned on and on. Bartholomew's thoughts began to wander. Instead of listening to the words Oliver was saying, he began paying attention to Oliver's expressions and how he moved about, emphasizing certain words with his paws. He noticed that from time to time Oliver would glance discreetly over to the hallway table. This was curious. And then, in a single brilliant moment, Bartholomew understood everything. He knew what his great adventure would be. He saw the underlying strings connecting all the seemingly random events. He thought his heart might burst at the perfection of it all. The marbles were bouncing, and each one was exactly where it should be. He stood up and walked quickly to the hallway table. He picked up the framed photograph of Clara and held it up in front of Oliver.

"This is an old and dear childhood friend of mine. Do you recognize her?"

It was like watching a snowman melt on a warm spring day.

"She is my sister, Clara Rabbit."

"Do you know where she is?"

Oliver's eyes filled with a sadness Bartholomew had

never seen in him before. He set down the operator's manual and said, "I will tell you all I know. Please understand these are painful memories, and it is very difficult for me to speak of them."

Bartholomew slid a chair over to Oliver, who nodded his thanks and sat down.

"When I mentioned I had lived in Lepus Hollow, there was a great deal I left out. In the summer before Clara's last year of school, our parents separated. It was devastating for all of us. My sister Sophie and I were older and went with our father. Clara, being the youngest, left with our mother. I never heard from them again and neither did Sophie. My father would never speak of them, something which bothered me greatly. I know now it was as painful for him as it was for me, but his manner of expressing grief was not the same as mine. Several years ago while I was looking for some papers in his study, I came upon a letter my mother had written to him the year after they separated. She and Clara were living on a small farm. The only clue to the farm's location was some sort of tree which was covered with eyes. I searched for two years with no success. I could find no reference anywhere to a tree of this description. I can only imagine that my mother simply did not wish to be found and invented a fictitious location." He paused. "This is the unsolved puzzle I live with every day."

There was a heavy silence in the room. Bartholomew put his paw on Oliver's shoulder. "Oliver, I have seen this Tree of Eyes. I have touched it. I know where it is. We can find Clara."

The look on Oliver's face was something Bartholomew would remember the rest of his life.

Once he had gotten over the shock of this revelation, Oliver could not stop talking about Clara. "To think I may see dear Clara again! I am simply astonished that you have been to the Tree of Eyes. And that photograph of Clara, right on the table where I could see it! Great heavens, just imagine if I had not come to visit, or if I had not met you in the Swamp of Lost Things. How astonishing that those awful Skeezle brothers played a part in leading us towards Clara. It is mind-bogglingly fantastic to think about. It's all so very curious. It certainly makes one wonder about fate and divine guidance. Perhaps there were angels looking out for us." He looked slightly embarrassed, as though he expected Bartholomew to laugh.

"Or suppose I had not answered your knock on the door?" Bartholomew tried to erase the memory of himself hiding under the table laughing. "Oliver, I suspect you might be right about some sort of invisible guidance from beyond. It seems to me there are far too many coincidences for it all to be chance."

Bartholomew heard the Cavern of Silence snort. "What? Do you mean to say this is not simply a series of random events combining with your excessively vivid imagination?"

They spent the rest of the day planning their search for Clara.

"I can take the train home in the morning and inform my supervisor of these recent events. He is an old and trusted friend, and when he hears about Clara he will have no objections to my extended leave. Once gear and provisions are packed, I shall return on the next train."

Bartholomew added, "Parfello and I will draw up

maps of the fastest route to the Tree of Eyes. There are no trains, so be certain to bring stout walking shoes. It could take several weeks for us to reach the tree. After that we are on our own trying to find Clara's farm." He thought carefully about how to phrase his next words. "Oliver, the Tree of Eyes is something more than an ordinary tree. There is a chance it may be able to offer us assistance in finding Clara. It's rather complicated, but once you see the tree I think it will become much clearer to you."

Oliver gave a quizzical look but said, "Bartholomew, in this matter I shall follow your lead. Without you, I never would have had this chance to find Clara. Once again, I am in your debt."

Chapter 4

The Search Begins

Four days later Bartholomew met Oliver at the Lepus Hollow train station.

"I trust you had a comfortable trip?"

"Quite so. Not to mention a lovely glass or two of a delightful wine." He laughed, then looked slightly embarrassed. "Of course I take no stock in such things, but as I napped on the train I had quite an unusual dream. It was about Clara, and was quite startling in its clarity – as though I were standing there in front of her. I was on a simply lovely island with Clara facing me. She smiled and said, "I am counting the days until I see you." He stopped, looking for signs of mockery on Bartholomew's face. There was none, and he continued, "I wrote down what she said next for fear I would forget it." He took out a crumpled piece of paper and began to read.

"Every atom, every molecule, and every bouncing marble is exactly where it should be at every moment in time."

After Oliver had gone to bed, Bartholomew sat in

the drawing room warming his paws by the stone fireplace.

"Cavern, who set this chain of events in motion? Did it start recently or was it long ago?"

"Bartholomew, the universe is infinite in size and infinite in depth. It is made up of dreams within dreams, worlds within worlds, and selves within selves. There are more forces at work here than you can know, but that knowledge is for another day. Now it is time to begin the search for Clara. I will warn you, however, finding her will be far more difficult than you can possibly imagine, and when this grand adventure is done, you will not be the same rabbit you are now."

There was a great flurry of activity the next morning as Bartholomew and Oliver prepared for their trip. Bartholomew carried only his adventurer's pack. It had served him well and he had grown quite fond of it. Oliver, on the other paw, had far different priorities. Sitting on the street in front of Bartholomew's house was a large three-wheeled metal wagon. Its wheels were coated with a thick layer of a dark substance resembling rubber. Strapped securely in the wagon was a towering stack of crates, boxes, and oddly shaped packages. Bartholomew stared in disbelief at the immense mound of gear and supplies.

"What in the world is all this?"

"These are the necessary supplies we must bring with us on our search for Clara."

Bartholomew gave Oliver the look he would give to a bunny who was building a wooden ship to carry him to the moon. "And you have a team of twelve horses to pull this colossal wagon?"

Oliver mirrored the look he had received from

Bartholomew. "A team of twelve horses? That would be an extremely inefficient way to move a wagon such as this. Think of all the food we would have to carry just to feed the horses, not to mention the water they would need. I have something far better. Using parts from a Prototype Mark III Electro-Vacuumator, I have constructed a duplonium powered steam motor which propels the wagon at speeds of up to ten miles in a single hour. I don't imagine we shall be walking any faster than that. Really, Bartholomew, you should take more of an interest in science. Horses, indeed." Oliver laughed his great booming laugh and then grinned. "Do you like it?"

Bartholomew was clearly dubious. "How does it work?"

"Lift up the handle and try to pull it."

Bartholomew walked around to the front of the wagon and lifted the long metal handle resting on the ground. He tentatively gave the wagon a light tug. It moved forward effortlessly with a hissing noise. His eyebrows raised slightly and he tried again. This time he pulled it to an incline in the road and attempted to pull it up the hill. It moved up the slope with absolutely no effort, matching Bartholomew's pace precisely. He turned the wagon around, guiding it back to Oliver.

"I believe I have underestimated you, Oliver T. Rabbit. This is truly a miracle."

Oliver gave an exaggerated frown. "There are no miracles, only science."

Bartholomew smiled. "If you say so."

Several hours later they were on their way. Oliver pulled the duplonium powered wagon behind him while Bartholomew studied the maps, giving directions when the path ahead became uncertain. Along the way they chatted about all manner of topics. Bartholomew was learning there was a great deal more to Oliver than just his position with the Excelsior Corporation.

"Since I was a small bunny I have been enormously interested in scientific matters. It's quite fascinating to observe the world and try to understand how all the parts and pieces work together in such perfect harmony. How do birds fly? How do fish swim? It may sound rather cold, but the bodies of these creatures are nothing more than well-designed pieces of organic machinery. Nature is the greatest inventor of all, and I am simply trying to copy or modify her existing creations. Of course, much of her invention is beyond my scientific understanding, but it's still science. Did you know that with our known laws of physical motion it should be impossible for a bumblebee to fly? And yet, every day I see the little devils flying about my yard, mocking my inadequate scientific knowledge." He laughed.

They gradually fell into a routine on their journey. Each night they would set up camp, and thanks to the duplonium wagon there was a comfortable tent to sleep in and hot meals for dinner. It soon became clear that Oliver was quite adept at cooking, a fact which did not surprise Bartholomew at all. In the morning they packed all their gear back into the wagon and continued on their way.

When they reached the mountain range, Bartholomew told Oliver about the deadly frigid mountain pass and his decision to avoid it. They turned west towards the narrow valley which cut through the mountains, paralleling the pass. Bartholomew listened to the quiet hiss of the wagon as it effortlessly moved up and down the hills of this rugged terrain. He might have to revise his current definition of miracles.

As they walked through the valley, they continued their long and sometimes ardent discussions. Some were weighty and some were not. Oliver was in the middle of a long dissertation on the proper way to cook the cream filling used in éclairs when he stopped, looking off into the distance. There was a small speck in the sky flying along the mountains that lined the valley. "That can't be a bird. At this distance I wouldn't be able to spot it. It has to be something much larger. I have no idea what it could be though." They both watched curiously as it slowly circled over the lower mountain peaks, then turned towards the center of the valley, gradually veering over in their general direction. "I think it might be heading this way."

"Excellent. We shall get a much clearer view of it. I do hope I shall be able to identify it, although no specific creature springs to mind at this moment. Perhaps it's a large vulture of some kind."

Bartholomew was not quite as enthusiastic about the approaching creature. He kept his eyes focused on the beast as it moved towards them. He could make out a huge pair of wings, but their motion didn't resemble that of a normal bird. It seemed to glide for a long distance, then slowly flap its colossal wings until its speed had increased enough for it to glide again. As it approached them it gradually gained altitude until finally it was circling high overhead.

Oliver shielded his eyes from the sun with one paw as he watched the creature soaring far above them. "This is amazing – it is more than amazing, it is astonishing. I believe I know what this is, although I fear my own senses are deceiving me. I spent one summer at the Lapinoric Museum of Natural History, studying all manner of prehistoric fossils and the remnants of long forgotten ancient civilizations. What you are looking at is a living pterosaur, though far larger than any of the fossilized skeletons at the museum. It is impossible, and yet it soars in the sky above us. These creatures lived and died over two hundred and fifty million years ago." Oliver's gaze never left the pterosaur.

Without warning the creature pulled in its wings and entered a steep dive, its speed increasing dramatically. It was shooting straight down towards Bartholomew and Oliver.

Bartholomew shouted, "Get under the wagon! We have become its prey!"

Chapter 5

Prey for the Pterosaurs

"How odd, I would not have supposed that a pterosaur would–"

"Oliver, get under the wagon now!"

Oliver abruptly realized the gravity of the situation and hastily rolled beneath the wagon, joining Bartholomew. Moments later the pterosaur passed mere feet above them, traveling at an incredible velocity. They could hear the roar of the wind from its gigantic wings. It shrieked loudly and headed back up into the sky, slowly circling around as it gained altitude for another dive.

Bartholomew thought out loud. "We have no defense against a creature like this. If it stops its diving attacks and lands next to us, we are doomed. It will simply reach under the wagon with its huge claws and pluck us out, one by one. We can't possibly run away, as it clearly flies faster than we could ever travel on foot."

"That's it! You've got it, Bartholomew. We can't outrun it on foot, but we can outrun the creature with the duplonium wagon!"

"How? We have to pull the wagon behind us. We can't run faster than the pterosaur."

"Have faith in the miracles of science, my friend. There are a few small details about the wagon which I failed to mention previously."

"Small details?"

"After the pterosaur makes its next pass, jump into the back of the wagon and strap yourself in as tightly as possible. This is going to be a rough ride, and I hope it's not our last. I so dearly want to see Clara once more before I leave this world."

"Don't talk like that. We'll find her. What happens after I'm strapped in?"

"You will know soon enough, my good friend!"

The pterosaur shrieked and roared past a second time, its claws scraping wildly against the side of the metal wagon. Its hideous cry was filled with rage and frustration at its second failed attempt to snatch them out from under the wagon.

Immediately after its pass they rolled out and leaped to their feet. Bartholomew scrambled into the back of the wagon and tied himself securely in. Oliver ran to the front and flipped the long handle up and backwards, latching it to the top of the wagon. He climbed between several of the crates in front and flipped open a small panel, calling out to Bartholomew, "I am switching off the regulator now. That's what limits the speed of the wagon. It's capable of traveling at far greater speeds, but since we decided to walk, I thought–"

"Just do it! The creature will be diving again at any

moment!"

Oliver flipped a small yellow lever and turned a red dial to the right. The wagon began to move forward, its speed increasing rapidly with each passing moment.

"We're moving now! I believe our maximum velocity will be close to forty miles in one hour. We should easily be able to outdistance the pterosaur at that rate."

"How do you steer it?" Bartholomew managed to shout out the question over the bumping and crashing of the crates and boxes. The wind was howling around him now as the wagon sped forward at ever increasing velocity.

"Steer it? I'm afraid that's quite impossible at this time. I hadn't planned on an event such as this and in my eagerness to get the wagon ready for–" His voice was drowned out by the roaring wind and the wild creaking and rattling of the wagon in its frenetic race across the rocky plain. Bartholomew hung onto the careening wagon with all his might. He was not thinking, he was only reacting, driven solely by his instinct for self preservation. In the midst of all this he heard Cavern's quiet voice. "How's this for an adventure?" Bartholomew howled uncontrollably with a manic laughter.

After many jarring and jolting minutes, Oliver turned the red dial to the left and their speed decreased. Eventually the wagon creaked to a halt. Bartholomew could hardly move, but turned and looked behind them. The pterosaur was heading back to the mountains on the far side of the valley. Bartholomew untied his ropes and climbed painfully out of the wagon. "Good heavens, I feel as though I have spent an hour in one of those mechanical paint can shakers. I'm not certain my bones are connected properly anymore."

Oliver closed his eyes and leaned back in the wagon. "This is adventuring business is quite exhausting, I must say." When he opened his eyes again he let out a blood curdling scream. A gigantic pterosaur was streaking down from the sky directly towards the wagon. Bartholomew turned just in time to see the creature's enormous talons grab the entire wagon, including Oliver, and carry it off into the sky. There had been two pterosaurs, not just one. The second one had circled around behind them while the first one distracted them with its false attack.

Bartholomew could do nothing except chase after the fleeing pterosaur. It was flying back towards the area where Oliver had first spotted them. Oliver's cries for help were barely audible now, and Bartholomew shuddered to think what might be in store for his friend. As he ran after Oliver he tried to think of something he could use as a weapon against the pterosaurs, but everything they had was in the wagon. He realized he was still holding the rope he had used to tie himself to the duplonium wagon. That was at least something. It might come in handy if he had to do any climbing to reach Oliver.

Bartholomew dashed across the wide plain towards the mountainside where the pterosaurs lived. He watched closely as the pterosaur descended behind a group of trees, noting to himself several prominent landmarks. Fortunately, it had landed below the tree line, which meant it would be easily accessible, and the dense grouping of trees might provide some protection from the pterosaurs.

He was exhausted and gasping for breath when he finally reached the other side of the plain. He was not used to running such long distances. Oliver was right – adventuring was exhausting. He forced himself to rest briefly, then looked up at the trees he had chosen for landmarks. There were two towering spruce trees about fifty feet apart with a stand of smaller trees growing between them. The pterosaur had glided in between the two tall trees, then disappeared down behind the shorter ones. Maybe there was a nest there. Did pterosaurs even have nests?

He still needed a weapon before he went in after Oliver. He looked at the rope in his paw and the image of an ancient rabbit warrior appeared in his mind – an ancient rabbit warrior carrying a sling. That could work. The rope he had was long enough, and he could make a pouch for the sling from a piece of his coat.

He scoured the area and found a shard of jagged rock which he used to saw the rope into two equal lengths, then tore off a square piece of his coat lining. Using the jagged stone he soon had two round holes drilled in the pouch, and tied one rope to each hole. His sling was complete. He found a round stone the size of a small egg and slipped it into the sling's pouch. Holding both ends of the sling in one paw, he swung it around in a wide arc. When it was going fast enough to make a low roaring sound he released one end of the rope. The stone shot out with a shrill whistling noise and streaked off into the distance. Unfortunately, it was traveling in exactly the opposite direction of the one he'd intended.

He tried again. And again. Eventually he could send the rock shooting out in the general direction of his choosing. The pterosaurs were huge and would make easy targets, so extreme accuracy wasn't paramount. He found himself calculating the odds that a flying stone would stop a gigantic shrieking pterosaur, and the odds did not seem to be falling in his favor.

Pushing his way through the dense trees, he emerged on the other side but found no nests on the ground and no sign of anything in the trees. Scanning the side of the mountain, he eyed a large black circle about fifty feet up the rocky slope and let out a groan. It was the entrance to a cave. After his experience in the Cavern of Silence, he had sincerely hoped he would never have to enter a cave again, never mind one housing prehistoric pterosaurs with a taste for rabbit. It only took one thought of Oliver's plight, however, to send Bartholomew scrambling up the rocky slope to the cave entrance.

Chapter 6

The Cave

Bartholomew crept into the cave, concealing himself behind a large boulder. Once his eyes were accustomed to the dark, he studied the layout of the cave. It was more of a tunnel than a cave, extending back a good distance then curving around out of sight. The cave floor had bones scattered across it, and Bartholomew did his best to avoid looking at them. Slipping a rock into the pouch of his sling, he crept forward, hugging the wall as he moved deeper into the tunnel. When he reached the curve he stopped, listening carefully. He could hear a snuffling noise and hoarse whistling sound. He inched forward and peered around the corner. There was a massive pterosaur curled up on the floor sleeping. Several hundred feet past the pterosaur lay the duplonium wagon, but he saw no sign of Oliver. Suppose the pterosaur had already... he couldn't finish his thought. Somehow, he had to get past the beast and find Oliver. He gingerly removed his boots, moving over to the wall farthest from the pterosaur. Trying to avoid even the slightest noise he crept forward, step by silent step making his way past the sleeping monster.

He'd done it. This wasn't so bad. If he found Oliver they could slip back out past the pterosaur.

The duplonium wagon sat almost a hundred feet ahead of him. He blinked several times, attempting to focus on the dark rocky wall behind the wagon. The wall looked as if it was moving slightly. Then the realization hit him – it wasn't a rocky wall, it was the broad wing of a second sleeping pterosaur. His heart started pounding. Could a thumping heart wake a pterosaur? He clenched his teeth and crept forward.

He was only twenty feet from the wagon when the pterosaur sleepily moved its huge wing. Like an oversized fan it sent a torrent of air towards Bartholomew, stirring up a great cloud of dust along the way. The dust flew into Bartholomew's nostrils and within seconds he knew he was going to sneeze. He made a dash for the wagon. Maybe he could climb inside before–

"ACHOOOO!!"

The pterosaur let out a horrific shriek, it's gigantic wings flailing about. Bartholomew raced towards the wagon. A voice cried out, "In here!" Oliver was still in the wagon. Bartholomew reached the wagon and leaped up onto it. He saw Oliver hidden between two stacks of wooden crates and slipped safely down just as the pterosaur's talons crashed onto the crates, splitting several of them open.

"Ah, just in time. I assume you are here to rescue me again?" Oliver grinned at Bartholomew.

"To be quite honest, I'm not precisely certain why I'm here. I thought I was on my way to find Clara, not to spend the afternoon in a cave filled with hungry pterosaurs."

"It's really not as bad as it seems."

"You have an escape plan?"

"No, no, nothing like that. But I've been having quite an enjoyable time studying the behavioral patterns of pterosaurs. The male always sleeps in the back of the cave and the –"

"Have you studied the part where the pterosaurs pull the two rabbits out of the duplonium wagon and snack on their crunchy bones?"

"Oh dear, I hadn't really focused on that aspect of their behavior. I suppose I was just trying to ignore it. Do you have an escape plan?"

"Nothing other than sneaking past them, and that didn't work especially well on the way in. Do they ever leave the cave?"

"One of them always stays here. I suspect they are guarding their... their..."

"Bedtime snacks?"

"Oh dear, I'd better think of something. All right, let me see, what do we have in the wagon? There is the duplonium powered electric motor which propels the wagon, and we have four Mark III Vacuumators. We have no weapons of any kind, and at any rate I would hate to destroy such magnificent creatures as these."

"Why in the world did you bring four vacuumators?"

"Not now please, I'm trying to think." Minutes ticked by while Oliver mumbled to himself using incomprehensible scientific jargon. Finally he said something Bartholomew could understand. "I have a plan. It's based on sound scientific principles, so it's certain to succeed." He twisted over sideways and reached inside one of the cracked wooden crates, pulling out two large rubber raincoats. “This should do nicely. Sit on this and put your paws inside the sleeves.”

“You’re expecting rain?”

“Stop being ridiculous and do what I say. Now, help me uncrate one of the vacuumators.”

Ten minutes later they had a vacuumator sitting in front of them. “Let’s see... where did I pack the electrical gear?” Oliver poked around some canvas sacks, finally pulling out an old leather satchel. He opened it, removing a few tools and a roll of wire. Soon wires were running from inside the vacuumator to the metal walls of the wagon. “Perfect. Here is my plan. We don’t need to sneak out. The wagon will carry us out of the cave. I have connected the electrical generator in the vacuumator to the wagon itself, sending a powerful electrical current through the metal walls of the wagon. As long as you remain seated on the rubber raincoat with your paws in the sleeves, you will be insulated. If you accidentally touch the metal wall or the floor of the wagon you will be instantly electrocuted.”

“Ah, your plan is sounding more and more enticing. I especially like the part about being instantly electrocuted.”

“Stop acting like a bunny and pay attention. I’m going to start up the vacuumator now and electrify the wagon. The noise will wake both pterosaurs, but we should be perfectly safe in the electrified wagon, unless they knock the wagon over, in which case we will both be electrocuted. That sounds quite bad until one compares it to being ripped apart and eaten by a pterosaur.”

Bartholomew began to feel light headed. “Please stop talking. Just do whatever you have to do.”

“Very well. I will start the vacuumator.” He flipped a small lever and the vacuumator’s tremendous roar filled the cave. The pterosaurs shrieked wildly, flapping their wings and clawing at the rocky floor. The gigantic male pterosaur behind them half leaped and half flew over the wagon, scrambling towards the front of the cave. Both pterosaurs moved out of sight past the curve in the cave.

“Fascinating. This is an unexpected and highly beneficial consequence. The sound of the vacuumator has scared the pterosaurs. It must resemble the cry of some fearsome predator. This is excellent. I will get the wagon moving.” He flipped a switch and the wheels began to turn. Unfortunately, it was moving in the wrong direction and bumped against the back wall.

“A minor setback – I will simply flip this yellow switch here, and push this button on the control panel and that should do it. Hold on, here we go again.”

Oliver turned the red dial and the wagon began rolling in the proper direction. When they reached the curve in the cave, Oliver turned the red dial down and the wagon came to a halt.

“Perfect. Now, you need to get out and turn the wheels so we are heading towards the cave entrance.”

“What? I have to get out? You do realize there are two hungry pterosaurs out there who think rabbits are delicious?”

“Of course I do. It will only take a moment. Leap out, push the arm towards the cave entrance and jump back in. Nothing to it.”

Bartholomew looked dubious, but said. “All right,

here I go."

"WAIT!! I need to disconnect the wires or... you know... zzzzzzt!" Oliver quickly unscrewed a connector and pulled the wire loose. "Go!"

Bartholomew leaped over the edge of the wagon and grabbed the long steering arm, lining it up with the cave entrance. The two pterosaurs shrieked and began moving towards him, angrily clawing at the cave floor. He leaped back into the wagon and slipped down between the crates. "It's done."

Bartholomew reconnected the wire, sending current through the wagon wall. The pterosaurs were almost upon them. One of them touched the wagon with its wing, sending out a brilliant shower of sparks. The pterosaur roared in pain and pulled back, flapping its wing angrily. Oliver turned the red dial and the wagon moved forward towards the cave entrance. The two pterosaurs were becoming increasingly agitated.

Bartholomew hollered out to Oliver. "I have an idea. Unhook the wires, turn the vacuumator up as loud as it will go and throw it out of the wagon. Maybe they'll attack it instead of us."

"Yes, that might work. Hold on!" Oliver disconnected both wires and turned the vacuumator to full power. The roar was deafening and the pterosaurs were leaping up and down, jabbing their long beaks towards the wagon. "Okay, help me throw it out." Together they picked it up, and hurled it as far as they could from the wagon. The vacuumator sent up a huge dust cloud, making it almost impossible to see. The pterosaurs could no longer control themselves and scrambled past the wagon to the roaring vacuumator. Oliver turned the red dial and the wagon shot forward out of the cave, bouncing and rolling down the steep slope until it crashed into the dense stand of trees. Luckily they were not crushed by the heavy shifting crates.

"Should we leave the wagon here?"

"No, it has all our supplies in it. I think we can go around the trees. The vacuumator should keep the pterosaurs busy for a while. Oliver tugged at the wagon and the large wheels gripped the rocks. "The coating on the wheels is my own invention and provides far greater traction than ordinary rubber."

Like a great awkward mountain goat the wagon crept over the rocks and boulders and down the slope of the mountain. At long last they found themselves on the flat plain again. They had escaped the pterosaurs.

"Let's go before they come after us."

The roaring vacuumator in the cave abruptly went silent.

"That's not good. The pterosaurs have destroyed the vacuumator. Do you think they've forgotten about us?"

"I don't think so." Bartholomew pointed above the trees. The two pterosaurs had taken to the air and were circling around to gain altitude, preparing for a dive.

"Should we hide in the wagon?"

"No, they'll grab it like they did last time. We can hide under it, but if they take the wagon away we'll be in the open." They rolled under the wagon, peering out at the pterosaurs circling overhead. Both pterosaurs pulled their wings in at the same moment, entering into a steep dive. Bartholomew could hear the whistling sound as they shot through the air towards them. He hoped the end would be quick.

When the pterosaurs were still about a hundred feet

above them a brilliant blue beam of light shot out from the side of the mountain and hit both pterosaurs. They shrieked and swerved wildly, opening their wings and ending the dive. Rather than circling around to gain altitude, they turned away, flying towards the other end of the valley.

"What was that blue light?"

"I have no idea." They rolled out from under the wagon and looked up at the mountain.

"There!" Bartholomew looked to where Oliver was pointing and saw a lone figure standing on a ledge halfway up the mountain. He wore a long green cloak with a hood pulled over his head. He raised one arm, pointing towards the end of the valley. A brilliant blue beam shot out across the plains and the figure vanished.

"I think he wants us to leave."

"I believe we should oblige him."

Oliver grabbed the wagon handle and they began their march to the end of the valley. They reached it by the time the sun was sinking below the mountains.

"This was a remarkable adventure, my friend. We escaped the clutches of two deadly pterosaurs with the aid of a mysterious cloaked figure who shoots beams of blue light from his paw to control the monstrous flying prehistoric beasts."

"You know, when you put it that way, it's probably best if we never tell anyone about this."

"Ha! You may be right about that. I know quite a number of rabbits at the Excelsior Corporation who would not be ready for a tale such as that. How about we make camp here and open a lovely bottle of wine to celebrate our escape?"

As they sat next to the campfire eating dinner, Oliver

couldn't stop talking about the pterosaurs.

"I am utterly baffled by the appearance of these creatures. The more I think about it, the more I believe I can categorically state it is impossible for them to exist. They simply cannot be. That leaves only one possible alternative." His voice had become strangely hollow. "They are magical flying demons from another realm." He waited expectantly for Bartholomew to respond.

"Good heavens, did you see that??"

Oliver's head whipped around. "See what? Is it a demon??"

"No, just a rather large bumblebee flying past."

Oliver frowned. "You are mocking me?"

"Regarding the magical flying demons from another realm?"

"Ah. Now I see. For an unscientific rabbit, you have a rather ingenious mind. You are saying that bumblebees cannot fly and the pterosaur cannot exist, and yet they do. Hmm, I never thought I would see the day, but you may have taught me a rather humbling lesson, Bartholomew. The things we find mysterious and magical are simply things which science currently does not understand. Once they thought lightning bolts came from Zeus, and now we have used that same force to escape the clutches of a modern pterosaur. I suppose there are colonies of them living in caves up there. This area has barely been touched by rabbits. Who knows how long the pterosaurs have been here. Maybe one day we will return to investigate the flying beasts of Pterosaur Valley."

"Pterosaur Valley it is, my friend."

"Who do you think the figure in the green cloak was?"

“I cannot even begin to imagine, but to me he is a far greater mystery than the pterosaurs.”

‘We will leave that mystery for another day. Would you care for a second glass of wine?”

“I think I will retire for the evening. This day has quite exhausted me. It’s not every day I manage to escape the clutches of a pair of magical flying demons.”

Oliver hurled a small stone at him.

Chapter 7

Oliver T. Rabbit vs. The Tree of Eyes

By the following afternoon they were looking down into the valley where the Tree of Eyes would be found. Bartholomew pointed to a distant section of the valley saying, "The tree is located in that area. It will take us at least two days to get there. I'm anxious for you examine it and give me your expert scientific opinion." He could barely keep a straight face. Oliver T. Rabbit versus the Tree of Eyes – it would be a momentous face to face meeting between science and the unknown. The irresistible force meets the unmovable object.

For the next two days they weaved their way through the vast forests on their way to the Tree of Eyes. On the morning of the third day, they parked the duplonium wagon next to the dense wall of trees surrounding the clearing where the Tree of Eyes grew.

"Oliver, why don't you go ahead in while I finish unpacking a few things. The Tree of Eyes is right on the edge of the lake. I should warn you that some rabbits say the Tree of Eyes may possesses the power of speech." It took every ounce of his self-control to maintain his serious expression.

"Very well, I shall use my vast array of scientific skills to examine this Tree of Eyes and determine its true nature. It shouldn't take long."

"Mmm hmm," was all Bartholomew could manage to say.

Bartholomew waited until Oliver disappeared into the trees, then crept in after him. He ducked down when he spotted the Tree of Eyes, crawling forward until he had a clear view of the tree. He rubbed his paws together with anticipation as Oliver approached it.

Oliver T. Rabbit stood staring at the Tree of Eyes. The eyes on the tree were motionless, hanging like heavy white fruit from the branches. Walking slowly around the tree, Oliver methodically appraised its characteristics from many different angles. He approached the trunk of the tree, rapping on it with his knuckles in numerous places. He gently poked one of the eyes with his paw.

"Sometimes I wonder about Bartholomew." He moved back a few paces and faced the tree again. For the sake of science and experimentation, he would conduct one final test, no matter how foolish it made him feel. "Good afternoon, Tree of Eyes. It is a pleasure to make your acquaintance. My completely mad friend, Bartholomew Rabbit, has told me you may possess the ability to speak. If this is true, please answer this question for me. What is the best way to prepare cream filling for éclairs?" The only sound Oliver heard was the distant buzzing of insects.

Bartholomew was furious. The wretched tree was

making him look like a fool in front of Oliver. It made him want to get out the firewood saw and scare the leaves right off this insidious creature. Then he stopped. Suppose something was wrong with the tree? It could be sick or even poisoned. It was a living creature after all. Maybe it needed his help. He rose up from the brush and stepped into the clearing.

"Ah, there you are. I'm afraid your Tree of Eyes is just an ordinary tree. I believe it acquired its name due to the nature of its white fruit and their uncanny resemblance to a pair of eyes. I'm afraid the tree will be offering us no assistance in our search for Clara." There was no mistaking the tremendously condescending tone of his voice.

"Oliver, you have to believe me, this tree is not what you–"

"MAGICAL FLYING DEMONS SHALL FEAST ON YOUR LONG FLOPPY EARS!! DID YOU REALLY THINK WE WOULDN'T KNOW YOU WERE HIDING THERE, BARTHOLOMEW RABBIT?? DID YOU REALLY THINK WE COULDN'T READ YOUR–"

"Shhh! What are you saying?"

"Oops, I forgot."

"Well, be careful. You'll ruin our fun."

"It doesn't work if they know how we're doing it."

"Be quiet! You're only making it worse!"

"Hey, what are you guys talking about?"

"Oh, bright eyes here almost told the rabbit we could–"

"ATTENTION ALL EYES!! STOP TALKING IMMEDIATELY!!!"

The eyes looked around nervously.

Oliver and Bartholomew had managed to crawl away after the horrific explosion of sound. Oliver sat up, his paws on his ears, a terrified look on his face. He gaped with wide eyes at the tree. Its eyes were now moving again. Bartholomew looked absolutely furious. He stood up, glaring angrily at the Tree of Eyes.

"What is wrong with you? Why do you have to treat rabbits like this?"

"Is that my little Honey Bunny? Is that my little–"

"Stop using that voice this instant! I will not fall for your trickery again. What were you talking about? What was that about reading something?"

The eyes darted about wildly. One set of eyes looked shrewdly at Bartholomew and said in a deep and professorial tone, "Reading? Ah, yes, we have been reading a small volume of collected short stories. Many of them contain delightful descriptions of the magnificent forests found in the upper regions of–"

"Silence! I must think." Bartholomew tried to recollect the tree's conversation. Something it said had struck an odd chord within him, something the eyes couldn't have known.

"How did you know about the magical flying demons?" There was no response.

"HOW DID YOU KNOW about the magical flying demons?" Still no response.

Bartholomew lost his patience. "HOW DID YOU KNOW ABOUT THE MAGICAL FLYING DEMONS?"

There was a collective gasp from the eyes.

"He asked the question three times in a row!"

"How could he know about the law?"

"We have to tell him. It's the law as set forth by the

Great Tree, you know it is."

"But a rabbit? Tell a rabbit?"

"It wouldn't be the first time. You remember the other one..."

"Of course I do, but that was different."

"I'm waiting for your answer. You have to tell me. As you said, it is the law." Bartholomew tried to look as stern as he possibly could.

"All right, I'll tell you if you wipe that ridiculous expression off your face."

"He's right, it does look quite silly. However, you are correct, it is the law and I will answer your question. We knew about the flying magical demons the same way we knew you were hiding in the brush and knew the sound of your mother's voice. We can read your little rabbit mind. Are you happy now?"

"You can read my mind?"

"He doesn't even understand the answer!" The eyes shrieked with laughter.

"I understand the answer quite well. I was merely thinking out loud."

"No need for that, we can read your mind." More high pitched maniacal laughter, followed by giggling and an odd cackling noise.

"I want you to teach me."

The eyes gasped in unison.

"Are you mad? We can't teach a rabbit to read thoughts."

"How do you read thoughts?"

"How do you read thoughts?"

"How do you read thoughts?"

"Please stop that. There's no need to be a show off."

"Really. Oh, look at me everyone, I can ask a

question three times in a row. Aren't I a clever little rabbit?"

There was snickering and guffawing from the eyes.

"You MUST answer the question. The law? Remember?"

A new voice emerged from the Tree of Eyes. It was powerful and humorless, exuding a sense of absolute power and authority.

"This your second warning, eyes. Do not pester me again. Bartholomew Rabbit, hold your paws out in front of you with your palms facing upward."

Bartholomew held out his paws. The Great Gem glowed brightly in front of the tree.

"As I thought. Stand still. This will not hurt."

Some of the eyes giggled.

A long tendril unraveled, snaking out towards Bartholomew. It wrapped itself around his head four or five times. It felt as though his thoughts, memories and feelings had been caught up in a ferocious whirlwind and were spinning wildly about inside his head. A moment later the bizarre sensation abruptly ceased and the tendril withdrew back into the tree.

"Oliver T. Rabbit, step forward."

Oliver had been sitting on the ground the whole time watching Bartholomew. He stood up, looking slightly dazed as he meandered over towards the tree.

"Bartholomew Rabbit, you will remain motionless."

The tendril extended out again. This time it had a single glowing red leaf on the end of it. The red leaf pressed against his forehead, then withdrew.

"Oliver T. Rabbit, you are well-schooled in the arts of science and mathematics, are you not?"

"I am, although there are certainly many things in

this world I–"

"I am completely aware of all your abilities. I am going to give you a mathematical problem. Solve it in your head, but do not speak the answer out loud. Is this clear?"

"Yes, quite clear."

"Here is the problem. Oliver has seven carrots and eats four of them. How many carrots does Oliver have left?"

Oliver could feel his jaw tightening.

"Have you solved the problem or do you need more time?"

"Of course I have solved the problem. A one year old bunny could have solved it."

"Temper, temper. No need for thoughts like that. Bartholomew Rabbit, look closely at Oliver's head and tell me what you see."

Bartholomew looked. To his amazement, a small pink cloud was coming out of Oliver's ear. It began floating towards Bartholomew. "I see a pink cloud."

"Touch the cloud, please."

Bartholomew walked over to the cloud and cautiously poked it with his paw. He heard Oliver's voice in his head and felt an unexpected rush of anger pass through him. "The answer is three carrots, you blithering bug-eyed buffoon."

"Did you hear the answer?"

"I did."

"You have successfully completed your lesson. The Tree of Eyes is required to answer only two questions per rabbit per lifetime, and you have had yours. That is the law as set forth by the Great Tree. Eyes, do not pester me with trivial matters such as this. If you contact me again before one hundred years has passed, there will be severe consequences. Are we quite clear on this?"

"Yes, Great Tree, we humbly apologize and will not pester you again."

The eyes all turned towards Bartholomew. "Thanks a lot, Bartholomew Rabbit. You got us all in trouble again."

"Yeah, thanks a lot."

"Who is the Great Tree?"

"Why should we tell you, troublemaker? You already had your two questions, so buzz off."

"Yeah, who died and made you King Rabbit?

There was a smattering of laughter among the eyes.

Oliver could tolerate the tree's rude and immature behavior no longer. He turned to the Tree of Eyes and said coldly, "If you can read my mind then you know what we are looking for, do you not?"

"Maybe."

"Would you prefer that I ask you three times how to read minds? I doubt the Great Tree would appreciate being pestered again five minutes after his warning."

There was angry murmuring among the eyes.

"Oh come on, we were just fooling around. You're such a meanie."

"Yeah, quit being a big bully, Oliver."

"Very well then. Now that you are in a more cooperative mood, I have a proposition for you.

"We agree to all of it."

"How can you agree to something you haven't heard??"

"Hello? We can read your mind? Remember?" There was giggling from a few of the eyes.

"Very well, but for the record, would you please state exactly what it is you are agreeing to?"

"We will find Clara's farm for you. After you find Clara you will return here and ask us lots of personal questions and study us and write books about the new species of tree you discovered and hundreds of rabbits will come to visit us and we can read all their minds and play ridiculous childish pranks on all of them."

"Not precisely the words I would have used, but it will suffice. You find this to be a satisfactory arrangement?"

"Yes, we already said we agree. And in return you will not make us contact the Great Tree for at least one hundred years. You don't even want to know what comes after the second warning."

"Very well. It seems we have an agreement. Where is Clara's farm?"

"We will show you."

The eyes began chattering among themselves. "Should we use the breadcrumb trail?"

"Yes, that will work best since the chubby one can't see thoughts."

"Don't call him chubby. He can still make us pester the Great Tree."

"Oh right, and then they'll NEVER find Clara's farm."

"Stop the bickering please. I just want them to leave."

"Bartholomew Rabbit, we will send out thoughts and shape them, leaving a trail both you and Oliver T. Rabbit can follow. We are sending the first thought now."

Bartholomew watched as a fluffy white cloud

emerged from the Tree of Eyes and floated across the clearing. It headed through the stand of trees in the direction of the duplonium wagon.

"Follow me, Oliver. They sent out a thought for us to track." They dashed after the small white cloud.

When they reached the duplonium wagon the thought was about thirty feet away, heading south. It slowed down and began swirling like a miniature whirlwind, becoming smaller and more opaque. Sinking lower and lower until it touched the ground, it vanished in a bright flash of light. Bartholomew walked over to where the cloud had been. Lying in the grass was a small irregular shaped piece of white cardboard with the image of an eye on it. It was Bartholomew's missing puzzle piece.

"Oliver, look at this!"

"Your missing puzzle piece. How on earth did they do that?"

Bartholomew shook his head. "I don't know. They seem to have transformed a thought into a physical object. This is impossible and yet there it is."

"Just like the bumblebee." Oliver turned away, grumbling to himself.

"What's wrong?"

"What's wrong? What isn't wrong? The pterosaurs are wrong. The Tree of Eyes is wrong, and now this puzzle piece is wrong. My world of science is crumbling like a bad cheese. I used to know where everything was and how the pieces fit together. I don't like these new things one bit. Not one bit."

Bartholomew thought carefully before making his reply. "Oliver, I'm sure you know you're not the first scientist whose world has been turned upside down by new discoveries. It's true these things we have found will shake the hallowed halls of science, but they also increase our understanding of the world around us. That's the true purpose of a scientist, isn't it?"

Oliver gave a rueful smile. "You're right, of course. After everything that happened when I was a bunny, change has always been difficult for me. It seemed to me when things changed it was never for the better. I'll try to remember your words the next time we run into a gigantic mind reading bumblebee."

Bartholomew watched a second white cloud float several hundred feet past the first puzzle piece, then sink to the ground with a flash of light.

"Time to go, my friend. The puzzle pieces are leading us to Clara's farm."

Chapter 8

The Diaries

"Any of the farms along here could be Clara's."

"But which one? The puzzle pieces ended after we passed through the woods and reached this road."

"We'll ask at the first farm."

"Clara's my sister, so perhaps you should stay with the wagon while I knock on the door. They'll be more receptive to a rabbit trying to find his long lost sister."

"Agreed. I'll wait here."

Bartholomew watched Oliver walk down the long dusty path to the farmhouse. It would not be as simple as knocking on a door and having Clara answer. He remembered Cavern's words. "Finding her will be far more difficult than you can possibly imagine, and when this adventure is done you will not be the same rabbit you are now." He had not mentioned any of this to Oliver, not wanting to alarm him.

Oliver approached the door and knocked on it. An elderly rabbit opened the door. Oliver spoke to her for almost a minute, then she stepped outside. At one point she put her paw on his arm and his head fell forward, his shoulders slumping down. Bartholomew saw a dense gray cloud float out of Oliver's ear. This did not look promising. Bartholomew had seen Clara on the Most Beautiful Island and was quite certain she was still alive, but now he was not so sure about Oliver's mother. He was filled with an overwhelming sadness as he watched Oliver turn and walk forlornly towards him.

Oliver's face was expressionless. "Clara's farm is the next one over. My mother is not there. She died over two years ago and Clara has not been seen for more than three months."

Oliver put his paws over his face and turned away from Bartholomew. The sobbing was almost more than Bartholomew could bear. When he turned around again Bartholomew put his paw on Oliver's shoulder. "I'm sorry, my old friend. I am truly sorry."

As they walked to Clara's farm, Oliver told him some of the stories he remembered from when his family had lived together in Lepus Hollow. Those had been happy years for Oliver, Sophie, and Clara.

"Her neighbor gave me the key and said we are welcome to stay at Clara's house as long as we wish."

"It will be a good place to rest, and hopefully we can find some clues to Clara's whereabouts."

Oliver unlocked the door and they entered Clara's home. On the entryway table was a photograph of Clara and her mother. There was also an old photo of the whole family. Oliver pointed to it. "I remember that day. We went for a picnic by the river. Mama baked an apple pie just for the picnic." He picked up the photograph, looked at it closely, then gently set it down again. "Let's see what we can find."

As they explored the house it seemed oddly familiar

to Bartholomew. Many of the books were the same ones lining his shelves. There was an Alexander Rabbit guitar identical to his. The walls were covered with artwork that he recognized. One of the chairs was the same chair he had in his drawing room. There were too many similarities for it to be mere coincidence.

"I found something." Oliver had opened a dresser drawer by Clara's bed. He removed four small leather bound books. Each one had the word "*Diary*" embossed in gold leaf on the front cover. He gave two of them to Bartholomew. "We can read these after dinner. They might be our only hope of locating Clara. And maybe I can get to know her again after all these years."

There was no food in the house so they brought in supplies from the duplonium wagon. Bartholomew lit the stove and got water boiling using a piece of duplonium. Clara's house was soon filled with the delicious aroma of Oliver's cooking. They ate at the small kitchen table, and when daylight began to fade Bartholomew lit the lamps. He imagined Clara sitting in the large stuffed chair reading the same books he had read. After dinner they went into the living room and sat on a colorful flowery sofa. They silently took out Clara's diaries and began to read.

May 3 – Mama and I arrived at the new farm today. I don't like it. I don't see any other bunnies around and I don't have anyone to play with. I miss Sophie and Oliver and Papa. I want to go home but Mama says we can't and we have to make the best of it. I don't want to make the best of it. I want to go home. They don't even have a school here. Mama says most of the rabbits work on the farms and learn at home. She said she will find me books to read and teach me all the things I would learn at school. I did see some nice horses at the next farm over that I hope I can ride.

July 7 – All we ever do is dig in the gardens and plant vegetables. I'm tired of eating the same food every day. Mama bought six chickens and they lay eggs for us. We sell some of the eggs to buy things from the store. The chickens are funny. Sometimes they chase me around when I am feeding them. I miss Sophie and Oliver and Papa. I miss seeing my best friend Bartholomew. I wish we had a school here and he was my friend here. I hope I can see him again. I told Mama I can talk to Bartholomew in dreams but Mama says that's only wishing.

July 29 – I think I'm going to name all the chickens. I was playing in the garden with them and I thought one was talking to me but I figured out it was an inside me talking to the outside me. It made a big jewel in my paw but Mama can't see it and told me not to make up stories. Mama always says I make up stories but I don't.

Bartholomew was astonished at this last entry. Clara had found her Great Gem when she was still a bunny. He read through more of the entries, most of which had to do with life on the farm and stories about the neighboring rabbits. Then something caught his eye – the word 'tree'.

August 19 - Mama sent me out to pick raspberries so she could make jam and a pie. Raspberry pie is my most favorite kind. Our neighbors at the next farm told us a good place to pick them at a lake. It's a long walk to get there but they said there were lots of them so the walk is worth it. There was a funny tree there. It looks like it has eyes on it. I told Mama the tree could talk and she laughed but said no more stories. I am going to show the tree to Mama so she'll know it's not pretend. The tree is silly and sometimes says funny things to me like Bartholomew used to say.

August 24 – I went back and saw the funny tree again. It says lots of things that make me laugh. I think I have a new friend now. It can do lots of tricks too. It made my bucket be filled with raspberries but I don't know how it did the trick. Mama bought more chickens today and said the farm is doing well and she is proud of me. She made raspberry pie again but told me not to talk to the tree. She said she didn't know if it was bad or not and it was best to stay away from things you don't understand. I don't want to stay away but I don't want to be a sneak when Mama said not to.

Clara had met the Tree of Eyes and had spoken with it. The tree had been polite to her and hadn't played its usual childish pranks on her. Why? He continued on, flipping through entries until he found another one mentioning the tree.

September 9 – I visit my tree friend lots now because I know he's not bad, but I don't tell Mama. I always come home with two buckets filled with raspberries and I don't have to pick any. I tell Mama I spent the whole time picking the berries. The tree showed me how to see little clouds. It made a pink one turn into raspberries in my bucket. When I took them home I saw some blue clouds come out of Mama's ear. It was kind of scary and I didn't tell her because she would think I was making up stories. One of them floated to me and landed on my paw and I heard Mama's voice in my head say she wished it would rain more so the crops would grow better.

This was astonishing. The Tree of Eyes had taught Clara how to see thought clouds and how to read them. It had showed her how to shape thoughts into objects, the same way it had made the trail of puzzle pieces. Bartholomew remembered something the Tree of Eyes said.

"Tell a rabbit?"

"It wouldn't be the first time. You remember..."

"Of course I do, but that was different."

They had to have been talking about Clara. How was it different with her? He flipped through the rest of the diary but there was no further mention of the Tree of Eyes. He opened the second diary. The writing looked as though she was older when she wrote this one. The first entry was about the Tree of Eyes.

April 4 – The tree is teaching me lots of things. I can fill the raspberry buckets myself now by turning the clouds into berries. I don't dare tell Mama anything more about the tree because it would be too scary for her. It's sort of magic but also not magic, just the way things are made. The tree says everything is energy, even rabbits and mountains. When we think something it makes a cloud of energy that floats out of our head. If we want we can send it to someone and they will know what we are thinking. But that only works if they know how to hear it. It was hard to make a cloud turn into a raspberry but the tree said I was trying too hard. When I didn't try, the cloud turned into raspberries. It was easy to make other things after that.

April 28 - I can make the clouds turn into lots of things now but I have to be very careful that Mama doesn't see me. I can't make things that Mama won't know where they came from so mostly I make extra food and lots of eggs. Everyone thinks we have the best chickens of all the farms. The tree is the only one who knows all the things I can do. Sometimes it has a grown up voice but he's not funny like the other ones. I still like him though and he likes to talk to me too I think. Sometimes it's kind of like having Papa with me again.

The other voice had to be the Great Tree. The Tree of Eyes and the Great Tree had known who Clara was the whole time, but had said nothing. They knew perfectly well where Clara's farm was. Why hadn't they said anything? Oliver looked up from the diary he was reading. "Clara was friends with the Tree of Eyes."

"Yes, I read that. This is all quite astonishing."

"She could manipulate thought clouds and make objects out of them, just like the Tree of Eyes did."

Oliver didn't reply. He was deeply engrossed in a diary. Bartholomew continued reading.

May 4 - Something bad happened today. I was sitting under the big tree in our yard reading a book Mama gave me and I was hungry but didn't want to go inside so I made an apple in my paw. I heard a crashing noise behind me and it was Molly Ann from two farms away. She was bringing us our milk but dropped one of the bottles on a rock. She had a scared look on her face and called me a shaper. I said I wasn't one I was just making an apple because I was hungry. She put the other bottles down and ran away. I'm afraid she might tell Mama and I'll get into trouble. I didn't like the way she was scared of me and thinks I'm something bad.

May 11 – Molly brought our milk today but she wouldn't look at me. She didn't say anything to Mama. She looked nervous and didn't stay to talk like she usually does. I want to ask Mama what a shaper is but then she might want to know how I heard about it. I'm going to ask the grown up voice at the tree to tell me. I'm going to hide my new diaries under the board. I still dream about Bartholomew and talk to him. Mama always tells me it was wishing, but I think it's real. He told me he always forgets what we talk about when he wakes up but doesn't know why.

Bartholomew turned to Oliver. "There are more diaries. She said she was going to hide them under the board, wherever that is."

"I have been trying to understand the science behind this. The tree said that everything is made of energy, which means that all matter is somehow composed of compressed energy. When we think a thought, we create an energy field which is invisible to us, just as many wavelengths of light are invisible to us. We know this invisible light actually exists because we can see it with special glasses."

Bartholomew thought about the Hallway of Doors in the swamp which he could only see through the dark glasses. He said nothing however, listening as Oliver continued.

"Somehow, the Tree of Eyes is able to see thought energy fields and can alter a rabbit's senses so they can see them too. This is incredible. This is no longer a bumblebee, Bartholomew. This is science. It has turned from magic to science. I still have no idea how the mind can compress a thought cloud into matter, or how a rabbit can hear thoughts just by touching the thought cloud. This is beyond anything I am familiar with, but I will come to understand it. It's only a question of time. It might even be possible to invent some sort of apparatus which would allow everyone to see thought clouds, or even to hear them. You could send a message to a friend instantly using only your mind. Astounding!"

"I'm going to look for the other diaries. My guess is they're hidden in Clara's room. Bartholomew stood up, leaving Oliver talking to himself. It was good to see him excited about something again.

Bartholomew's eyes roamed around Clara's room. The walls and floors were constructed of boards, but Clara had said *under* the board, not *behind* it. They must be under a floorboard. He got down on his knees and began prodding the floorboards. None of them moved at all. He stood up and looked around the room. Where would a young rabbit hide something? Under the mattress? Under the bed! He hadn't checked the floorboards under the bed. He pulled it away from the wall and pushed at the floor boards. One of them wobbled. Using his pocket knife he pried up the loose board and found a single booklet stuffed into the space beneath the floorboard. He pulled it out and looked at it. Written in pencil on the cover were the words 'Clara Rabbit's Diary'. He opened the diary and flipped through it. She was much older when she wrote this one. He sat on Clara's bed and began to read.

March 13 – It's been almost two years since Mama died in the epidemic. Many other rabbits in the area also succumbed to the dreadful disease. I'm still not sure what I shall do. I could stay and tend the farm as I have been doing, or I could sell the farm and return to Lepus Hollow in the hopes of finding Bartholomew. I am at a crossroads and not certain which direction to take. It has been so long since Molly Ann called me a shaper but still I am afraid to ask the tree if that's what I am. I don't want Bartholomew to find out I'm a shaper if it's something dark and evil. Molly is a good soul but she seemed so afraid of me. All I did was make an apple.

July 9 – I visited the tree today. It seems odd going there without buckets but I make the raspberries at home now with Mama gone. I still miss her dreadfully. The tree said many funny things that made me laugh, but I will admit sometimes its humor gets just a tiny bit tiresome. It was funnier when I was little, but it is still my dear friend no matter what. I asked to speak with the grown up voice and he said I should call him the Great Tree now. That is his real name. I got the courage to ask him what shapers are and if I was one. He said I was a shaper and one of the most naturally talented ones he has ever seen, and he has seen many. He told me shaping is a skill, like building cabinets or playing the guitar. He seemed especially kind today and told me not to worry, that I was a good rabbit and would express that goodness through my shaping. He said most rabbits are afraid of shapers because they don't understand it, or because they have heard tales about shapers who have done bad things. The Great Tree told me there is a Shapers Guild that has existed for many centuries. If I chose to join the Guild the Great Tree would tell me who to talk to.

Bartholomew could barely contain his excitement. A Shapers Guild? There was a large group of rabbits who could do this? He flipped the page to the next entry.

August 15 – I have decided what to do. Before I find Bartholomew I am going to join the Shapers Guild. I need to better understand the nature of this gift (or curse) I have. It seems to be growing stronger every day. I have spoken at great length with my secret voice, and we are in agreement. The voice said it is my destiny to do this and if I do not, it will negatively effect many future events. I trust the advice of my secret voice above all else. I will talk to the Great Tree tomorrow.

August 16 - I visited the Great Tree this morning. I told him I wanted to join the Shapers Guild. He seemed very pleased and told me if I followed this path I would become an extraordinary shaper. He told me to speak with a rabbit named Morthram in the village of Penrith. Morthram Rabbit is the Guild Master of the Penrith Shapers Guild.

August 27 – Once the crops have been harvested I will leave for Penrith. It is far north of here on the Halsey River and will take me almost two weeks to walk there. Before I leave I am going to sell the chickens. It makes me sad because they remind me of my days with Mama.

Bartholomew turned to the last entry in the diary.

Sept 20 – I am leaving today for Penrith. I'm not certain when I will return, but when I do, I hope and pray Bartholomew will be with me. My secret voice has told me it is Bartholomew's destiny to meet the Great Tree. I can only guess he will be my equal in shaping, as we are in all other things. In the event I do not return and fate brings my Bartholomew to be reading this, I have left a gift for you in the dark wizard's castle. I know you will use it wisely, my dearest friend.

Chapter 9

Clara's Gift

Bartholomew was glad Oliver wasn't there to see the tears in his eyes. At last he knew where Clara had gone. He read the entry again and smiled. When they were young, he and Clara would play knight and princess. Bartholomew always insisted there should be a dreadfully scary wizard he must fight. The wizard's dark and foreboding castle was always his closet.

Bartholomew walked to the closet. He was almost afraid to open the door, to find out what Clara had left for him.

"It is your destiny." It was the Cavern of Silence.

He gripped the door handle tightly and pulled it open. The closet was empty. Had someone taken Clara's gift? He stretched as tall as he could and looked on the partially hidden upper shelf. He jumped back with a loud yelp, skittering across the room. There was something moving in the corner. It began to edge forward. When it reached the light Bartholomew gave a nervous laugh of relief. It was a thought cloud, but unlike any he had ever seen. It was not a single color, but many colors all swirling about. It floated down from the shelf and hovered in front of him, the colors whirling and changing. He could see small yellow flashing sparks in the center of the cloud. How could Clara have created something like this? He took a deep breath and touched the cloud. He was standing in the Garden with No End. Clara stood in front of him.

Bartholomew thought his heart would burst. “Clara!”

“I am not Clara, I am only a thought from Clara. Her gift to you is the gift of knowledge. I am here to teach you everything Clara has learned about thought clouds and shaping. We can stay in this garden as long as you like. When you return to Clara’s house no time will have passed. Time does not exist here on the island.”

Bartholomew could not stop staring at the image of Clara. He reached out with one paw and gave her arm a small poke. His paw passed right through her. He gave a sigh.

“One day you will find her.”

“I know.”

“Shall we begin?”

“I’m ready.”

A pink cloud floated out of Clara’s ear. “Touch the cloud.”

Bartholomew smiled to himself. He already knew how to read clouds. He reached out to touch the cloud, but it darted several feet away. When he moved closer it darted out of his reach again. Soon he found himself chasing it madly about the garden. Finally he stopped.

“I assume there is something to be learned from this exercise?”

“Sit down, please.”

Bartholomew sat on the ground.

"Suppose you see a thought leaving a rabbit's ear and you want to read it. What do you do?"

"Walk over to it and touch it."

"And if you are in a situation where that is not possible? Let's say a rabbit is on the other side of a deep chasm."

"Hmmm... that would present a problem."

"Look at the small pink cloud you were chasing. Now simply imagine it's heading towards you."

Bartholomew looked at the thought cloud and focused his thoughts, clearly seeing in his mind the cloud moving toward him. To his great surprise the cloud did exactly what it was supposed to do. A moment later it was hovering in front of him.

"Now make it float around the perimeter of the garden. You can bring thought clouds to you and send your thought clouds to others if you know where they are. But of course whoever you send it to must be able to read thought clouds."

Before long Bartholomew had complete control over the cloud, making it leap and fly about the garden.

"Very good. As Clara suspected, you are a quick learner. You have a remarkable natural ability for this."

"Now comes a more difficult task. We are going to learn about shaping. Shaping is not achieved by using the self you are used to. This makes it harder in some ways, but far easier in others. You will be using your inner self. I can see the Great Gem in your paw so I know you are familiar with your secret voice within."

"Yes, I call it the Cavern of Silence."

"Very good. We will begin by shaping something you love, something you are emotionally attached to.

That is the easiest type of object to create. Think of something which means a great deal to you but has a simple form."

"Done."

"This is what I want you to do. See the object clearly in your mind. Turn it around, feel the weight and depth of it, and feel the love you have for this object. Then I want you to simply send it to your Cavern of Silence and ask him to bring it into your world."

"I'll try."

Bartholomew closed his eyes and saw a small red wooden heart Clara had given him on the Valentine's Day before she had left Lepus Hollow. He still had the heart in his desk drawer at home. He moved the heart around in his mind and viewed it at different angles. When the image was sharp and clear he said, "Cavern, this is the wooden heart Clara gave me. Please bring it into this world."

He opened his eyes. A large pink thought cloud had come out of his ear. It floated down in front of him and began to whirl around. Faster and faster it spun, getting smaller and denser as it got closer to the ground. There was a small flash of light and the spinning cloud vanished. Lying on the ground in front of Bartholomew was a small oddly shaped lump of purple wood.

"Again, please."

Bartholomew sighed. This was going to take longer than he thought.

It took Bartholomew seven more tries before Clara's red wooden heart sat in front of him.

"You are indeed gifted. That simple task has taken some shapers many, many years to master. You were successful after only eight attempts."

"Now, I want you to imagine an apple."

Bartholomew smiled. He knew it was only a thought of Clara, but it was wonderful to see her there talking to him.

"Pay attention please. I will remind you again I am not Clara. Now, the apple?"

Bartholomew once again had no idea how long he had been there. There had been so many lessons with Clara. Had it been an hour or a hundred years? He did not think he would ever get used to being in a place where time did not exist.

Shaping was becoming a natural reflex for Bartholomew. He could quickly create almost any small object now, even complex ones. The last object he shaped surprised both him and Clara. He had made a working pocket watch with almost thirty perfect little spinning gears. He had a thought as he looked at the watch. What would a clock do in a place where time did not exist? He watched the second hand slowly move around the face of the clock, but soon forgot how long he had been watching it and how many times it had gone around. After several tries he gave up and put the watch in his pocket.

"You have done exceptionally well, Bartholomew. There is one more lesson for now. We have shaped things which exist. Now we will shape things which exist only in your mind. I want you to imagine a white ball the size of an egg. When you throw the ball it will softly burst in the air and one hundred yellow flowers will fall to the ground forming the shape of a star."

Bartholomew just stared at Clara. "Clara can do this?"

"Clara could do this when she was a bunny."

Bartholomew rolled his eyes. “Of course she could.”

A minute or a hundred years later Bartholomew was still sitting in the Garden with No End. In front of him were fifty spinning green clouds. Each cloud gradually transformed into a shiny round ball, then the balls all changed colors and moved to form a single large rotating circle. The circle began to close. When the balls reached the center they merged into one large multicolored ball, which then expanded. As it grew in size, its color faded until it was almost transparent. Bartholomew stood up. The invisible sphere moved toward him and gradually enveloped him. He vanished from sight. When the sphere moved away from him he became visible again. Clara nodded her approval.

“That was your last lesson for this session, Bartholomew. You have every right to be proud of what you have accomplished. There are many, many other forms of shaping, but those are for another day. Some of them are extremely dangerous and the ethics of some are still being debated among shapers. I will send you back now, but whenever you wish to learn more, you may simply touch Clara’s thought.”

Clara paused for a moment. “There is one last gift from Clara before you return to your world. Clara wanted you to know she has loved you always.”

Before Bartholomew could react he was back in Clara’s bedroom. He missed her more than ever.

Bartholomew found Oliver in the living room scribbling madly on a piece of paper. He looked up at Bartholomew. “Did you find the other diaries?”

“There was only one diary. Clara went to the village of Penrith to join the Shapers Guild. It will take us about two weeks to walk there. There’s something else.

I think it's time we talked. Would you care for a freshly baked molasses cookie from Dorothy Rabbit's Bakery in Lepus Hollow?"

"That's a very peculiar question to ask. Are you feeling all right?"

Bartholomew held out his paw. There was a brief flash of light and a large warm molasses cookie appeared on it. Oliver looked up at him in surprise. "Yes, we should talk."

Bartholomew sat down on the couch next to Oliver. "Do you remember when I told you I had stayed on a lovely island during my time in the Swamp of Lost Things? There was more to it than that. The place I discovered is called the Most Beautiful Island, and time as we know it does not exist there..."

An hour later, Oliver sat staring at Bartholomew with an intensely curious look.

"This Cavern of Silence tells you things that you don't already know?"

"Yes, he said he exists outside of space and time and I am guessing this allows him access to events which will occur in the future and events which have happened in the past. It's still confusing to me, but I do trust everything he says and he has never broken that trust. Sometimes his messages are cryptic, but in time the meaning becomes clear. I often get feelings from him rather than words, which in some ways is a much more efficient way to communicate."

"This is all so interesting. A year ago I would have laughed at you, but the impossible things we have seen have changed me, probably more than I am aware of. There are scientists today who say time is malleable and does not always move at the same speed. That would mean it's not outside the realm of scientific possibility for a place like your island to exist where there is no time at all. I declare, this world of ours gets stranger every day. Or more precisely, the world stays the same, but my understanding of it is always changing."

"I fear it is more than any us can ever completely fathom."

"To think you are turning thoughts into physical matter. Amazing. I wonder if the reverse would be possible. Could physical matter could be turned into a thought?"

"I hadn't thought about that. If that were possible, you could convert an object into a thought, send the thought far away and convert it back into matter again. It might put all the moving companies out of business though." Bartholomew laughed at the image of rabbits turning all their household goods into big puffy thought clouds.

"I dare not even think about the future of our world."

Bartholomew stood up. "Speaking of the future, we should prepare for our journey to Penrith. Once we arrive there, we'll be one step closer to finding Clara."

"I do hope we find her safe and sound at the Shapers Guild."

Bartholomew said nothing. He knew Clara would not be in Penrith.

It took Bartholomew and Oliver a full day to prepare for the trip. They cleaned and tidied Clara's house, leaving everything as they had found it. As he was cleaning Clara's room, Bartholomew had an idea. Could he take Clara's thought with him? Could he carry a thought with him the same as you would carry a tin of cookies?

"Oliver, do you have a large empty tin? I want to pack a few things in it."

"There's one somewhere in the back of the wagon."

Bartholomew walked out to the duplonium wagon and rummaged around looking for the tin. He noticed three long crates beneath the other supplies, and pushed one aside so he could see the label stenciled on the crate. It read, 'One Excelsior Model Mark III Electro-Vacuumator'. They had been dragging these vacuumators around behind them for weeks. What was Oliver thinking? He hollered out to Oliver, "You never did tell me why your brought along all the vacuumators."

"To sell them, obviously. I shall be making some sales calls along the road to Penrith."

Bartholomew shook his head but said nothing. He found the empty tin in the back of the wagon and carried it into Clara's room. He opened the closet door. Remembering Clara's instructions, he imagined the thought floating down from the shelf and into the empty tin. It did exactly that. The multicolored thought cloud hovered silently in the tin. "Stay in this tin until I open it again." It might be possible for him to use the thought cloud as a means of traveling to the Most Beautiful Island, but he wasn't certain if he could then leave the island through the Hallway of Doors. He put the top back on the tin and packed it carefully in the wagon.

The next day Oliver returned the house key to Clara's neighbor and told her they would be leaving, but were not certain when they would return. He said Clara had traveled to Penrith on business and they hoped to meet up with her there.

Bartholomew waited for Oliver in Clara's house. He walked through the rooms one more time and found a recent photograph of Clara which he put in his coat pocket. It might help them find her, and it would also be a great comfort to him during his travels. He went into her room, opened the closet door, and sat down on the bed. A pink cloud floated out of his ear and up to the top shelf of the closet, moving back into the corner where Clara's thought had been. It was for Clara, in the event he was unable to return.

He locked the front door behind him and found Oliver waiting out on the dirt roadway. "It's a long journey, but not as difficult as our trip to the Tree of Eyes. Once we reach the Halsey River, there is a well-traveled road which runs along the river all the way to Penrith. Clara's neighbor said there are some small villages along the way, but not many."

Oliver walked to the front of the duplonium wagon and picked up the handle. The wagon moved forward with a soft hiss.

"Every step we take brings us closer to Clara."

Chapter 10

The Road to Penrith

The weather was lovely and the walk through the lush green farm country was delightful. Bartholomew could understand why Clara's mother had decided to settle here. As they strolled along, rabbits would often come out of their houses to get a closer look at the duplonium wagon. Oliver would launch into a lengthy explanation of precisely how the duplonium engine worked. Some of the rabbits found this fascinating, but others had very droopy eyes by the time he was done. He did make one sale to a farmer who planned to use the vacuumator to power his farm machinery.

After several days of traveling through the bucolic farm country, they reached the banks of the Halsey River. It was a wide river with a strong and steady flow, which was unfortunately moving in the wrong direction. Their journey to Penrith would have been far quicker if they could have traveled there by river barge.

The road along the river was well traveled, and occasionally a rabbit would walk along next to them and begin chatting about the weather, the river, and other such topics. In the evenings they parked the duplonium wagon on the side of the road and Oliver would prepare dinner. Often times the delightful aromas of his cooking would attract neighboring campers, and Oliver was always happy to share his meals with those who were less fortunate.

On their second day of their journey, a tall rabbit strode up alongside them. He nodded politely and said, "Good afternoon, friends, I trust your day is going well?"

"Indeed it is, good sir. A lovely day to be out walking."

"And where might you be heading?"

"Ah, our destination is Penrith."

"Oh dear, have you not heard about the rock slide?"

"Rock slide?"

"Indeed so, sir. The road to Penrith has been blocked by a terrible rock slide. A section of canyon wall collapsed into the river, completely blocking the road. It's far too steep to safely climb over, and it would be quite impossible to navigate your marvelous wagon across the rubble. Large rocks in the river are preventing the barges from passing through. Anyone traveling to Penrith is being forced to take a lengthy detour around the mountains and through a pass leading to the other side of the range. I am told it adds nearly three weeks travel time to their journey. I'm sorry to be the bearer of such disappointing news, but that unfortunately is the current situation. I wish you nothing but good luck on your journey." He tipped his hat and soon had left them far behind.

"We have to get to Penrith sooner than that. There must be something we can do. Perhaps a small boat could make it past the rock slide?"

"Hmm..." said Oliver, "you have given me something to think about." He was silent for the next hour except for an occasional mumbled technical phrase. Bartholomew knew better than to bother him while he was thinking.

Finally Oliver spoke again. "I may have a solution to this impasse. Our two remaining Mark III Vacuumators will play a crucial role in this endeavor. Are you familiar with Isaac Rabbit's third law of motion?"

"Let me see... everything which is moving upwards... uh... those things which move..."

"Oh good heavens, did you attend even a single day of school? It's quite simple. 'Every action has an equal and opposite reaction'."

"Ah, yes, I see. Those words will certainly help us to navigate the river."

Oliver gave him a pitiful look. "When you fire a shotgun, the gun pushes back against your shoulder. The action is the projectile being shot forward, and the reaction is the gun being pushed backwards into your shoulder. Is this clear to you?"

"Yes, that much is clear."

"Fine. I constructed the duplonium wagon so it will float in water. I thought it would be useful in the event we needed to pull it through swampland or across a shallow lake. Now, imagine if you can, two Mark III Electro-Vacuumators bolted to the duplonium wagon with the polarity reversed on the magneto oscillators."

"Magneto what?"

"The Vacuumators will blow air out instead of sucking it in. Would it help if I drew some colorful little pictures for you?"

"There's really no need for that tone of voice. I quite understand what you are saying. The Vacuumators will blow air out the back of the duplonium wagon and, like a balloon which has been released, it will shoot forward. But hopefully not in the same fashion as a wildly out of control balloon."

"I've taken all that into consideration of course. By converting the front wheel into a rudder, we shall have complete control over the craft. We simply turn the wagon around and the rudder will be at the back of the boat where it belongs. It will take us a few days to modify the wagon, but it should save us three weeks of travel time. The wagon is certainly small enough to pass between the large rocks deposited by the rock slide. The current is strong, but it's not dangerous."

Bartholomew was initially dubious, but the more he thought about it, the more sense Oliver's plan made. He was also quite aware that Oliver was a renowned scientist and a highly regarded inventor.

That evening when they parked the duplonium wagon Oliver said, "I'm afraid you will have to play the role of chef tonight, as I shall be busy drawing up final plans for the duplonium wagon modifications. I will also prepare drawings for a number of new parts we'll need." He gave a knowing look to Bartholomew. "Are you capable of fabricating such things?"

Bartholomew looked at him with a bemused expression. There was a small flash of light and a large wrench appeared in his paw. "Just say the word. If you need me, I shall be preparing dinner." Bartholomew stepped behind the duplonium wagon. There were several flashes of orange light and a moment later he strolled out carrying a tray filled with an assortment of freshly baked pastries. "I thought we would begin dinner with dessert."

"Your methods are quite irregular, but I shall take full advantage of the situation nonetheless. Can you tell me how you prepare your éclairs?"

Later that evening, Oliver brought Bartholomew drawings of all the parts needed to modify the wagon. Bartholomew went into the tent where the flashing lights would not draw attention, emerging an hour later with a wooden crate full of shiny new parts. He set the box down in front of Oliver, who carefully sorted through all the pieces.

"Yes, these will do nicely. We should arrive at the rock slide late tomorrow afternoon and I can begin modifying the wagon in the morning. With these new parts, it won't take me as long to convert the wagon as I had anticipated. We should be ready to launch within a day.

After breakfast the following morning, they loaded their gear into the wagon and set out on the river road. They could see the mountains rising up ahead of them and the deep recess where the Halsey River had cut through the range, forming a narrow canyon. As they walked towards the distant peaks, Oliver explained again in great detail how he planned to modify the wagon. Bartholomew was quite relieved when they finally arrived at the canyon.

Chapter 11

The Adventurer

Their tall rabbit friend had been accurate in his description of the event. A large section of the canyon wall had slid down over the road and into the river. They couldn't see the entire rock slide, as the river made a sharp turn farther back into the canyon. The road had been carved into the base of the canyon alongside the river, but was of course was now blocked by the rock slide.

There were a few other rabbits in the area who had stopped to gawk at the landslide, but by dinnertime they had all gone home. Oliver and Bartholomew set up the tent and retired early, to be fully rested for the next day's labors. The conversion of the duplonium wagon would be a difficult and time consuming task.

After a hearty breakfast, work on the wagon finally began. They uncrated the two vacuumators, attached both brackets, then bolted the vacuumators to what was now the rear of the wagon. Oliver attached special modified exhaust nozzles of his own invention which would greatly increase the force and velocity of the air being expelled from the vacuumators. They added large flat metal sheets to the front wheel, bending and bolting everything together to form a smooth and functional rudder. Oliver replaced the long straight metal arm on the front of the wagon with one that curved up and backwards over the crates and boxes. This would allow them to maneuver the rudder while sitting in the wagon. Bartholomew would steer while Oliver operated the vacuumators. After securely tying everything down, Oliver walked around the wagon several times, poking and prodding to make sure nothing was out of order.

They maneuvered the wagon over to a shallow sandy area by the river, then rolled it into the water. Bartholomew checked carefully for leaks and found none. Oliver tested the two vacuumators, first reversing the polarity of the magnetos with a small yellow lever. When he turned the red dials, the vacuumators roared like two small hurricanes. The wind almost knocked Bartholomew off his feet when he accidentally stepped in front of the nozzles. Finally, when they were both satisfied with every detail of the wagon, they rolled it out of the water.

"I think we've done it, my friend. Everything is working flawlessly. My guess is it will take us only an hour or so to make our way upriver through the canyon. Who knows, if this works as well as I suspect it will, the ship might even carry us all the way to Penrith."

"I believe we should celebrate her completion with a bottle of fine pinot grigio."

"A sound proposition, indeed."

After a delicious dinner, Bartholomew and Oliver discussed their plans for Penrith. The first item on their agenda would be to find Morthram, Guild Master of the

Penrith Shapers Guild. If Morthram didn't know where Clara was, they would be back to square one.

A beautiful starry evening found Bartholomew sitting by the river. As he sat watching it flow past, his mind was filled with a soft and melodic tune from long ago. It was a song his grandfather used to sing to him when he was a bunny. The words had a far different meaning to him now.

There's a clock in my room with two silver hands,
Moving so slowly, it's hard to understand,
How the time is flying by.

There's a tree on my street, tall and grand,
Growing so slowly, it's hard to understand,
How the time is flying by.

Two silver hands won't slow down,
Time is a river, and love is to be found
While the time is flying by.

Bartholomew rose early, his mind whirling with thoughts of their impending journey on the Halsey River. He examined the wagon one final time, checking and rechecking to make sure nothing was amiss. He turned his eyes to the river, then up to the mountains and the clear blue sky above. It seemed like a lifetime since his first visit to the Cavern of Silence. So much had happened. The possibility of finding Clara had changed everything. Cavern was right, he was not the same rabbit he had been before, with his naive ideas about adventuring. He wondered how the years had changed Clara. From what he had read in her diaries, they seemed to be growing in the same direction. He had a feeling when he saw her again it would be as if no time had passed.

Oliver emerged from the tent an hour later, fully dressed and ready to go.

"I'll make breakfast and then we can launch the wagon."

As they ate, they discussed tactics for maneuvering the boat upriver.

"I believe we should stick close to the other side of the river, staying as far away from the rock slide as possible. Once we have passed the slide area, we can find a sandy shore to land the craft, or if things are going well, we can continue on upriver."

Bartholomew agreed. "A sound plan if ever I heard one."

"Shall we take our leave?"

They cleaned up the remains of breakfast and doused the fire, then headed over to the wagon and rolled it into the river. Bartholomew held up his paw for Oliver to stop. "One last thing before we leave." There was a small flash of light and a bottle of champagne appeared in his paw.

"You can shape champagne? Why have you not told me this?"

"Ha! A bunny could do it!" Bartholomew raised the bottle and swung it into the side of the wagon, smashing it to pieces. "I christen thee, *The Adventurer*."

Oliver nodded. "I like it. *The Adventurer* she is. For the record, I have absolute faith in *The Adventurer's* seaworthiness and for our successful voyage up the river."

"All aboard who's going aboard!"

They climbed onto the wagon, which was now bobbing up and down in the water. Oliver took his place in the back of the craft and started both vacuumators. Soon they were roaring loudly, shooting out two powerful jets of air behind the boat. Bartholomew sat in the center of *The Adventurer* and took command of the rudder, which moved smoothly in both directions. "Cast off, Captain Oliver!"

Oliver laughed. He turned both vacuumator dials to the right and the roaring sound increased threefold. Bartholomew could scarcely hear Oliver's voice above the thundering vacuumators. *The Adventurer* moved into the river, gaining speed with each moment. Bartholomew swung the rudder to the left and they were heading upriver towards the opposite shore. They were on their way.

The Adventurer performed flawlessly as it made its way across the Halsey. Oliver gave the thumbs up sign to Bartholomew, who quickly returned it.

Bartholomew pulled the rudder gently to the left, making a slight correction to the ship's course. Without warning, the world around him became a silent one, the sounds of the vacuumators and the river simply fading away to nothing. He was familiar with the sensation and knew what would come next. Seconds later, the Cavern of Silence spoke.

"You will soon have to make a terrible decision. There will be two choices facing you. Whichever one you choose will mark the beginning of an unalterable chain of events."

The roaring of the vacuumators returned. Bartholomew didn't want to think about decisions which would begin a chain of unalterable events. Not now, anyway. He would talk with the Cavern of Silence after they had safely passed the rock slide.

He returned his focus to *The Adventurer*. She was moving easily against the current. Once they had crossed to the other side of the river, Bartholomew swung the rudder over and headed directly upriver. *The Adventurer* pushed its way past the first section of the rock slide and entered into the canyon. When they rounded the curve in the river he could see the rock slide was far larger and longer than they had initially suspected. It had slid farther into the river here, greatly narrowing the passageway. Bartholomew looked back at Oliver, who had a worried look on his face. He hollered out to Bartholomew.

"Are you familiar with Bernoulli Rabbit's principle?"

"What?"

Oliver shook his head. "The river is getting narrower, which means the speed of the current will increase enormously. I'm not certain we have enough power to overcome it!"

"I don't think we have a choice. We don't have enough room to safely turn the boat around."

Oliver nodded and pointed ahead. They would continue on. He turned both dials to the right as far as they would go. The vacuumators were running at full power now. Their thundering roar echoed through the canyon as *The Adventurer* plowed ahead through the rushing torrents of water.

The boat forged its way deeper into the canyon. The current was increasing in speed as the river narrowed, but the enormous power of the vacuumators kept the craft moving forward at a steady pace. Oliver gave the thumbs up sign again.

That was when Bartholomew noticed the rocks ahead.

Chapter 12

Bartholomew's Choice

The rocks were protruding just above the surface of the water, creating enormous swells of white foam as the river raged and churned around them. He shouted out a warning, but Oliver did not hear him over the deafening vacuumators. *The Adventurer* hit the rocks with a terrible grinding sound, tipping wildly to one side. Water rushed into the craft through a huge gash in floor. Bartholomew tried to move the rudder but it had been too badly damaged. He saw the desperate look on Oliver's face. In a matter of moments *The Adventurer* would succumb to the raging river.

He heard the Cavern of Silence again. "Clara's thought."

The tin! If they could touch Clara's thought cloud in the tin, it would instantly transport them to the Most Beautiful Island. He crawled across the crates until he found it. He wrenched the tin out and pulled off the lid. The thought cloud was still there.

Oliver shut down the vacuumators and hollered to Bartholomew.

"What should we do?"

Bartholomew crawled frantically across the crates towards him. "Touch the thought cloud! It will take us to the Most Beautiful Island."

"There's nothing in the tin."

"Put your paw in it."

Oliver jabbed his paw into the tin. Nothing happened. There was a terrible sound of tearing metal as *The Adventurer* moved several feet farther across the rocks. Bartholomew realized Clara's thought would only work for someone who could read thought clouds. Oliver could not use it.

"It doesn't work for me. You must save yourself. Touch the thought cloud. I'll be fine."

Time seemed to stop. This was what the Cavern of Silence had warned him about. He could save himself, but he would be leaving Oliver to face the deadly river alone. He looked at his friend, who was still gesturing for him to touch Clara's thought cloud. He thought about Clara and the kind of rabbit she was, and the kind of rabbit he wanted to be. She had not created this thought cloud so he could use it to abandon his friend.

"No, I am staying with you. We will find another way." With a flash of light a long rope appeared in his paw. There was a three pronged metal hook tied to the end of it. He whirled the heavy hook over his head and sent it flying toward the rocks at the edge of the river. It landed between two boulders. He pulled the rope tight. The hook was trapped securely between the two jagged rocks.

"Grab the rope and don't let go!"

Bartholomew pulled himself up and forward until he was standing up on the side of the shuddering craft. A moment later Oliver stood next to him gripping the rope.

"We must jump into the river as *The Adventurer* slides off the rocks or we shall go down with her." Oliver nodded.

There was a final terrible rending of metal as the ship began lurching off the rocks into the raging river.

"Jump!"

Still gripping the rope they both leaped into the water, desperately pulling themselves toward the rocks on the shore. Less than a minute later they lay panting on the edge of the rushing river. They were alive, but *The Adventurer* was gone, along with Clara's thought and all their supplies. They inched their way up the steep jagged rocks. When they were safely above the river, Bartholomew pointed farther into the canyon.

"We can follow the canyon wall until we reach the road."

They clung to the rocks, moving like crabs from one to the other until finally arriving at the end of the colossal rock slide. Clambering down the jagged mountain of debris they were soon standing on the road below. The river was wide here, its slow and steady current giving no hint of the terrible rapids they had barely survived.

"Bartholomew, without your help I would not have..." Oliver didn't finish the sentence.

"Not a word. You would have done the same for me. That's what friends do. Now, let's find our way out of this dreadful canyon."

They walked along the road, hugging the canyon

wall. Neither of them wanted to get too close to the river.

"What in the world is this?"

Bartholomew had found a doorway cut into the side of the canyon. The door was constructed of heavy iron bars, resembling something from the Age of Darkness. It was locked shut with a massive padlock.

"I suppose it's a tunnel of some sort left over from the construction of the road."

Bartholomew peered through the bars. It was not a tunnel, but a shaft, going straight down into the earth. It was round and smooth, about fifteen feet across. This was not a natural formation. Someone had built it, but there were no clues who that might have been. With a flash of light a bright sphere appeared in front of him, floated between the bars and then downward, lighting up the interior of the shaft. After several hundred feet he could see where the tunnel turned, and the glowing sphere disappeared from sight. He had learned nothing about the shaft except it was long and deep.

"It looks as though we've stumbled onto still yet another mystery."

They continued on towards the end of the canyon. When they finally emerged into the open fields, they were close to exhaustion. Their wet clothes had soon dried in the warm sun, which did much to improve their mood. As they were hobbling along, Oliver spied a wooden structure in the distance, partially hidden by trees. When they drew closer they could see it was a two story building constructed entirely of logs. It seemed tidy and well kept. The was large colorful sign on the front which read:

THE FERILLIUM INN
A Welcome Haven for Weary Travelers

"Perfect. This is exactly what we need. It will give us time to rest, and in a day or two I can shape more supplies."

"Not be a purveyor of gloom, but we have no money. Everything we had went down with *The Adventurer.*"

A look of panic appeared on Bartholomew's face. "My dark glasses!" He reached into his pocket and found them still there. "We have the dark glasses, but no coins. I believe I can remedy that situation." He opened his paw and five gold coins appeared in a flash of light.

"Ah. I keep forgetting your unusual ability. Onward to the inn then."

Chapter 13

Theodore Rabbit

They pulled open the front door of the inn and entered. It was warm and cozy, and the air was filled with the delightful aroma of baking bread.

The rabbit behind the counter greeted them cordially.

"A good day to you, sirs. If you are looking for a room you have come to the right place. The rock slide has greatly diminished our normal traffic, and consequently we have numerous rooms available."

"That is welcome news, my friend. We are quite weary from our travels. Our supplies were lost to the river, but we are at least able to pay for food and lodging."

"Excellent. I shall place you in a large room with a lovely view of the Halsey."

"Perfect, although I fear we have already seen more than we care to of that river."

The dinner served that evening was excellent, and Oliver commented several times how tasty it was. Afterwards they took a short walk around the inn, then retired for the night. They slept late the next morning, resting up from their exhausting experience on the river. Breakfast was waiting for them when they arrived downstairs.

The innkeeper's name was Theodore Rabbit, and he had lived most of his life along the Halsey River. "We really have no idea what caused the terrible rock slide. Some rabbits say they heard a low rumbling noise right before it occurred. The only thing I can guess is there was a small earthquake, although it would be quite unusual for this area. Speaking of which, I don't recognize you as being from around this area. Do you live far from here?"

"Yes, quite far indeed. I live in a small village called Lepus Hollow. We are heading towards Penrith on business. My friend Oliver is a scientist employed by the Excelsior Electro-Vacuumator Corporation."

"I am currently the head of research and material acquisitions."

"How wonderful to have such a distinguished rabbit at our humble inn. I suppose all your family members are breathlessly following your exploits?"

"That is unfortunately not the case. We are trying to find my sister. Last we heard she was in Penrith, so that is our destination."

"Ah, I see. I certainly wish you the very best of luck in finding her."

Bartholomew suddenly felt very cold. He paid close attention to his feelings now, but could find no good reason for this one. After a few moments the feeling vanished. Perhaps it had just been his overactive imagination.

"Oliver, why don't we take a walk outside. I should

like to see some of this area while we're here."

"Excellent idea. A brisk walk after breakfast is quite good for one's constitution."

They both stood up and excused themselves.

"Let's walk over through those trees. We need a secluded area where I can shape new supplies for our trip to Penrith. It would take too long to create a new duplonium wagon, so for now I'll just shape a simple wooden cart we can pull behind us. We'll also need food and new clothing."

"Yes, and several bottles of champagne."

"Thank you for reminding me. I would hate to forget something as crucial as champagne."

"At last we have found some common ground."

Bartholomew gave a loud snort. He turned his focus to the work at hand and soon had fabricated a basic wooden cart. Next came the shaping of the supplies they would need for the trip. Several hours later everything was carefully packed in the wagon, including two bottles of a very fine champagne. Oliver found branches and leaves lying about the area which he collected to cover the wagon.

"I believe I have something which will be slightly more effective than branches."

There was a flash of light in his paw and a green ball floated down to the ground. It quickly grew in size, its color fading rapidly. As it floated towards the wooden wagon, it continued to grow until it was nearly twelve feet across. The sphere had become completely transparent and was enveloping the wagon. The sections of the wagon which were inside the sphere disappeared. Soon the whole wagon had vanished.

Oliver was astonished. "How did you make the

wagon disappear?"

"The basic idea is when light hits the sphere, instead of bouncing off, it travels around to the opposite side of the sphere, then continues on in the same direction it was going when it first hit the sphere. When you look at the sphere you see everything that's behind it, but not what is inside it."

"How marvelous. I do believe there is a glimmer of hope that one day you might become a fine scientist."

"And perhaps I shall teach you to read thought clouds."

Oliver laughed. "I'm afraid I make a far better scientist than a thought reader."

With the wagon safely hidden, they headed back to the inn. Upon their return they discovered there were three new guests. Two rather rough looking rabbits were seated at one table, and a third rabbit was sitting by himself. His clothes were well tailored, but strangely out of fashion.

Oliver was his usual gregarious self and greeted the new guests.

"Good afternoon, my friends, I do hope you are having a wonderful day. I'm quite certain you will enjoy your stay here at the inn. I can tell you from personal experience the food is delicious."

The two rough looking rabbits looked up at Oliver. One of them gave a small grunt in reply to Oliver's greeting. The well dressed rabbit gave a painfully insincere smile.

Oliver turned to the innkeeper. "Good sir, I have a question which will not seem to leave me alone. Your inn is called the Ferillium Inn, and as a scientist I am quite familiar with a rare element which bears the same name. Is there a connection between your inn and the element known as ferillium?"

"Ah, a question I have been asked before. The answer is no. Ferillium is simply the name of the inn's original owner. An odd name to be sure, but that is the truth of the matter."

"My thanks to you, sir. I shall no longer have that question pestering me at all hours of the day."

"Might I inquire how much longer you will be staying with us here at the inn?"

"We shall be leaving for Penrith in the morning, so this will be our last night here. It has been a most enjoyable diversion from a rather distressing journey."

"Very good. I shall plan a special farewell dinner for our two esteemed visitors."

Bartholomew shivered. The cold feeling was worse than before. "Oliver, perhaps we should head upstairs and prepare for the trip tomorrow?"

When they were back in the room, Bartholomew confessed his feeling of dread to Oliver. There was nothing he could point to as the source of this sense of foreboding, but the feeling was growing stronger. Oliver suggested it might be nothing more than a residual uneasiness from their perilous experience on *The Adventurer*. Bartholomew did not think so, and after some discussion they found themselves no closer to an explanation. Oliver decided he would take a nap and Bartholomew followed suit. When they arose, Bartholomew shaped them each a change of clothing and they went downstairs for dinner.

As promised, the innkeeper had prepared a lovely meal for them. Oliver was supremely impressed with the innkeeper's culinary expertise and they spent quite some time discussing various recipes. When they had finished the main course, the innkeeper brought out a freshly baked apple pie.

"This is an old and secret recipe of mine, and I promise it to be an apple pie you will not soon forget." He smiled graciously and put the pie down on the table in front of them. He cut each of them a large slice, carefully sliding it onto their plates. Then he poured a small amount of warm cream on top of the pie.

"Enjoy, my friends. It has been a pleasure having you as our guests." He smiled and walked around the bar into the kitchen.

Bartholomew's bad feeling was stronger than ever. The pie was delicious, but something was not right. He could not stop shivering.

Oliver looked up from his empty plate. "An extraordinary pie, but I'm afraid all this food has made me quite sleepy, even after my long nap. I'm rather embarrassed to say I could take another nap this very moment."

Bartholomew glanced over at the two rough looking rabbits eating dinner. A dark gray thought cloud floated out of one rabbit's ear. Bartholomew pulled the cloud across the room to him. He was instantly filled with a cruel, heartless feeling, and heard the words, "Them little rich pants rabbits will be sleeping like bunnies in another minute. They'll be shakin' paws with Mr. Ferillium before the day is done."

Bartholomew leaped to his feet. The innkeeper had drugged the pie. Oliver fell across the table with a loud thud, sound asleep. The door to the kitchen opened and a frightful face peered out. It was a shadow like the Skeezles. There was a flash of light and a white sphere appeared in Bartholomew's paw. He raised his arm to throw it towards the two rough looking rabbits. The last thing he remembered before everything went black was someone shouting, "Look sharp, he's a shaper!"

Chapter 14

Descent into Darkness

The first thing Bartholomew became aware of was a rhythmic rattling noise and a terrible headache. Next he noticed he couldn't move his arms. He struggled briefly, then drifted back to sleep, hoping the pain in his head would go away. The rattling sound grew louder and woke him again. This time he managed to open his eyes. He was riding in some sort of cart. He turned his head. Oliver was next to him, sound asleep, his arms and legs tied up with heavy rope. Bartholomew looked down at his own arms. He was tightly bound just as Oliver was.

"Wakey up, little rich pants rabbit. You has a lovely nappy?"

Bartholomew heard crude laughter from whoever was pushing the cart. He twisted his head around and saw two rat creatures who closely resembled the Skeezle brothers. He remembered the Skeezle's words, "We are shadows, but there is no cause to be afraid." These must be the real shadows. They were hideous. Behind them was the tall rabbit from the inn who wore the outdated clothing.

"What are you doing with us?"

One of the shadows pointed his paw at Bartholomew. "You goes to new working place, rich pants. No more fancy corporation or such for you. You working for Mr. Ferillium. I hope you don't *mine*."

The second shadow burst out with high pitched screeching laugh. "I hope you don't *mine*? I get joking. Is a good joking, Merkel." He turned towards Bartholomew and said loudly, "Yeah, I HOPING YOU DON'T MINE."

"Ain't so funny if you says joke a lots. Only first time is funny."

"Funny if I says it louder."

"Maybe some."

Bartholomew peered over the top of the wagon trying to see where they were. It looked like they were on the river road as it headed back into the canyon. Oliver began to stir.

"Uhh... can't move my arms. I declare, this is a very odd —" He opened his eyes and looked at his arms. "Good heavens, why am I trussed up like some wild beast?" He managed to focus his eyes on their captors. "Who are these creatures? Hold on, it's those dreadful Skeezle brothers. Are you still angry about that duplonium incident at your house? I will gladly reimburse you for any damage we may have caused. Furthermore, I demand you release us this instant or you shall pay dearly."

"Oh goodness Merkel, we is paying dearly. The fear is filled in me now."

"You cracking me up, Zobo. I hope you don't MINE."

"No mine joking no more. It not funny now."

"Still funny."

The tall rabbit pushed his way past Merkel and Zobo.

"Good Lord, enough of your ridiculous jabbering. Your very presence is an assault to my senses. I want to hear nothing but silence from both of you." He looked at Oliver and Bartholomew. "Allow me to introduce myself. I am known as Mr. Ferillium. I can deeply appreciate what you must be feeling at this time. How distressing to awaken from deep slumber and find yourself tied up in a cart headed for who knows where. Fortunately, I know precisely where you are heading. You will be joining the rest of my captive workers deep underground in King Oberon's personal ferillium mine. I'm quite certain you will simply love it there and won't ever want to leave. You may be assured you never will."

Bartholomew was now fully awake. He tried to shape a pocket knife to cut his ropes but felt only a violent shock to his left ear.

"A valiant effort, little shaper. You are unfortunately wearing a rather unique mask created by an ingenious employee of mine who also happens to be a gifted shaper. As I'm sure you have noticed, thought clouds cannot pass through it. The only thing you will produce is a rather painful shock to your ear. We will be removing this mask at a later date, but sadly it will be after you have departed from this lovely world of ours. I might add that not a single shaper in the mine has ever managed to remove their mask, and many have tried, some with rather gruesome results."

Bartholomew turned his head towards Oliver, who

had a terrified expression on his face.

Finally the cart creaked to a halt. Bartholomew peeked out between the slats and saw the same heavy iron door they had examined when they exited the canyon.

Merkel and Zobo rocked the cart back and forth, tipping it over onto its side. Oliver and Bartholomew tumbled out onto the roadway. Mr. Ferillium took a large brass key from his coat pocket and opened the padlock. The iron door swung open with a loud squealing noise. Reaching his arm up behind the doorway, Mr. Ferillium pulled down the end of a heavy rope which had a long hook attached to it. The rope appeared to be wound around some sort of pulley apparatus.

"Great heavens, you're not going to drop us down into that ghastly hole are you?"

"You say you are a scientist and yet you display a stunning lack of curiosity. Do you not want to discover what lies at the bottom of the shaft? No matter, you will both find out shortly."

Merkel grabbed the long hook and slid it through the ropes tied around Bartholomew and Oliver's feet, while Zobo untied the ropes binding their arms. Mr. Ferillium pulled out a silver whistle hanging from a thin gold chain around his neck. He poked his head into the doorway and blew three short bursts on the whistle. Moments later a distant clanking noise echoed up through the shaft. The rope began to tighten, dragging Oliver and Bartholomew feet first through the doorway. Oliver let out a loud yelp as they swung out into empty space several hundred feet above the bottom of the shaft.

"Farewell, my esteemed guests. We shall meet again soon, but unfortunately it will be under far less pleasant circumstances."

Mr. Ferillium gave the whistle one long blast. The rope shuddered slightly and the clanking sound started up again. Bartholomew and Oliver began their long descent into the darkness below.

After several terrifying minutes, they reached the bottom of the shaft. Bartholomew untied the ropes around his feet, then untied Oliver's. They heard the clanking noise again and the long rope snaked back up the shaft.

Oliver's eyes roamed the shadowy tunnel. "What is this dreadful place? He said we would be captive workers in a ferillium mine. I daresay, I am not the least bit interested in that sort of thing. Is there some way we can escape, now that we are free of the ropes?"

"I don't see how. We can't climb up the shaft, so our only option is to go in the other direction. Perhaps along the way an opportunity will present itself. I've tried several times to shape objects, but with no success. I've also attempted to remove this fiendish mask, again with no luck. It's unnaturally strong and is attached to my head in a way that is quite incomprehensible to me. It feels as though it has become part of me."

Oliver sighed deeply. "I suppose you're right. All we can do is move forward and discover what fate has in store for us. In hindsight, I do wish we had paid more attention to your feelings of dread at the inn. Theodore Rabbit was a dastardly and fiendish innkeeper. Although, in his behalf, he was also quite a marvelous chef. I sincerely believe that was the tastiest apple pie I have ever eaten."

There were times when Bartholomew found Oliver's mind to be completely baffling. This was one of those times. They walked forward into the darkness, following the shaft as it sloped deep beneath the mountain range.

The shaft seemed to go on forever. Their only sense of progress was from the distant sounds echoing up through the tunnel which gradually grew louder the farther they traveled. Finally, they saw light coming from around a curve in the tunnel far ahead. As they turned the sharp bend, the shaft dropped off unexpectedly, causing them to lose their footing and tumble down through the shaft out onto an enormous mound of straw. Bartholomew rolled off the pile of straw and looked around. They were inside a large cage made of heavy iron bars. What lay outside the cage was astonishing.

They were sitting at the edge of the largest cavern Bartholomew had ever set eyes on. It appeared to be at least a mile or more across in both directions. There were hundreds of wooden buildings sitting on the floor of the cavern, giving it the feel of a small city. Roads were carved into the sides of the cavern, spiraling around it all the way up to the roof. He could see hundreds of rabbits walking along the roads, pushing heavy wooden carts in front of them. The cavern was lit by thousands of glowing spheres floating high above its rocky floor.

"Oliver, I believe we have found King Oberon's ferillium mine."

Chapter 15

R75

"Good heavens, this mine is gargantuan. I've studied large mining operations for the Excelsior Corporation, but they all pale in comparison to this. To think this was sitting under our feet the whole time we were at the inn. It's quite fantastic."

Bartholomew was not as enthralled with the mine as Oliver was. He was more focused on finding an avenue of escape. He examined the cage but found it quite solid. Hanging from the top of the cage was a bell with a string dangling down from the clapper. "It looks as though we're supposed to announce our arrival. I suppose we can't stay in here forever. Shall I ring the bell or would you like to?"

"I will let that honor be yours."

Bartholomew pulled the string sharply, producing a loud clanging noise. Moments later the door to a nearby building swung open and a tall rabbit emerged. It was Mr. Ferillium.

"Ah, I see our guests have arrived." He gave another of his exaggerated and obviously insincere smiles.

"Might I ask how long you will be staying with us at the mine? Hold on a moment, I remember now, you'll be staying here forever." He pulled out his whistle and blew a long blast on it.

Two shadows scurried out from the building. Bartholomew didn't think they were the same ones who had pushed them to the mine shaft, as one of them was wearing a long blue hat. They walked over to Mr. Ferillium and one began to speak rapidly, using a curious combination of squeals, squeaks and clicking noises. Mr. Ferillium gave a loud sigh. "I am afraid your squeaks and squeals are quite incomprehensible to me. Would you care to try again?"

The rat creature with the blue hat stamped his foot and said, "Should I take the prisoners to Bunkhouse R?"

"Only the smaller rabbit will be going with you. The larger one stays with me. His new home is the mechanical engineering compound and his new employment is repair and maintenance of the duplonium powered diggers. I also have a number of personal projects for Mr. Oliver T. Rabbit. A great mind should not be wasted on such menial tasks as physical labor. Take the other one to Bunkhouse R. Come along, Oliver."

The rat creature looked at Bartholomew. "I am Fen. I strongly advise you to cause no trouble."

Bartholomew called out to Oliver, "Don't lose hope." Oliver turned to look back at Bartholomew. His face already wore a hopeless expression.

Bartholomew walked along behind Fen as they weaved their way through the maze of wooden buildings on their way to the bunkhouse. He decided to attempt a conversation with him.

"You're a Grymmorian shadow?" The rat creature stopped in its tracks, then turned to Bartholomew with a terrible scowl on its face.

"I am a muroidian from Grymmore. The word you used is despicable. If you use that term with one of the guards, they will kill you before the word is out of your mouth."

"Oh dear, I do apologize. I had no idea it was offensive to Grymmorians."

Fen gave a sniff and made a clicking noise. "Follow me." He turned his back to Bartholomew and walked forward. After many twists and turns through the narrow alleys they finally stopped at a long structure on the far side of the cavern. Painted on the front of the building was a large letter 'R'.

"This is Bunkhouse R, your new home. Do not forget this. Wait here. If you try to run you will more than likely be killed by the guards."

Fen walked up to the door and pounded loudly on it. A moment later it was opened by a large scruffy rabbit wearing a tattered red vest and carrying a wooden stick about two feet long.

"Fresh rabbit, eh? Bring him in."

Bartholomew greeted the rabbit wearing the red vest.

"Good day to you, I am–"

The rabbit lashed out with the stick. It made a loud cracking noise as it whipped across Bartholomew's arm. He gave a yelp, backing away from the rabbit who had hit him.

"You talk when I tell you. Clear?"

Bartholomew nodded.

"I'm called Simon, and them shadows put me in

charge of Bunkhouse R. That means I'm in charge of you, rabbit. You do what I say when I say it."

Fen had not taken his eyes off Simon. When he had used the words 'shadows', Fen's foot imperceptibly moved up and down. Bartholomew made a mental note that Fen did not think very highly of Simon.

Fen waited while Simon signed his papers, then gathered them up, turning to leave. He looked at Bartholomew as though he was going to say something, then thought the better of it and walked away.

"Follow me." Bartholomew trailed behind Simon into the bunkhouse. The main room was at least one hundred feet long, with four rows of beds running down the length of it. Each bed had a wooden chest in front of it. Bartholomew followed Simon down one of the aisles. He stopped and pointed to a bed. "You sleep here. Number 75. Don't forget. They ask you, you're R75. Bunkhouse R, bed 75. Clear?"

Bartholomew nodded.

"You work every day, seven in the morning till seven at night. Pick up your lunch from the kitchen in the morning and take it with you. Your clothes and gear is in the box by your bed. You work hard and do what them shadows says. Make me look bad and you'll be getting worse than this stick. Clear?"

Bartholomew nodded again. It was at that moment he knew he and Oliver had to escape.

Simon left Bartholomew sitting on his bunk. He lay back, closing his eyes.

"Cavern, why am I here? I didn't abandon Oliver in *The Adventurer.* If I did what was right, why did you send me to this hideous underground world?"

"Like the bouncing marbles, you are exactly where

you are supposed to be. I cannot tell you more than that right now. I can only tell you not to give up hope. Remember to show kindness and respect to all living creatures. Each has its own Great Gem and it is their destiny to find it."

The door to the bunkhouse opened and rabbits streamed in. One by one they found their bunks and lay down. Some of them were asleep in moments. A tall, thin rabbit lay down on the bunk next to Bartholomew's. He was wearing a shaper mask.

"You're a shaper?"

"I've dabbled in it. And you?"

"I suppose I am. I haven't joined the Shapers Guild, but I have learned to shape some things. We were on our way to Penrith to look for an old childhood friend of mine when we were taken captive by the innkeeper at the Ferillium Inn."

"Theodore Rabbit. Many prisoners are here thanks to him. He is paid handsomely by the Grymmorians for his services."

"You don't call them shadows?"

"I do not."

Bartholomew was getting a very good feeling about this shaper.

"My friend who was also captured is a scientist and is working on the duplonium powered diggers, whatever those are."

"You'll see them tomorrow. Come with me in the morning and I'll teach you everything you need to know about mining ferillium. It should take you about five minutes to learn it all. I haven't been here long and sad to say, I'm an expert. By the way, I'm R74 as you can plainly see. It's a pleasure to meet you, R75."

"Those are the names we use here?"

"Only if you wish to avoid Simon's stick, or far worse from the Grymmorian guards."

"How did you come to be in the mine?"

"I was betrayed by someone I trusted. There are good shapers and bad shapers, as I'm sure you are aware."

"To be completely honest, I've never spoken to another shaper before. Would you mind if I asked you some questions?"

"Ask away."

"What are these?" He pulled the dark glasses out of his pocket and held them in front of R74.

"Put those away! Are you trying to get us killed?" R74 looked around to see if any of the other rabbits had seen them.

Bartholomew stuffed the glasses back into his pocket. R74 moved closer to Bartholomew and began talking in a low voice. "Never show those to anyone. Plenty of rabbits have lost their lives over a pair of World Glasses. They are of enormous value. You're fortunate I'm not an unscrupulous shaper like the one who sent me here."

"When I was wearing them I found something that looked like a hallway filled with doors. What was that place?"

"They are called World Doors, and very few shapers have had the opportunity to see them. I will try to explain it, but it's a complex subject. My very basic understanding of it is that there are many worlds occupying the same space. Our world is one of them. There is also a place called the Void. The Void is the dark space which separates all the worlds. No matter where you are in the Void, you are one step away from any of the worlds. The hallway you spoke of is in the Void, and each door leads to another world. World Doors are ancient beyond our understanding. That is the extent of my knowledge."

"There was a symbol on the door knob. It was a single eye. Does that mean anything to you?"

"A single eye? You saw this yourself?

"I did."

R74 looked around the room again to make certain they were not being watched. He reached inside his coat, opened a hidden pocket and withdrew a gold ring, cupping it carefully so only Bartholomew could see it. It had a single eye on it with a small diamond in the center. It was the same eye Bartholomew had seen on the World Door.

"This is a Shapers Guild ring." He slipped it back into his pocket.

"That's the same symbol I saw. Do you think shapers built the World Doors?"

"I doubt it. It's far more likely shapers adopted the symbol from an ancient culture or another world."

There was a stirring at the end of the room. Simon had entered. "Dinner for rabbits who want it!"

R74 stood up. "Time to eat, my friend. The bad news is the food is ghastly. The good news is there is plenty of it."

After dinner the rabbits all returned to the bunk house, as they were not allowed outside in the evening. Most of them lay down on their bunks and went to sleep. The twelve hour work days were exhausting. Bartholomew lay down, deciding to rest up for the next day. Sleep did not come easily with the coughing and snoring sounds that echoed throughout the bunkhouse, but eventually it did come.

He awoke abruptly the next morning to the sound of a clanging bell and Simon shouting, "Breakfast for rabbits who want it!" Bartholomew followed R74 into the dining area. Breakfast was the same as dinner but served cold. He ate as much as could, knowing he would need his strength for the day's work.

Simon rang the bell again and breakfast was over. The rabbits swarmed back to the bunkhouse and changed into their mining gear. Bartholomew found a canvas mining suit in his wooden chest, and put it on over his clothes as he had seen the other rabbits do. He followed R74 out the front door. Hundreds of rabbits were pouring out of the bunkhouses like ants, heading towards the roads which spiraled up around the outer walls of the mine. Bartholomew followed R74 up to the second tier of roads.

"This is where we work. It's not complicated. There are huge machines called diggers. That's what your friend is working on. They're shaped like fifty foot long cigars but have mammoth grinding wheels in the front. The digger bores into the side of the cavern, usually a hundred feet or so, sometimes more. The rock it grinds up passes through the main body of the digger and comes out the back. Once the digger stops, we move in. Our job is to shovel the rock fragments into wagons, then dump the ore onto the conveyor belts. I'm not sure where the belts take it, but it must go someplace where they process it to remove the ferillium. Once we clear away enough rocks to free the digger, it backs out, rolls over about twenty feet and the whole process starts over again."

"What do they do with all the ferillium?"

"The short answer is nobody really knows. I've heard rumors about something called a ferillium crystal, but there are always rumors being passed about. Here's your shovel. It'll be your friend for the next twelve hours. Keep moving no matter how slowly. The guards are far worse than Simon ever thought of being. Never make eye contact with them, and do whatever they say."

Bartholomew took the shovel from R74 and walked over to where the digger had bored into the cavern wall. He began shoveling rocks into the wagon, matching the pace of the other rabbits in the area. When his wagon was filled, R74 showed him where to take it. They rolled it onto a catwalk, then latched it to a hinged platform. R74 pulled a lever and the wagon flipped over, dumping the ore onto a monstrous conveyor belt below.

"That's it. You now know everything I know about mining ferillium."

Bartholomew laughed. "I suppose it is good exercise, with no annual club dues to worry about."

He was not in such a jovial mood at the end of the day, when he painfully dragged himself back to the bunkhouse and collapsed in a ragged heap on his bed. Day one was over, but it was only the first of many long torturous days to come.

Bartholomew gradually became accustomed to the routine of the mine. He grew stronger with time and was not so exhausted in the evenings. The food was dreadful, but it was nutritious. The Grymmorians needed the miners to be strong enough to work. A sick and hungry worker meant a decrease in the ferillium output.

Weeks passed by with only one notable event. Bartholomew was walking back to the bunkhouse at the end of his shift when he heard a commotion high above him. He looked up and saw a prisoner on one of the catwalks facing an angry Grymmorian guard. The guard was pointing and shrieking at the prisoner, but Bartholomew couldn't make out what he was saying. The guard put his paw on the prisoner's chest and pushed him off the catwalk. There was a dreadful cry, then silence. Bartholomew felt sick. The prisoner had fallen to his death. A group of rabbits gathered around their fallen friend, but there was nothing to be done. A Grymmorian guard sauntered over and eyed the dead prisoner. He gave him a sharp kick.

"No more work for this one. All you rabbits move along."

As they stepped away, Bartholomew got a clear view of the fallen prisoner. He was wearing a mask. He was a shaper. The guard took a small bottle out of his pocket and dripped a thick orange liquid onto the rabbit's mask. The viscous fluid spread out across the fabric of the mask and seconds later the mask relaxed, draping loosely over the rabbit's head. With one smooth motion the guard pulled the mask off. Bartholomew quickly turned and walked away, barely able to contain his excitement. This was the first glimmer of hope he had felt since his arrival. He needed to find out more about the orange liquid.

Bartholomew's second glimmer of hope arrived several days later at his work site. Early one morning as he stepped up onto tier two he noticed a digger sitting about fifty feet away from his section of cavern wall.

The digger was not running, and a group of rabbits and Grymmorian guards were standing around it, pointing and talking. One of the rabbits was Oliver.

Bartholomew desperately tried to think of a way let Oliver know he was there. He stepped behind his mining cart where the guards couldn't see him and smashed the wooden handle of his shovel against a sharp metal corner piece. The wood split badly. He carried the shovel over to the nearby site, making sure he stood close to Oliver.

"I am R75. Anyone have a spare shovel? This one is broken." He held the shovel up for the guards to see. Oliver turned to look at him. He had immediately recognized Bartholomew's voice. He reached out and took the shovel from Bartholomew.

"Take one from the wagon, R75. There's no need to waste a good shovel. I will repair this and leave it at your site in the morning." He turned back towards the defective digger.

By using the name R75, Bartholomew had told Oliver exactly where to find him.

When Bartholomew arrived the next morning, the repaired shovel was leaning against his mining wagon with a note tied to it. "The handle may still be slightly loose."

Bartholomew picked up the shovel and walked out of the guard's line of sight. He twisted the grip at the end of the handle. It turned. He twisted it more and it unscrewed from the wooden shaft. When he removed the handle he saw the shaft was hollow and had a rolled up paper inside. He stuffed the paper into his pocket and screwed the handle back on. He would read it when he was back in the bunkhouse.

Chapter 16

Oliver's Plan

After dinner, when all the other rabbits were lying on their bunks, Bartholomew slid the paper out of his pocket and silently unrolled it. As he had expected, it was from Oliver.

I was so glad to find you were safe and well, my old friend. I have been worried quite sick about you. I am fine, I assure you. My work is not as physically taxing as yours. I repair broken diggers and any other malfunctioning mechanical device they send my way. Mr. Ferillium has me building some small duplonium powered machines. Duplonium is in extremely short supply here and I suspect Mr. Ferillium is using these machines to line his own pockets. I'm quite certain he is selling them to buyers who visit him at the inn.

Here is the real news. I have devised a plan for our escape and I am in the process of implementing it. It involves the diggers. Do you remember the shaft which brought us to the mine? As it turns out, that shaft was made by a malfunctioning digger. It didn't stop when it was supposed to, but continued boring and turned upwards, eventually exiting at the surface. It took them months to clean up after the incident and they had to close the road so travelers would not see the digger. My plan is to modify a digger with a compartment inside where we can hide ourselves. I will add a second set of controls which override the existing ones. We can essentially drive the digger up to the surface and emerge as free rabbits. I am quite certain this will work. There is a very small chance the digger could get stuck between here and the surface, but I fear it is a risk we must endure. The digger modifications will be complete in several weeks. Please destroy this note and leave your reply in the shovel handle.

Yours truly,

Oliver

Bartholomew tore the note into tiny pieces, scattering them across the grounds on his way to work the next morning. On the way back from work he broached the subject of escapes with R74.

"Has anyone ever escaped from the mine?"

"Shhh. Lower your voice when you say that word. I don't know for certain. I have heard stories, some with happy endings, but most with very bad endings. Is this simple curiosity or is there some other reason you are asking me this question?" He looked pointedly at Bartholomew.

Bartholomew hesitated. He trusted R74, but he was not certain how much room there would be in the digger. "For now let us say it is simple curiosity."

"Simple curiosity it is then. If it turns out to be more, please let me know. I would be happy to assist in whatever venture you might be entertaining."

Bartholomew gathered scraps of paper from around

the bunkhouse and borrowed a small pencil from Simon when he was not looking. He wrote his reply to Oliver.

Oliver, I can think of no better solution to our mutual problem than the one you mentioned. I believe we should move forward with your plan. Is there any possibility there would be space for a third rabbit in our party? I have a friend who is interested. He has similar skills to mine. Also, I have seen a thick orange liquid which the guards use to remove the shaper masks. Please let me know if you can learn anything about the nature of this material. I am certain you can see the obvious benefit if we were able to obtain some of this substance.

—Bartholomew

Once Bartholomew had proven himself to be a reliable worker, Simon was not as harsh with him. He would occasionally allow Bartholomew extra privileges, and in return Bartholomew ran errands for him. Bartholomew didn't mind this at all, since it got him out of the bunkhouse. In the evenings he often ran paperwork to the various offices as prisoners were moved from one location to another. He was getting familiar with the basic configuration of the mine and knew the location of most buildings. It was on one of these errands that he ran into Fen, the Grymmorian who had first taken him to Bunkhouse R. Bartholomew was on his way to Bunkhouse L when he saw Fen standing in a narrow alleyway. He recognized him from the long blue hat he wore. Fen was leaning against a wall, his head hanging down in front of him. Bartholomew did not need to read Fen's thoughts to know he was unhappy.

"Fen?"

Fen recognized Bartholomew. "R75, the rabbit who calls me Grymmorian."

"Is something wrong? To be honest, you look... as though you'd lost your last friend."

"It's that obvious? I am homesick. There is great turmoil in Grymmore, but it is my home and I miss my friends."

"I understand how you feel. I miss my friends also. Won't they let you go home for a visit and then return?"

Fen gave him a look of surprise. "You misunderstand my role here. I am a prisoner just as you are. I would not be a party to the mining of ferillium or the use of slave labor."

"You're a prisoner? But you're a Grymmorian."

"There are good Grymmorians and bad ones. King Oberon's guards took me from my home and brought me to this place. Most of my family was killed."

"I'm very sorry to hear this, Fen. I had no idea. The Grymmorian King sounds quite despicable. He must be, to have created a place like this. Why did he create it? Does anyone know?"

Fen looked around cautiously. "All I know is, in the wrong paws even the most benign substance can be used for evil purposes."

This short conversation had a profound affect on Bartholomew. All the horror stories he had been told about Grymmorians when he was a bunny seemed silly now. Fen was not like the vicious Grymmorian guards, and if there was one Fen, there were thousands of others just like him. There was a quality about Fen that Bartholomew could not quite identify. A moment later it occurred to him what that quality might be.

Bartholomew held out his right paw, palm facing upwards. The Great Gem glowed brightly in the dark alley. Fen stared at it mutely, then held out his own paw. His Great Gem glowed brightly next to Bartholomew's.

He said to Bartholomew, "You have found the Jewel of Barsume."

"I call it the Great Gem."

"There are many names for it, but names do not change its true nature. The Jewel has told me of your escape plans. If you wish I will assist you, but only if you allow me to go with you.

"You would help me escape?

"If I am included in your plans."

"Fen, there is something you can do which would help immensely, but before I can promise you passage with us I have to find out if there's room. I will leave a mark on the wall when I know for certain. An X means yes, a Y means no."

A week later Fen handed Bartholomew a vial of the thick orange liquid. Bartholomew decided not to use it until they were in the digger. Even with his mask removed he would be no match for the hundreds of Grymmorian guards, many of whom might also be shapers. He wrote to Oliver about including a fourth passenger on the digger, also telling him he had obtained the orange liquid. When he retrieved Oliver's reply it said there was more than enough room inside the digger shell for R74 and Fen. The modifications were almost done and the digger would be ready to travel in four days. Oliver proposed they leave at night while everyone was sleeping.

Two days before their departure, Bartholomew was

sent out to deliver paperwork. He went to his secret meeting place to mark an X on the wall, but found Fen waiting there. Bartholomew gave him the good news and the specifics of their escape plan.

R74 received his good news the following morning at their worksite.

"Remember when you asked if my question was simple curiosity?"

"I do."

"It is no longer simple curiosity. If you are still interested, I would not plan on getting any sleep two nights from now."

"I am not a rabbit who needs much sleep. Let me know and I will do whatever you need done."

"You need only to follow me when the time comes."

Bartholomew lay awake most of that night going over and over the details of their escape plan. He didn't know if a real adventurer would be as scared as he was, but he suspected they would be. He dearly hoped Oliver knew how to operate a digger. He tried not to imagine what would happen if the huge machine stalled on the way to the surface. To be trapped inside the digger forever was a bridge he had no desire to cross.

Departure day started out like every other day in the mine. They had breakfast, changed into their gear, walked to the site, and shoveled ore for twelve hours. At the end of the day they walked back to the bunkhouse. R74 did not seem noticeably anxious.

"You're not worried about this evening's activities?"

"Worrying will not make the digger go faster or the trip any safer. What I do know is one way or another I will soon be free of this place."

"You're right, of course, but let's hope it's one way

and not the other way that frees us."

Their plan was to meet Oliver and Fen at the tier two worksite. Oliver would have the digger in position and ready to go. They would arrive at midnight and be inside the digger within three minutes. Two minutes later Oliver would start the duplonium engines. The Grymmorian guards would be unable to stop the digger once it was boring into the rock. There was always the possibility they could resort to duplonium projectiles, but Bartholomew didn't think they would waste their valuable duplonium on a few escaping prisoners.

Well before midnight Bartholomew and R74 slid out of their beds and padded quietly down the length of the bunkhouse. It was not unusual for rabbits to get up in the night to use the latrine, so even if they were seen walking in the bunkhouse it would not arouse much suspicion. Once they were out in the yard it would be a very different story. Simon was snoring loudly when they slipped past him. Bartholomew gingerly opened the door to avoid squeaks, then carefully closed it behind them. They kept to the shadows, silently threading their way between the dark buildings, ever on the alert for Grymmorian guards. This was the most dangerous part of the plan. If they were caught trying to escape it meant certain death. At last they reached the road which led up to tier two and the digger. They kept to the edge of the pathway, being careful not to dislodge any rocks which might roll down the hill and alert the guards. When the digger was in view, Bartholomew reached into his pocket and pulled out the small bottle of orange liquid, showing it to R74.

He whispered, "Fen gave this to me. It's what they use to remove the shaper masks. A drop or two on the mask and a few seconds later it can be removed."

R74 stopped abruptly, staring at Bartholomew.

"What??"

"This is what they use to remove the shaper masks."

"Open it."

"We still have several minutes until–"

"Open it now."

Bartholomew took the lid off the bottle, dripping a small amount of the viscous liquid on his paw. He touched R74's mask and then his own. Seconds later he felt the mask relax its hold and he pulled it off his head. R74 did the same.

"We don't need the digger."

"What do you mean?"

"Just what I said. With my mask off we don't need the digger."

Before R74 could fully explain they had reached the site. Two figures stood silhouetted in front of the digger. Oliver and Fen had arrived before them.

Oliver hurried over and whispered, "The doors on the other side of the digger are open. Climb in and–"

He was interrupted by clanging alarm bells from tier one. A cluster of glowing spheres high in the cavern flared brilliantly and shot down towards them. The entire area was as bright as a summer afternoon. They heard shouting and the sound of Grymmorian guards frantically running up the hill, some blowing whistles. Fear shot through Bartholomew's entire body.

R74 turned and faced them. "Form a circle and hold paws. Do it now!" He grabbed Bartholomew's paw. In less than a second the circle was closed.

"Over by the digger! Seize them!"

There was a blinding flash of light followed by a

violent whirling motion.

Chapter 17

Morthram

When the whirling stopped Bartholomew found himself standing on a busy village street. Oliver, Fen, and R74 were standing next to him. Wagons and carts were clattering by as rabbits strolled down the walkways talking and laughing. The sky was a beautiful clear blue and a warm summer sun shone down from above.

R74 turned to them. It was the first time Bartholomew had seen him smile.

"Welcome to Penrith, my friends. I am Morthram, Guild Master of the Penrith Shapers Guild. Follow me and I'll take you to the Guild hall. You're welcome to stay there as long as you want."

Bartholomew couldn't stop staring at the sky as they walked behind Morthram. He had forgotten how blue it was.

"You will surely run into a lamppost if you keep gazing up to the heavens like that."

"Oliver, my friend, that is a risk worth taking. It is far too pleasant to see blue sky over my head instead of rocks."

"Do you know why the sky appears to be blue and not another color?"

"Shall we save that scintillating conversation for another day?"

Oliver laughed. "Very well then, perhaps tomorrow."

Bartholomew snorted, turning to Morthram. "How did you do it? How did you bring us to Penrith? I've never seen such shaping before."

"I will teach you if you wish, R75. I am in your debt. Without your help we would not have made it out alive."

"It was Fen who gave me the vial of orange liquid. Oh, my name is Bartholomew by the way. I left R75 back in the mine."

"Forgive me, it's the only name I have known you by, Bartholomew. Ahh, here we are."

Turning down a narrow alleyway, they stopped alongside a long, low brick building. Morthram flicked his paw and a blue liquid splashed onto the wall. It spread out rapidly, taking on a rectangular shape. Seconds later a large wooden door appeared. Morthram twisted the knob and swung it open.

"Welcome to the Penrith Shapers Guild, my friends."

Fen remained outside. He was cautiously touching the door, his eyes fixed on Morthram.

Morthram looked at Fen curiously. "You've never seen shaping before?"

"The Grymmorian King banned shapers from the kingdom when I was young. The guards took the shapers away and they were never heard from again. I have not seen shaping until now. Would you teach me to do these things?"

"You would not be safe in Grymmore, not with King Oberon in power."

"No, I would not be, but I feel drawn to it in a way that is beyond my understanding."

Morthram looked closely at Fen. "I will teach you. I will provide room and board and in return I ask that you perform any needed repairs or maintenance to the Guild hall. You will agree to follow the rules of the Guild?"

"I will."

"We can start whenever you wish."

Morthram showed everyone to their rooms, which seemed luxurious in comparison to their recent accommodations. After a bath and a clean change of clothes, Bartholomew decided to talk to Morthram about Clara. He found him in the dining hall.

"Morthram, I told you we were on our way to Penrith to find a lost friend, but what I didn't say was that you may be the only one who knows where she is. We were coming to Penrith to talk to you. As so many things are, being taken captive in the mine was a great blessing in disguise. If Theodore Rabbit hadn't ensnared us, we never would have found you. I am reminded of words I once heard from a very close friend of mine.

"Every atom, every molecule, and every bouncing marble is exactly where it should be at every moment in time."

A look of realization flashed across Morthram's face. "Clara Rabbit spoke those very words to me. You're looking for Clara, and you are the Bartholomew she talked so much about. You're quite right, this is far more than a coincidence." He pursed his lips, studying Bartholomew carefully for several long moments. "This puts everything in a new light. You will need to stay here for at least a month or more. Your time here will not affect Clara's safety, but the skills you learn will be of immeasurable value to you later on."

"You know where she is?"

"I know where she is. She is safe, but I won't tell you where to find her now. I will tell you when the time is right. To have any chance of bringing her back unharmed, your shaping abilities must be far superior to what they are now."

"I will stay until you say it's time to go, and I would be more than grateful for anything you can teach me."

"Excellent. We start tomorrow morning. There is one more thing. You must agree to certain Guild laws and guidelines regarding the ethical use of shaping. Shaping brings with it great power, and it goes without saying you bear the personal responsibility of using that power wisely. The general intent of the Guild laws are twofold. First, you may cause no harm to any living creature. All living things have the sacred life force within them. You will come to understand that the physical form of a creature makes no difference, and their behavior, whether you perceive it as good or bad, makes no difference either. Killing another creature means permanent expulsion from the Guild, unless it is under the most dire of circumstances.

"Secondly, you may not shape items for your personal enrichment. There are times when such actions may be necessary, but the general intent is as I stated. Can you abide by these guidelines? I assure you there have been shapers who could not."

"These sentiments echo my own."

"Excellent. I expected as much after my conversations with Clara. She is of the same mind as you. Are there any questions I can answer for you?"

"The World Glasses I showed you in the mine – do you know more about them than you already told me?"

"Not much. Dare I ask where you got them?"

"In the Swamp of Lost Things. Oliver and I were held captive by the Skeezle brothers, a pair of Grymmorians who waylay visitors and steal their possessions. We managed to escape using a piece of duplonium I had found, and on the way out I picked the glasses up. I had no idea of their value at the time, I simply needed a pair of dark glasses to protect my eyes from the glaring sun."

"You had mentioned you saw one of the World Doors with these glasses?"

"I did, but when I entered the hallway only one door would open. It led to a place I call The Most Beautiful Island. It was there I got to know my secret inner voice and found my Great Gem."

"I'm assuming you are referring to the Isle of Mandora. It's a gateway area outside of time and space. Did time seem to act differently there?"

"There was no time."

"Then you were on the Isle of Mandora. Did you stay on the island the whole time?"

"I never left it."

"A wise decision. The island is the entrance to a world created by creatures who are very different from us, creatures who have evolved beyond our understanding. It would have been impossible for you to even see them."

"Do you know anything about something called the Tree of Eyes?"

Morthram looked surprised. "How did you hear about that? Clara spoke of this tree also."

"My inner voice told me to seek it out."

"Indeed. You were able to locate it?"

"Yes, I discovered a journal under my sofa titled *Dr. Mazlow's Guide to Unusual Trees*. There was a map in the book which led me to the Tree of Eyes. Have you ever heard of this Dr. Mazlow?"

"I can truthfully say I have not. You have no idea how the book came to be under your sofa?"

"No, it's still a mystery to me."

"There is the possibility it was shaped by someone who wanted you to find the tree."

"I never thought of that. Who would do such a thing?"

"Who indeed. What did the Tree of Eyes say to you?"

"It showed me how to read thought clouds. To be entirely accurate, it was the Great Tree who taught me."

"You spoke with the Great Tree? What did he say?"

"Mostly that he doesn't like being pestered by the Tree of Eyes."

"No, he does not like to be pestered."

"What is the Great Tree?"

"I'm not altogether certain, but I can tell you very few shapers have ever talked to him. I've heard stories, but it's hard to know what to believe. Bartholomew, it's remarkable that your inner voice told you to seek out the Tree of Eyes. More than ever I believe you to be a very special rabbit, as is Clara. The forces at work here are beyond me, but I will do my best to be guided by them. Having said that, it's time we move on to other tasks at hand. If you like, you may keep your World Glasses in the Guild vault. They are of extraordinary value and every precaution must be taken not to lose them."

Bartholomew handed him the glasses. Morthram waved one paw and a massive black vault appeared in front of him. He pulled a brass lever in the center of the door and it swung silently open, revealing hundreds of doors of every shape and size inside the vault. Flipping open a small round door, he slid the glasses into a velvet lined compartment.

"They will be safe here. Just let me know if you need them."

Several guild members entered the hall and appeared to be waiting for Morthram, so Bartholomew excused himself and went off in search of Oliver. Following the delightful aroma of baking, he tracked Oliver to the kitchen and found him standing next to a tray of pastries.

"Laugh if you will, but no shaped éclair can compare to the quality of my own freshly baked pastries."

"You know, Oliver, éclairs are fine, but what I would really like is a pie. Would you dash back to the Ferillium Inn and get that apple pie recipe from Theodore Rabbit? I know he would be happy to share it with you."

Oliver snorted loudly.

After a wonderful dinner, Morthram introduced Bartholomew and Oliver to a group of Guild members who had stopped by to visit. Bartholomew thoroughly enjoyed talking with the other shapers and listening to them swap adventure stories. Fen sat spellbound, soaking up every word of the shapers' tales.

As Bartholomew sat in his chair watching Fen, something very unusual happened. A ghostly second image of Fen gradually appeared over the first one. This veiled second image was of an older Fen who was standing in front of a cheering crowd. The image grew clearer and sharper and more solid while the present image of Fen and the Guild hall faded away. Bartholomew was standing in the midst of Fen's future. In a single moment he knew Fen would become the King of Grymmore, and it would be Fen who ushered in the return of shaping to his kingdom. Bartholomew had no idea how or when this would happen, but he knew it would. The future image gradually faded away and was replaced by the present. Bartholomew found himself back in the Guild hall, watching young Fen listen to the shapers. It was the first time Bartholomew had experienced anything like this. In the past, such information always came to him through the Cavern of Silence, never directly to him. It was a subtle difference, but a meaningful one. It dawned on him that his inner self was gradually merging with his outer self.

Chapter 18

Blinking

Bartholomew woke early the next morning, his mind filled with thoughts of the rabbits still held captive in the ferillium mine. It was a helpless feeling knowing there was nothing he could do, but he had high hopes these circumstances would change. He rose and dressed, entering the Guild hall where he Morthram waiting for him.

"Ah, there you are. Are you ready to begin your training?"

"I am."

"Excellent, follow me and we'll find an empty practice room."

Morthram led him to a large room, empty except for two chairs facing each other about ten feet apart. Morthram took a seat in one and Bartholomew took the other.

"I know you are capable of shaping objects which exist, and objects solely of your own invention. This is more than most shapers will learn in their lifetime. That being said, we can move on. The next step is to reverse the process – to convert a physical object into a thought cloud." A wooden block appeared on the floor between them. "How would you convert this block back to a thought cloud?"

Bartholomew shook his head. "I had wondered if that was even possible. I have no idea how to do it."

"All right, let's back up and I'll explain exactly what shaping is. All things that exist are made solely of energy. A wooden block, an apple, a rabbit, a planet; all made of nothing but compressed energy. In truth, physical matter does not actually exist, only energy exists. The physical matter we love so much is more or less an illusion. When we touch an object it is actually one energy field pushing against another energy field. Now, Bartholomew Rabbit is made up of two parts – there is your physical self and your mind. Your physical self is no different from a chair, or an apple, or a bird. Your mind, and I am *not* talking about your physical brain, is very different. Your mind exists outside of space and time, like the Most Beautiful Island you spoke of.

Your mind can exist without your physical body, but obviously to interact in this world of ours you need a physical presence. When you create a thought cloud, you are simply creating an energy field with your mind. When you shape something, you are using the infinite power of your mind to compress an energy field into a physical object. To reverse that process you use the power of your mind to decompress the energy which makes up the physical object, converting it back into a thought cloud. Shapers refer to these two different states of energy as *thought clouds* and *thought forms*. Thought clouds can be turned into thought forms and vice versa. Does all this make sense to you?"

"It does. I can see I have been shaping without any real understanding of what I was doing."

"You are not the first rabbit to do that, I assure you. Do you want to try again?"

Bartholomew studied the wooden block on the floor. Closing his eyes he spun the block around in his mind. When it had become almost real to him, he imagined all the atoms and molecules breaking apart and returning to their original state as a cloud of energy. When he opened his eyes, half the block was gone and there was a small blue cloud floating nearby.

"A good first attempt. Now, try it again and see the block clearly changing back to an energy field. Don't forget to release that thought into your inner self."

By the end of the day Bartholomew was able to convert the block into a thought cloud. He spent the next two days switching the block back and forth between a thought cloud and a thought form.

"You must make your conversions faster. In a life and death situation you will not have the luxury of time. Practice this over and over until you can make the block rapidly blink in and out of its physical state."

One week later Morthram was satisfied with Bartholomew's progress.

"This is excellent, Bartholomew. The next step is to move the block to a new location every time it flips into its physical state. Practice this for the rest of the day and tomorrow."

By the end of the next day Bartholomew was exhausted, but he could convert the block to a thought cloud, move the cloud across the room, and convert it back to a block in a split second. He left the practice room and headed to the kitchen for dinner. Along the way he ran into Fen.

"Bartholomew, look what Morthram has taught me!" Fen held out his paw and with a small flash of light a wooden block appeared in it.

"Congratulations, Fen. That's wonderful you can shape an object after such a short time."

"Morthram is a great teacher."

"He is a great teacher with an excellent student. You have done well, my friend."

The next day Morthram greeted Bartholomew in the practice room.

"The time has come for you to transfer a living rabbit from one location to another. It is what shapers call 'blinking'. I will be the rabbit you transfer. I want you to blink me around the room just as you did the wooden block. There is only one irreversible error you can make. There is a limit to how long a shaper can stay in the thought cloud state and still be able to convert back again. It is not long, several seconds at most. This is another reason why speed is vitally important. There have been shapers who were too slow and could not return to their original form. These are tragic events, but it is a harsh reality of shaping. This time limitation also puts a limit on the distances we can travel in thought cloud form. Our escape from the mine and travels to Penrith took less than a second.

"You're sure I'm ready for this?"

"No need to worry. If you are taking too long, I will convert myself back into physical form. So yes, I'm sure you are ready."

Bartholomew opened and closed his paws a few times then took a deep breath. A moment later

Morthram blinked out and was gone, reappearing a split second later in a far corner of the room."

"Perfect! That was marvelous. Again, please."

After he had successfully blinked Morthram around the room numerous times, Bartholomew's final test came.

"I've saved the most difficult task for last, of course. You must blink yourself around the room. It will be a novel experience for you to be in the thought cloud state. You will be able to see and hear and think, but you will have no physical body. You move about using your will. Think where you want to go and you will be there. Once you arrive, simply convert your thought cloud self back to its physical form. You must remember, as pleasant as it is to be in the thought cloud state, remain there no longer than one or two seconds."

Bartholomew took a deep breath and looked down at his feet. A second later they vanished, along with the rest of him. It was a brief but intensely blissful experience to be floating in empty space. He willed himself to the other side of the room and blinked back into the physical world.

Much to Bartholomew's embarrassment, Morthram gave him a great hug.

"Congratulations my friend, you have accomplished something remarkable today. There are not many shapers in the world who are capable of this feat. Come with me, there is something I have been waiting to give you."

Chapter 19

The Ruby Ring

Bartholomew followed him to the main hall. The Guild vault appeared in front of Morthram and he swung the great door open, removing an object from a narrow red drawer.

He faced Bartholomew. “Extend your right arm.” Morthram slid a heavy gold ring onto Bartholomew’s paw. “Congratulations. All hail the ruby ring.”

Bartholomew looked down at the gold ring. On the face of the ring was a single eye with a red stone set in the center of it.

“The stone is a ruby. There are ten ring levels in the Shapers Guild, each with its own stone. The eighth ring is ruby, the ninth is diamond, and the tenth level is emerald.” Morthram held out his paw and showed Bartholomew the diamond on his ring.

“Are there many shapers who wear the emerald ring?”

“There is only one emerald ring, and I will not tell you who wears it, so don’t ask.”

“From the bottom of my heart I thank you,

Morthram, for all you have done to help me. Truly, I am in your debt."

"I am the one repaying a debt, my friend. I would still be rotting in that cursed ferillium mine if not for you. Don't thank me yet, though. You still have much to learn before you leave." Morthram grinned, adding, "If you think that ruby ring means you're done here, you are sadly mistaken. But for now, let's go and show off your new ring to Oliver and Fen."

They walked down the hallway to the Guild library. The main reading room was at least fifty feet long with twelve foot tall ceilings. Bookshelves covered all four walls. Bartholomew had never seen so many books in one place.

"Are all these books about shaping?"

"Good heavens, no. The Guild expects its members to be knowledgeable on a wide variety of subjects and disciplines, not just shaping. Members must be familiar with the customs of countless other cultures and worlds. A high level shaper will often be called to distant realms, and must be able to appropriately interact with the inhabitants. Not fully understanding another culture's beliefs and conventions could prove disastrous."

Bartholomew glanced across the room and saw Oliver engrossed in a book. He waved to him, calling out his name. "Oliver!"

Oliver looked up from his book. "Hello, my friend. I hope your shaping lessons are going well. I'm afraid I have not been very good company since I discovered this library. There are an enormous number of scientific volumes here which are quite fascinating. Many are new to me, including some which attempt to explain the science behind shaping. These are theoretical texts of course, but most interesting. Now, what is this surprise Morthram has been telling me about?"

Bartholomew walked across the room and held out his paw, showing Oliver his Guild ring.

"You are a Guild member. This is wonderful news! Wait, I just read about this yesterday. The ruby ring represents the eighth level, does it not? For you to enter the Guild at the eighth level is quite remarkable. Congratulations, my friend."

Fen overheard their conversation and stepped out from behind a large chair, a wide grin on his face. He held out his paw, displaying his new amethyst Guild ring.

"You are making amazing progress, Fen. In a few short weeks you are already a level two amethyst." Bartholomew looked as though he was about to say something, then stopped.

"What is it?"

"I'm not quite sure how to say this, Fen, but I think it's something you should hear. The other day when you were listening to the shapers' stories, I saw you simultaneously in the present and in the future. In the future, you were the King of Grymmore, and the one who brings the return of shaping to your kingdom"

Fen chose his words carefully. "I have good reason to believe what you have seen may come to pass, although there are many events still to unfold. I do know you have a part to play in a great number of these events. I have heard this from the Jewel of Barsume."

Bartholomew looked at Fen curiously. "You're certain?"

"I am certain. Our meeting in the ferillium mine was

not mere chance, just as your meeting with Morthram was not mere chance."

"It's a long and complex chain of events which has brought us to this place."

"It is indeed."

Morthram interrupted their conversation. "Did I forget to mention there was one more surprise? Bartholomew, if you would look over to the other side of the room, would you please tell me what you see?"

"I see the other half of the library."

"And now?" Morthram waved his arm and a blast of light flew across the room. Two dozen rabbits blinked into view.

"All hail the ruby ring!"

Morthram continued. "The presentation of a ruby ring is no small occasion in the Shapers Guild. These Guild members have come to meet and congratulate you."

The visiting shapers surrounded Bartholomew, introducing themselves one by one. Many of them had heard the stories of Morthram's captivity in the ferillium mine and the daring escape they had made.

Fen seemed to be having more fun than anyone talking to the shapers and listening to their stories. The tales seemed to get wilder as the evening progressed, and Bartholomew suspected someone had shaped a little something extra into the punch bowl. As the evening wound down, the guests shook Bartholomew's paw again and congratulated him before departing. This day would long remain a cherished memory for Bartholomew.

As he fell asleep that night he thought again about how much he had changed since he set out for the

Cavern of Silence. He didn't need a worn pack to make him feel like an adventurer now. He had become what he set out to be. He was Bartholomew the Adventurer. Sleep carried him away while his eyes were still on his new ruby ring.

The next morning Bartholomew rose early and hurried to the practice room. Morthram had told him they would begin working on advanced defense skills. Bartholomew arrived first and entered the darkened room. He walked over to one of the lamps, but abruptly stopped, his ears perking up. There was a barely audible rustling sound coming from the corner of the room. He looked into the shadows, trying to isolate the source of the sound. Before he had time to think, a dark creature leaped up and over one the chairs, charging wildly toward him. It let loose a horrible squealing shriek, raising a wicked looking dagger. The creature's claws scratched and tore at the floor as it scrambled madly towards him. Bartholomew gave a loud yelp, skittering backwards and tripping over the chair behind him. He stumbled and fell, his head thudding into the door. He sank to the floor in excruciating pain. The beast reached him as he was desperately trying to drag himself out of the room. Looking up in horror he saw a vicious Grymmorian guard, dagger raised high. "I kill rabbits who escape!" The dagger plunged down towards Bartholomew's chest. It stopped about six inches before it reached him.

"Would you care to tell me all the things you did wrong?" Morthram's voice was coming out of the guard's mouth. Bartholomew could make no reply. Finally he managed to speak.

"Morthram?"

"Indeed." The guard's body rippled and blurred, transforming into Morthram's familiar form.

"What? How could you..."

"Shapers call it formshifting. It's very useful when trying to avoid detection in another world. In such places there is always the danger of an unexpected deadly attack. You must be able to react without thinking, and react in a manner which causes no harm to your assailant. I'm afraid you did none of those things today."

Bartholomew's head throbbed for the rest of the day, but it was a good reminder of how poorly he had responded to the assault. It brought back embarrassing memories of the rabid wolf, but this time there had been no tree to climb.

"Let's begin with altering your appearance. You are now adept at converting your physical self to a thought cloud and then back again. You are also able to shape objects created only in your imagination. If we combine those two things we have formshifting. You convert your physical self to a thought cloud, and when you convert that cloud back to your physical form you merely create whatever form you wish to be."

"Could I convert myself to an object like a chair or a lamp?"

"You could. You would be quite undetectable, but you would suffer the great disadvantage of being unable to see or hear."

As the days slipped by, Bartholomew learned many new skills from Morthram. He could now create energy spheres, fireballs, frost storms, duplonium projectiles, and any number of defensive orbs. One of the more interesting orbs was an archaic one called a time shell, used to protect the shaper from arrows. At the first sign of archers, the shaper creates a time shell around himself. When the arrow hits the shell and begins to pass through it, time is altered for the projectile. It takes almost a full minute for the arrow to make its way through the wall, giving the shaper ample time to simply move out of the arrow's path.

Morthram's final lesson focused on sending thought projections to rabbits who are unable to read thought clouds, which is also a rather elegant way to communicate with creatures who don't speak your language. He explained that thoughts are not made of words, but of formless ideas and concepts. When an idea is projected to another creature, its mind converts the idea into its own language. If you happen to resemble the creature through formshifting, you can, with practice, pass for one of its own kind. Bartholomew spent the greater part of a week working on this skill. He was even able to successfully convince Fen he was a visiting Grymmorian.

That evening after dinner Morthram took Bartholomew aside to speak with him.

"Bartholomew, you have learned far more quickly than I had imagined you would. Only one other student has progressed at such a rate, and of course that is your friend Clara. We still have several weeks before you must leave, and I have a proposal for you. I have been kept awake many nights by thoughts of the rabbits still being held captive in Oberon's ferillium mine. I can no longer stand idly by without attempting to free them. On my own I fear my limited powers are not enough for what I have planned. There is a method I can teach you where two or more shapers link minds, magnifying their power. If we work together, I believe we could free the prisoners and close the ferillium mine."

Chapter 20

The Recipe

"I will go with you. I have been haunted almost daily by similar thoughts."

"This is welcome news, my friend. Over the last week I have been making short exploratory visits to the mine in the form of a Grymmorian guard and have learned much about its operation. I discovered their conveyor belt system carries the ferillium ore to the entrance of a huge tunnel. The ore is dumped into enormous wheeled wagons and rides through the tunnel on rails, eventually arriving in Grymmore. Honestly, I can't imagine the time it must have taken to create such a tunnel, or the cost in lives and in coin.

"My plan begins with us entering the mine as Grymmorian guards. In the event we are questioned by guards, we can read their thoughts and project our answers back to them. After that, things get more complicated."

Bartholomew listened for the next hour as Morthram revealed the rest of his scheme.

"I can find no flaws in your strategy, my friend.

When do we leave for the mine?"

"It will take us a day to practice linking minds, and a day to practice the necessary shaping. As an aside, I still don't understand King Oberon's need for such massive quantities of ferillium, but I do think it bears looking into. I thought perhaps you could speak to Oliver and see if he has any thoughts on this. With his background in science, he may be aware of some little known use for ferillium."

The next morning Bartholomew found Oliver in the library.

"Oliver, during your time with Mr. Ferillium, was there any mention of why the Grymmorian King needs such vast amounts of ferillium?"

"I asked Mr. Ferillium that question, but the vagueness of his reply led me to believe he did not know. I had the sense he was pretending to know more than he did, not surprising behavior for someone of his nature. As far as I know, ferillium has no practical applications. There have been several scientists who were able to create tiny ferillium crystals, but to what end I don't know. I do know the process does require large amounts of raw ferillium, which may or may not be significant."

"Interesting. After we have closed the mine we should investigate this further. Morthram had mentioned some rumors about these ferillium crystals, but he knew nothing substantial. Perhaps these crystals have a use unknown to us."

"I will search the texts in the library and try to find some answers. If I find nothing in the scientific volumes, perhaps the shaping texts will contain some clue to any hidden properties of ferillium crystals."

The following day was spent in the practice room as Bartholomew and Morthram finalized the details of their assault on the mine. By the end of the day they felt confident their endeavor would be successful. In the morning they would blink themselves to a dark corner of the mine and begin their liberation of the prisoners and the permanent closure of Oberon's mine.

They rose before sunrise and found Oliver had breakfast prepared for them. He wished them well. "I have not the slightest doubt you will be successful in closing this fiendish mine. What chance does a group of dunderheaded Grymmorian guards have against two of the most powerful shapers alive?"

Bartholomew laughed. "Your faith in us is most uplifting, my friend. Is there a message you would like to give to your old friend Mr. Ferillium, should I happen to see him?"

"I'm afraid any message I have would not fall within the ethical boundaries of the Shapers Guild."

"Ha! I'll try to think of something more suitable then."

After breakfast Bartholomew and Morthram walked to the center of the Guild hall. Fen arrived just in time to wish them luck. He looked on in wonderment as they formshifted into ragged and vicious looking Grymmorian guards. Moments later they blinked out and were gone.

They reappeared in a dark corner of the Ferillium mine, a spot carefully chosen by Morthram.

"We'll make our way to the center of the mine. In the event we're stopped by guards, you know what to do."

They sauntered out of the shadows onto a rocky path

leading to the main square. Their demeanor exuded the arrogant confidence of two Grymmorian guards, giving no hint of the trepidation Bartholomew was feeling. His return to the mine had rekindled painful memories of the many brutal acts he had witnessed. They began to pass prisoners walking along the pathway, but the prisoners avoided any eye contact. The guards Bartholomew and Morthram passed simply ignored them. Before long they reached the central plaza of the mine. It was surrounded on all sides by wide rocky streets and long, low wooden buildings. Dozens of prisoners could be seen passing by as numerous groups of guards stood watch over them.

"Are you ready?"

"I am."

A large transparent sphere blinked into physical form around them. They were safe inside the sphere, for no physical object in existence could penetrate it.

Bartholomew clasped Morthram's paw and they closed their eyes, falling into a deep state of concentration. Bartholomew held up his right paw and Morthram held up his left. Moments later blindingly bright lights appeared in each of their paws. They stood motionless as the lights grew even more intense. Guards ran towards them, paws shielding their eyes. Hundreds upon hundreds of small glowing red spheres poured out from Bartholomew's paw, followed by thousands of bright yellow spheres from Morthram's paw. The spheres shot through the wall of the protective shell, flying straight upwards to a height of several hundred feet. Like bees from a hive they spread out in all directions, their speed becoming blurringly fast.

The guards reached the transparent protective

sphere. The first guard smashed into the invisible barrier, squealing in pain and falling backwards to the ground. The other guards stopped. One reached out to touch the sphere and became enraged when he felt the invisible barrier. He pulled out a long dagger, stabbing at the sphere in an attempt to crack it open. When his dagger didn't even mar the surface, the guard shrieked in anger and pounded his fists on the shell until one of the tiny red spheres landed on his uniform. He jumped back, trying to swat the sphere off his jacket, but the sphere turned to liquid, spreading rapidly through the fabric of his coat. Seconds later he fell to the ground motionless. He was sound asleep and would remain in that state for more than a week.

Bartholomew watched as guards everywhere were struck by the red spheres, each one collapsing to the ground as the first one had. Prisoners watched in confusion as the guards fell, uncertain what they should do. One of them cautiously approached a sleeping guard and prodded him gently. When there was no response he tried again, this time giving him a sharp kick. The guard did not move. The prisoner raised both arms high into the air and cried out one word. "Escape!" Before he could yell it again, a yellow sphere landed on his heavy canvas mining suit. Like the guard, he tried in vain to brush the sphere off him. The sphere liquified and spread across his canvas coveralls. He blinked out and vanished in a flash of yellow light.

Bartholomew flicked his paw and the protective sphere around them dissipated. The guards were no longer a threat. He and Morthram watched as the prisoners ran about trying to avoid the yellow spheres. It was an impossible task and soon every prisoner had vanished from the mine.

Far above them, in the open fields surrounding the Ferillium Inn, a very different scene was unfolding. Hundreds upon hundreds of prisoners from the mine were blinking back into their original physical form. It only took a few moments for them to realize they were free of the mine. The cacophony of their triumphant cries echoed through the nearby canyon. Some of them recognized the Ferillium Inn and began running towards it. Drawn out by the uproar, Mr. Ferillium and the innkeeper Theodore Rabbit emerged through the front doorway. They took one look at the dozens of rabbits racing towards them and realized their predicament. Leaping over the porch railing, they began sprinting madly across the fields in the opposite direction. It was the last anyone heard of either of them. There were rumors of them living deep in the Swamp of Lost Things, but there are always rumors.

Back in the mine, Bartholomew and Morthram walked past the hundreds of sleeping guards. Morthram led Bartholomew to the entrance of the mammoth Grymmorian tunnel. A long train of empty wagons sat on the tracks. Each wagon was at least forty feet long and fifteen feet wide.

"Ready?"

They raised their arms and the bright yellow spheres again flew out. They spread quickly throughout the mine, each sphere landing on a sleeping guard. The guard vanished, only to reappear in one of the huge wooden rail wagons. Once all the guards in the mine had been blinked to the wagons, Morthram directed Bartholomew to a small control house.

"The metal tracks provide electrical power to the

wagons. That power comes from a duplonium powered steam generator which also powers the rest of the mine. This red lever controls the motion of the wagon train."

Morthram pushed the lever. With a shrill screeching noise the train of wagons began to move forward.

"It will take several hours for the wagons make their way through the tunnel. In the meantime, I would like to search Mr. Ferillium's office and see what we can find out about the mine."

They walked through the eerily silent streets and alleys to the main offices. As they passed the empty bunkhouses, Bartholomew was filled with a deep satisfaction knowing the mine would never again be filled with prisoners.

Finally, they stood facing Mr. Ferillium's building. Bartholomew made a quick detour, walking around to the side of the structure. The large metal cage where they had first arrived was still there. He touched the padlocked door. "They have trapped their last rabbit."

Once inside the offices, Bartholomew and Morthram began searching through the stacks of paperwork. Most of it dealt with the day to day operations of the mine. There were lists of prisoners and their bunkhouse locations, lists of payments made for the purchase of prisoners, and lists of prisoners who died in the mine. Many of the payments were to Theodore Rabbit. They also found ledgers recording shipments of ferillium ore to Grymmore. It appeared the mine had been in operation for over ten years. They found no clues as to the actual purpose of the mine or what Oberon was planning to do with the ferillium.

Bartholomew opened a door to a connecting room. A gray vault stood against the far wall. Morthram flicked his paw and a red liquid splattered onto the vault door. The door crumbled to dust. They examined the contents of the vault, which appeared to belong to Mr. Ferillium. There were dozens of boxes filled with row upon row of neatly stacked gold coins. Piles of gemstones lay in black velvet cases. Morthram flipped open a silver box and found a pair of World Glasses.

"We should take these for the Guild."

"Good idea. What's this?" Bartholomew pulled out a small ornate metal box. When he opened it he found a heavy six sided silver medallion attached to a thin chain. Around the edge of the medallion were symbols which he could not identify, and in the center of the medallion was a round blue gemstone.

"Those symbols look Grymmorian to me. It doesn't look especially valuable, but perhaps it has some other purpose. Bring it back to the Guild and we can have Fen decipher it."

They left the offices and spent several more hours searching through other buildings in the mine, finding nothing of any significance. Morthram looked at his watch. "The wagons are through the tunnel by now and well on their way to Grymmore. It's time to finish what we've started."

They walked back to the Grymmorian tunnel entrance. A bright green light appeared in Morthram's paw, then snaked out like a long rope down the length of the tunnel. The glowing green line began to grow, gradually transforming to a dark gray foam which quickly expanded until it filled the tunnel. A red beam shot from Morthram's other paw into the foam. Seconds later the foam solidified with a peculiar grinding noise. Bartholomew put his paw on the gray substance.

"It worked. It's solid granite, impossible for the Grymmorians to drill through. Shall we go up to the surface?"

Bartholomew and Morthram blinked out and reappeared in front of the large iron door on the canyon road.

"May I?"

"Indeed you may, my friend."

Bartholomew held his paw out. A green cube appeared, floating between the heavy iron bars and down into the shaft. Fifteen minutes later the same dense gray foam pushed its way up to the top of the shaft. Bartholomew shot out a bright red beam and the foam became solid granite.

"The mine is gone, filled with shaped granite. May rabbits never again suffer as they did in King Oberon's ferillium mine."

"Shall we head back to Penrith?"

"I'd like to search the Ferillium Inn before we go."

They strolled along the river road until the Ferillium Inn came into view. Some of the freed rabbits were still wandering about, but most had left the area. Bartholomew saw quite a few shaper masks laying on the grass as they made their way to the inn.

"Transferring the orange liquid into the spheres worked quite well."

"I should bring some masks back for Oliver to examine. I'd like to learn how they prevent thoughts from passing through them."

"The Guild would also be more than interested in knowing how they work. Perhaps we could create a countermeasure to use against them other than the orange liquid."

Bartholomew put a half dozen of the masks into his pocket.

The interior of the inn was a shambles. The freed rabbits had torn it to pieces, venting their anger at Theodore Rabbit. They spent an hour searching through the remains but found nothing. If there had been anything of importance the freed prisoners would have taken it. Bartholomew and Morthram blinked back into the Guild hall and found Oliver and Fen waiting to greet them.

"You were successful?"

"The mine is no more. The prisoners have been freed and the guards have been returned to Grymmore."

"Then we have a cause for celebration."

Bartholomew looked at Oliver with a grin. "Perhaps this will be even more of a cause for you to celebrate." He handed Oliver a wrinkled piece of brown paper.

Oliver took it with a puzzled expression. He looked at it closely, reading to himself. His eyes lit up and he roared with laughter.

"Theodore Rabbit's secret recipe for apple pie!"

"Just promise me you will leave out the sleeping potion."

Chapter 21

Morthram's Betrayal

"I've found something!"

Bartholomew looked up from the reference book he was reading in the Guild library. Oliver stood over him holding an ancient leather volume.

"What is that?"

"It's called *Shapres Wisdome,* and it's almost four hundred years old. Morthram suggested I look among the rare books for references to ferillium, and I found this. Read this section right here." He gingerly handed the heavy tome to Bartholomew, pointing to one specific paragraph. Bartholomew began to read.

Such crystals within the Circle of Shapres do bear the name Fendaron's Revenge, thusly called in sacred remembrance of the Great Loss. Argule the Alchemist, trusted diamond within the Circle has written of knowledge long hidden within the Tales of Fendaron. By truth, Fendaron's Revenge, when standing beside crystals of Aurachalkym are as one. Fendaron did perform this conversion from the dust of Aurachalkym to crystalline form. By his wielding of the Aurachalkym crystal, Fendaron drew inward to the crystal the totality of thoughts and powers from the multitudes of the Circle, allowing for their brutal slaughter by his warriors.

"It's hard to understand the old writing. It's something about a group of shapers who were massacred? Who is Fendaron?"

Oliver stared blankly at Bartholomew. "Who is Fendaron? It makes no difference who he is. This clearly explains why the Grymmorian King created the ferillium mine."

"I saw no mention of ferillium."

The inside of Oliver's ears grew bright red.

"Good heavens, Bartholomew, it's blindingly obvious. Aurachalkym is the ancient name for ferillium. Fendaron converted aurachalkym dust into a crystal. The crystal absorbed all the thoughts and powers of shapers, rendering them helpless against Fendaron's warriors."

"Oliver, this is amazing. I am starting to believe your scientific mind is a miracle in itself. The Grymmorian King must be creating a massive ferillium crystal which can absorb the thoughts and power of shapers. But why would he do this? There are no shapers in Grymmore, and certainly there is no threat of invading shapers. He has gone to enormous effort to create this crystal and yet we are no closer to understanding what he plans to do with it."

Bartholomew and Oliver showed the book to Morthram, who read it several times over before saying anything.

"We should go to the library. It's time I told you Clara's story and the story of my betrayal."

Morthram led them through the main reading room to an empty side room. He closed the door behind them.

"We will have privacy here. You are not to share this story with anyone. Do you both agree to this?"

"We do."

"Very well. The story begins almost six months before Clara arrived. I had been Guild Master to the Penrith Shapers Guild for almost ten years. One of my goals was to increase the Guild's membership to bring shaping out of the shadows and dispel the fear it causes in so many rabbits. One day a rabbit entered the Guild hall and introduced himself to me. He wore a level five sapphire Guild ring and said his name was Thaddeus Rabbit. When I asked if he was here to advance his shaping skills he laughed, saying he was quite happy being a sapphire, and had no inclination to advance beyond that. He had moved to Penrith from a small village far to the east where he had spent much of his life. He told me he had reached an age where he felt he should expand his horizons and see more of this world. He left his home and traveled for many months, eventually finding his way to Penrith. He quickly became a fixture around the Guild. All the members enjoyed his company, and when there was work to be done he was the first to volunteer. All in all, he was a welcome addition to the Guild.

"When a rabbit receives their level one garnet ring, they usually undertake a quest which is more of an informal tradition than it is a real quest. The initiate is always accompanied by a more experienced shaper, and the quest they are sent on involves little or no danger. They could be sent deep into the mountains to find a rare flower, or to bring back a unique crystal of some sort. It is designed to pose no threat, its only purpose being to impart a sense of belonging, a sense they are now valued members of the Guild. Thaddeus Rabbit made a perfect quest companion for the initiates. He was congenial and treated them with respect, never parading his skills in front of them as some rabbits do. He seemed sincerely humble and was a favorite among the new members. He went out on many first quests, never once failing to return with the required item. Many of the stories he told about the initiates were quite heartwarming. I felt it was a loss to the Guild that he chose not to advance beyond a sapphire, but I kept those thoughts to myself. He seemed happy with his lot, and a rabbit can't really ask for more than that.

"Thaddeus had been there for almost half a year when Clara arrived. I remember clearly when she walked through the door. I don't know how she did it, but she managed to simultaneously look woefully uncertain and supremely confident. When she approached me I quickly sensed she was no ordinary rabbit. I could almost feel the vibrations of her shaping power. She had an inborn shaping ability rivaled only by Bartholomew's. What she lacked was an understanding of what shapers are, and how they fit into the world. She had several bad experiences when she was young which affected her deeply. We spent many long hours discussing the true nature of shaping, and she finally came to understand that shaping in itself is neither good nor evil. It is the actions of the shaper which are good or evil. Her skills were remarkable, many of which she had discovered on her own, but some with help from the Great Tree. To be tutored by the Great Tree is an unparalleled honor, as I have told

Bartholomew any number of times.

"When Clara received her first Guild ring it was a ruby, as Bartholomew's was. There was no need for her to go on a first quest, but she felt it might send the wrong message to the other members if she didn't go. Thaddeus Rabbit volunteered to go with her. I had absolute faith in his integrity, and Clara seemed to like him so I allowed it. They were to go west to the Brycin Mountains and bring back a bloom called the Night Blossom. It's usually found at the lower elevations of the range and isn't especially hard to find. We expected the entire trip to take about two weeks. On the day she was leaving with Thaddeus, Clara took me aside and gave me a hug. She said if for some reason she didn't return, she wanted me to know she was grateful for all the help and understanding I had given her. She said she finally felt at home being a shaper. That was when she spoke the words I also heard from you, 'Every atom, every molecule, and every bouncing marble is exactly where it should be at every moment in time.' I believe now she knew what was going to happen, and knew the universe meant for her to be a part of it.

"Two weeks passed and they did not return. After another week, we became fearful that something had happened to them. We were making plans to send out search parties when Thaddeus returned. He was badly wounded, with dreadful claw marks running across his chest and arms. He was almost delirious from fever but did say Clara had been killed, the victim of a mountain bear. She had gone looking for firewood early in the morning and he awoke to the sound of her screams. He ran to her and saw the bear attacking her. As he rushed towards them he tried to create a protective shell around

Clara, but couldn't make it work properly. The bear turned on him, raking its gigantic claws across his arms and his chest, knocking him backwards into a boulder. His head hit the rock and he was knocked unconscious. When he awoke Clara and the bear were gone. He searched for several days but could not find her. He was all but certain she had been killed. When he finished telling us the story Thaddeus wept, as did many of us.

"The weeks went by and his wounds from the bear were healing nicely. I had offered to heal him with shaping, but he declined. He said the wounds helped him to remember Clara and to remind him how short life can be.

"Several months after that everything changed. It was the middle of the night, and I was sound asleep when a voice woke me. I don't know where it came from or whose voice it was, but it was loud and it was clear. The voice said, *'Clara is being held captive by the Grymmorian King. You must save her before it is too late'*.

"At first I thought it was just a wishful dream of mine that Clara was still alive, but as I gave it more thought I came to see it as truth. I believe the knowledge came from the self within me, although the voice was unfamiliar to me. I felt strongly that I had to go to Grymmore and rescue Clara. I told the other shapers about the voice I had heard and Thaddeus immediately volunteered to accompany me. The other Guild members were not as quick to offer help. Most did not want to risk their life over something that may or may not be true. At the time, it made little sense to anyone that Clara would be held prisoner by the Grymmorian King. In hindsight, it was because we all believed the story Thaddeus had told us.

"Thaddeus and I began preparations for the trip. I tried to teach him a few new shaping skills which might come in handy, but he had a difficult time with them. He was not what you would call a gifted shaper, but he did make up for it with his enthusiasm. He didn't doubt for a moment we would return safely with Clara. Once everything was packed and we had mapped out our journey, it was time for us to leave. Thaddeus didn't know how to travel in thought cloud form so I held his paw and we blinked our way to the Grymmorian border. We wouldn't be able to use shaping unless absolutely necessary once we entered Grymmore, since being caught shaping is essentially a death sentence there. The guards take you away and that is the end of it.

"We crossed over into Grymmore but kept our rabbit forms since Thaddeus had no training in formshifting. I will admit I had a great deal of trepidation when we first entered Grymmore as rabbits, but the worst that happened were some curious looks we received along the way. Not once did I feel in any serious danger. We found a few inns and shops along the way which catered to rabbits, and I will say I was quite moved by the kindness of many Grymmorians. We were given rides in wagons, places to sleep, food to eat, and more significantly, friendly conversation. I had heard so many stories growing up of how dreadful and cruel Grymmorians were that I had come to believe it, but it could not be further from the truth. There are good and bad rabbits and there are good and bad muroidians.

"Our destination was Malgraven Castle, home of Grymmore's King Oberon, and my plan was quite

straightforward. When we reached the castle I would formshift and enter as a lowly Grymmorian servant. While I scrubbed the floors and walls, I would pull the thoughts of whoever walked past me in an attempt to learn what I could about Clara's location. Thaddeus would stay outside the castle, since he had none of the necessary skills to avoid detection. In hindsight, I should have made the trip alone, but at the time I believed Thaddeus truly blamed himself for Clara's disappearance and wanted to make amends.

"Eventually we arrived at Malgraven Castle. I have seen a number of castles, but nothing like this. It is monumental both in size and in architectural complexity. I had no idea how I would find my way around it once I was inside, even if I knew where Clara was being held.

"Nevertheless, I formshifted into a rather sad looking Grymmorian servant who was unlikely to be noticed. I armed myself with a bucket of water and a pile of rags, and blinked into the castle early in the morning before most muroids had risen. I left Thaddeus sitting in a tent on the outskirts of the castle grounds. Fortunately, no one witnessed my arrival. Within seconds I was on my knees scrubbing the floor. As the day progressed, any number of Grymmorians passed me by. I don't think a single one ever looked at me. I pulled many thoughts to me. Most were quite mundane, about their personal lives or castle politics or what they were going to have for dinner.

"Towards the end of the day a rather frightening Grymmorian guard walked past me. I pulled his thoughts and struck gold. When I pull a thought to me, it's not like reading a book. It's not a linear string of words, but is a complete bundle of knowledge which all arrives simultaneously. I know everything at once. The guard was thinking about the King's throne room. He was on his way there to transport several valuable prisoners to the Lost Fortress in the Fandor Mountains. I could see their faces, and one of the prisoners was Clara.

"I made a split second decision. I would follow the guard to the throne room and scrub the floors there, slowly making my way over to the prisoners. Once I was close enough, I would grab Clara's paw and blink us both out of the castle. It seemed like a foolproof scheme, but I could not have been more wrong.

"I trailed along behind the guard, keeping my head down and making no eye contact with anyone. After weaving through the halls and corridors, the guard reached a set of tall bronze doors and pushed them open, entering into the room beyond. I followed him in, quickly kneeling down to scrub the floors, doing my best to remain inconspicuous. The room was magnificent, and was obviously King Oberon's throne room. At the front of the room was a long raised dais covered in red velvet, with an ornate golden throne sitting in the center of it. Seated on the throne was none other than the Grymmorian King, Oberon himself. In front of him stood the guard and two rabbits with burlap sacks over their heads. One of them must be Clara, but I had no idea which one.

"I stood up and began polishing the brass fittings along the wall, gradually making my way down the aisle to the front of the throne room. No one seemed to notice me. When I got close enough I could hear the King talking to the guard."

"Take the one named Clara to the Lost Fortress for safekeeping, and make sure she is comfortable and well fed. Hold on, I have a better idea. Take her down to the dungeons and execute her." He threw his head back and roared with cruel laughter. His grin turned quickly to a scowl. "Take this filthy shaper out of my sight and make sure I never see her again."

"I felt I must make my move while there was still only one guard present, so I made my way around to the rear of the throne, polishing fixtures as I went. Then, using the throne to block their line of sight, I sneaked up behind King Oberon. Clara stood only six feet away from me. All I had to do was touch her and we could blink out of the castle."

"Guard, take the sack off her head so I can give her a few final words of kingly advice."

The guard reached over and pulled the burlap bag off Clara. My heart dropped. It was not Clara.

"My final words of advice to you are... *never trust a rabbit named Thaddeus*."

"A large black thought cloud shot out of Oberon's ear. In a fraction of a second I had pulled it to me and read it.

"What I didn't see was the guard standing behind me. I never even felt the shapers mask slip down over my head."

Oberon was howling with laughter. "I do love a good betrayal."

"I turned around and found myself standing face to face with the guard I had followed. He began to ripple and blur, transforming into Thaddeus. I raised one paw to form a protective sphere around me but was rewarded only with a violent shock to my ear. It was my first experience wearing a shapers mask."

"Ah, Morthram, whatever are we going to do with you? Oh, I remember – we're going to add you to the King's rather extensive collection of shapers. First, however, I will have the distinct pleasure of watching you shovel rocks in the King's ferillium mine. You have no idea how weary I have become of your endless drivel about compassion for living creatures. Perhaps the guards in the mine can teach you a few lessons about compassion."

He rippled and returned to his form as the fiendish looking Grymmorian guard. "Here's a surprise for you. There never was a Thaddeus Rabbit, there was only me. Did you like my gruesome mountain bear wounds? It took me at least five seconds to formshift them. But I forget my manners, I have not properly introduced myself. I am Zoran, personal shaper to King Oberon of Grymmore and an avid collector of powerful shapers. Do you like my ring?"

"He held out his paw. His Guild ring had an emerald in the center of it. I spoke the words I knew to be true. 'I'm not surprised you bear the emerald. But know this, Zoran – as all others who have worn the emerald ring before you were, you also shall be destroyed'."

"Ah, that sounds remarkably like a threat. Perhaps my little friend Morthram Rabbit will be the next shaper to wear the emerald."

"Zoran reached out and pulled the shaper's mask off my head. I instantly shot up an impenetrable defensive sphere around me. A blistering red beam of light shot out from Zoran's paw and the sphere vanished. I have never seen anything like it."

"Well, that didn't seem to work very well for you. How about I stand here and you try with all your might to destroy me? I know you have such a difficult time taking a life, but know this – if you don't take mine I shall destroy every rabbit you hold dear to you, beginning with your little friend Clara."

"I was at a loss, at a crossroads. Evil such as this demanded a different set of rules. I reached deep inside the center of my being and pulled forth every ounce of shaping power I could muster. There was a single explosion of brilliant blue light and a blinding beam shot out from my paw. Halfway between my paw and Zoran's black heart the beam simply stopped in mid air. The light turned into solid matter and a myriad of small cracks appeared in it. Seconds later the beam crumbled to glowing dust and floated gently to the floor."

"Morthram, you are a sad little bunny dabbling in things beyond your comprehension and you are wasting my time with your foolishness."

"Zoran slid the shaper's mask back on my head and touched my arm. We blinked to the ferillium mine. When we arrived the guards took me to Bunkhouse R, bunk 74. What Zoran did not know was I had read the King's thought and discovered where Clara was being held."

Chapter 22

The Plan

Bartholomew looked at Morthram. "Where is she?"

"She is in the Lost Fortress. It's an ancient Fortress discovered only ten years ago by a party of the King's guards. No one is quite certain how old it is, but their scientists think it was built at least several thousand years ago. I saw glimpses of it in the King's thought. It's massive. His scientists are building a machine there which I could not identify, but I do know the ferillium crystal is crucial to its operation. I saw a room filled with hundreds of shapers, all alive, but frozen in time. There were other rooms filled with shapers, all wearing masks. That is where I saw Clara. We must rescue her and put a stop to whatever Oberon is planning."

"How?"

Morthram shook his head. "I don't know. Let's all think about it for a day. I'll talk to Fen. He's familiar with Grymmore and may be able to advise us. Perhaps together we can come up with a workable plan."

They left the library and headed to the dining room where dinner was being served. While they were eating,

Bartholomew asked Morthram about the emerald ring.

"Morthram, what do you know about the emerald ring Zoran was wearing? Why would the Guild give their highest level ring to someone like Zoran?"

"The emerald ring is not given, it is taken. For hundreds of years the ring has gone from shaper to shaper. When the wearer of the ring is defeated in battle, the victor takes the ring. Only a certain kind of shaper desires such a ring. The moment the ring is on your paw is the moment other shapers will try to destroy you. As I said, I was not surprised to see Zoran wearing the ring. It suits him well."

After dinner Bartholomew returned to the library. He was curious about the history of the emerald ring and found a lengthy written account of the shapers who had possessed it. None of them seemed very likable, and all of them had met untimely ends. He was engrossed in the tale of a particularly brutal shaper named Forzan, when there was a sudden flickering motion on the floor next to his chair. Bartholomew leaped to his feet, a protective sphere instantly forming around him. He stared in wonderment at the object floating in front of him. It was Clara's thought.

He circled around the thought cloud, studying it closely. It looked the same, with its swirling colors and the yellow flashing sparks in the center of it. But what in the world was it doing here? Clara's thought had gone down with *The Adventurer* in the Halsey River. Could it somehow have found him on its own? Could thoughts do that? There was only one way to find out. He ran out of the library, past the main hall and dining room, down the narrow hallway leading to his room, and bolted inside. He closed the door behind him and sat on his bed, waiting to see if the Clara's thought would follow him.

Ten minutes later it floated through the wall and glided over towards him. It hovered silently several feet away from his bed.

"This is something I have never seen before. Clara's thought is drawn to me." It struck him that this was not such an unfamiliar concept. How many times had he heard the phrase, "My thoughts will be with you." Clara's thought was with him. It was a comforting feeling when he thought about it that way.

The following morning Clara's thought still hovered by his bed. As he watched the swirling colors and the flickering sparks an idea came to him. Opening a dresser drawer, he rummaged through his clothes and pulled out one of the shaper masks. The masks didn't allow thoughts to pass through them. Could he trap a thought inside it?

He held the mask wide open and willed Clara's thought to enter it. It floated towards him and entered the bag, shrinking to fit down inside it. He tied the mask shut and returned to the library, where he sat and read for almost an hour. Clara's thought did not appear. When he returned to his room the thought was still inside the mask. His idea had worked. He tied the mask to his belt and tucked it into his pocket. It was barely noticeable. He smiled to himself. If he found himself in a desperate situation, he could slip his paw inside the mask in his pocket, touch Clara's thought and be instantly transported to The Most Beautiful Island.

Morthram spoke with Fen, telling him everything he had learned from reading King Oberon's thought. Fen readily agreed to meet with them the next morning to plan their assault on the Lost Fortress. Bartholomew spent the rest of the day in the library reading about the Grymmorian culture, while Oliver examined the masks and the orange liquid from the mine.

The following morning they all met in the library. Morthram was the first to speak.

"Each one of us has a unique set of skills. To successfully rescue Clara and stop Oberon, we will need to use all of our skills in concert. Bartholomew and I are high level shapers. We worked together to close the ferillium mine, freeing the prisoners and sending the guards back to Grymmore. Unfortunately, The Lost Fortress is not the ferillium mine, and Zoran is not Mr. Ferillium. We cannot overcome the forces in the Lost Fortress with brute shaping power. We are two shapers against the Emerald Ring and whatever forces he might have at his disposal. Zoran will have any number of strategically placed defenses to deter us. Even with surprise on our side, we will surely fail if we attempt to use force alone. The only viable option I see is the use of stealth. We must secretly infiltrate the Lost Fortress."

"I could not agree more," said Fen. "I know a great deal about the politics and intrigue which takes place within the King's palace. I grew up in that world. I knew Oberon before he was King, and I know the sort of muroidian he is."

"You grew up in Malgraven Castle?"

"I did, and I suppose it's time you knew the truth. I was put in the ferillium mine because I am the last rightful heir to the throne of Grymmore. My uncle was King Loran before Oberon took power. Oberon was his close advisor and staged a violent coup, killing the royal family and most of their heirs, including my parents. He is absolutely ruthless, craving only power. I was young when the coup took place. One of the guards was sent to kill me, but when he saw I was a bunny he sent me to the ferillium mine instead. I suppose he thought I wouldn't survive.

"You have all heard the stories of how much Oberon hates shapers. That is pure propaganda. He uses the muroidians' fear of shaping as a tool to keep Grymmore and Lapinor from becoming allies again. In private, he uses shaping to his advantage in every conceivable way, including having his own high level shaper.

"The truth is that Oberon wanted to be a shaper himself, but had no aptitude for it. This is not unusual – many are not meant for a life of shaping, but it was his own lack of ability that infuriated Oberon. He was denied the power he so utterly craved. Many of his teachers wound up in the ferillium mine, or worse. It's safe to say whatever Oberon does, he does in his insatiable quest for power.

"We can assume whatever machine lies beneath the Lost Fortress was created to bring more power to Oberon. Morthram, you read Oberon's thought and saw hundreds of shapers being held in the Fortress. We know the ferillium crystal absorbs the thoughts and power of shapers. If we combine Oberon's hunger for power, his desire to be a shaper, the ferillium crystal, the hundreds of captive shapers, and the infernal machine they are building, there seems to be only one logical conclusion. Oberon is building a device which will allow him to become the most powerful shaper in the world. I don't wish to sound unnecessarily dramatic, but it's very possible the fate of Lapinor itself rests in our paws. Oberon only pretends to despise shapers, but his absolute hatred for rabbits is quite real, I assure you."

Bartholomew looked at Fen grimly. "This chain of events we are caught up in has no end of surprises. There are forces at work here beyond our understanding, and they are pulling on the strings which lie beneath the physical world. What is crystal clear is that something or someone wants us to stop Oberon. I believe this force has brought us all together for that purpose alone."

It was Oliver's turn to speak. "I have examined the shaper masks and the orange liquid brought back from the mine. This has led me to a number of ideas for inventions which could help us bring Clara home safely and put a stop to Oberon. The devices I have in mind do not require the user to be a shaper and would work even if you were wearing a shapers mask. I would like to set up a small lab here at the Guild. The equipment I need could easily be shaped by Bartholomew. I am not an adventurer and shaper like Bartholomew, but I am a scientist and this is what I can do to help."

"Anything you need is yours. There is a large room off the main library you can use. I would also offer my assistance in the shaping of any laboratory equipment you might need."

"Thank you, Morthram. I'll start working on plans for the lab tonight."

Morthram continued,"We have all agreed the use of stealth is our best hope for defeating Oberon, but how precisely should we use it? What is our plan?"

Oliver responded first. "You said you saw scientists building a machine of some kind in the Lost Fortress. If

I could join Oberon's team of scientists, perhaps I could sabotage the machine."

"How would you get them to hire you?"

"I thought about that. I could let it be known I was working on a similar machine which would allow anyone to shape their thoughts. I have been thinking a great deal about just such a machine. There really is no reason why one couldn't be built. The texts in the library have given me any number of ideas for its construction. With my credentials, Oberon would be a fool not to hire me. Or at the very least, kidnap me and force me to work for him."

Fen responded, "I'm quite certain that would work. I know how Oberon thinks. He must always have the best, and in the world of science, you are the best. I could send letters to a number of Grymmorians who support Oberon and will more than likely pass the letters on to him. I will say you are designing such a machine here in Penrith, and will also mention your credentials as a scientist. It won't be long until they contact you."

Bartholomew stood up and said, "I can infiltrate the Fortress using my shaping skills. Using invisibility spheres and formshifting, I shouldn't have too much trouble finding Clara, although I have no idea what traps Zoran may have in store for us. As much as I would like Morthram's assistance, I think in this case we should work alone, neither of us knowing the plans of the other. In the event one of us is captured, we will have no secrets to reveal. I also have a number of ideas for a few items which do not require active shaping." He told them about Clara's thought and how it could be used to escape from the Lost Fortress.

Morthram spoke up. "Fen, what about you? Is there any need for you to go to the Fortress? Your knowledge of Oberon has already helped us immensely."

"My place is not in the Fortress, it is talking to the Grymmorian general council. When Oberon is removed from power, I want to be certain he is not replaced by someone just like him. We have suffered under this tyranny long enough. It's time for the countries of Grymmore and Lapinor to again become allies."

Morthram nodded. "Excellent. I believe we are on our way to a viable plan. Our next tasks should be building Oliver's lab and sending the letters announcing Oliver's shaping machine."

Oliver's lab was soon functional, and he spent all his waking hours there, leaving only for meals and sleep. Bartholomew visited the lab several times, but had little understanding of what he saw. The room was filled with beakers, flasks, and glass tubing, most of them filled with a strange assortment of boiling liquids and gooey, bubbling concoctions. There were blinking electrical devices and shelves lined with mysteriously labeled jars. Bartholomew quickly became lost when Oliver tried to explain any of it to him. It appeared to be more magic than science to Bartholomew.

Fen anonymously sent letters to six prominent Grymmorians who were on friendly terms with Oberon. He said he was afraid Oliver's machine might spell the downfall of Grymmore, adding that Oliver was not concerned with politics, only science. He would work for whoever would be the most helpful in advancing his shaping device.

Bartholomew discovered a fatal flaw in his plan to use Clara's thought as a means of escape. If he was wearing a shapers mask it wouldn't work. He remembered the small yellow spheres he and Morthram had shaped in the mine. If one was trapped inside a secret compartment in a ring, the wearer could flip the ring open and the sphere would fly out, transporting him to a predetermined location.

He decided to seek Oliver's help and headed down the long hallway leading to the new lab. He heard footsteps behind him and turned, but saw no one. Curious. Perhaps it had been the echo of his own footsteps? He continued down the hallway and heard the footsteps again, louder this time. Before he could turn around, an invisible pair of paws slipped a shapers mask over his head. He tried to pull the mask off but it was too late – it had already attached to him. What he saw next was completely unexpected. The air rippled and swirled in front of him, the blurry figure of a rabbit flickering in and out. Seconds later Oliver stood in front of him, wearing a ridiculously large grin.

"Poof! Surprised?"

"Oliver? What have you done?"

"Oh, just a little project I have been working on with Morthram." He handed Bartholomew a ring.

Bartholomew looked at it. It was a plain silver band with a small green stone set in the center.

"Touch the ring to your head."

Bartholomew looked puzzled, but did as Oliver asked. The shapers mask he was wearing released its grip on him. He pulled it off his head.

"How did you do that? And how did you make yourself invisible?"

"After I analyzed the orange substance you brought back from the mine, I was able to synthesize it. I discovered I could combine the de-masking agent with molten silver, and when the silver solidified it formed a ring which would release a mask. As for becoming invisible, that came about by understanding the nature of ferillium crystals. Ferillium crystals are a highly efficient way to store vast amounts of energy, but since I had none, I settled on a crystal with a somewhat similar structure. The green stone on the ring is a breonium crystal. Morthram was able to store an invisibility thought cloud in the breonium crystal which is released when the stone is tapped three times. The breonium crystal cannot store much shaping power, so the invisibility cloud can only be used once, and will only last for about three minutes."

"This is amazing, Oliver, and right in line with something I wanted to ask you about."

By the end of the day Bartholomew was wearing a heavy silver ring with an inset breonium crystal. The silver was infused with the de-masking agent, and inside a hidden compartment was a small yellow sphere which would transport the wearer fifty miles away even if they were wearing a shapers mask. By the end of the next day Oliver, Morthram, and Fen were all wearing the new escape rings. Oliver showed several interested shapers how to fabricate the rings, and they would soon be available to all Guild members.

Fen's prediction of Oberon's behavior proved to be quite accurate. A letter arrived for Oliver from one of Oberon's master scientists. He spoke enthusiastically of the work they were doing on their own shaping machine, and what a benefit it would be to both rabbits and muroidians. They wanted Oliver to come and work collaboratively with them. Oberon would pay Oliver twice whatever the Excelsior Corporation was paying him. Once the device was complete, a duplicate machine would of course be constructed for Lapinor. If Oliver wanted the position he should promptly reply and Oberon would send a carriage to meet him at the border. The letter didn't mention anything about the Lost Fortress or the hundreds of captive shapers.

Oliver wrote back saying he would happily accept the position and would be at the Grymmorian border gatehouse in three days.

He had one last project to work on with Bartholomew. Together they created two small sacks made out of shaper masks, each one holding a single thought cloud within it. One thought was of a bright green color, the other of a bright red color. When the bag was opened, the thought would find its way back to Bartholomew like a homing pigeon. If Oliver arrived safely at the Lost Fortress without incident, he would release the green thought. If he was being held captive or had otherwise run into trouble, he would release the red thought. Once they received either thought, Morthram and Bartholomew would leave for the Lost Fortress. What would happen after that was uncertain at best.

They held a party for Oliver the evening before he left for Grymmore. It was a cheerful event, with much laughing and any number of delicious pastries, but beneath the laughter and camaraderie lay the sobering awareness that this could be the last time they saw him. He was going to the Lost Fortress to work for King Oberon, and there was nothing certain about any situation involving Oberon. Oliver, however, seemed supremely confident and genuinely excited to see

Oberon's machine. He carried the red and green thoughts with him when he left in the morning.

Bartholomew shook his paw as Oliver stood next to the waiting carriage. "Have a good trip, and please be careful. Above all else, stay safe."

"Indeed I will, my friend. I have far too many inventions rattling around in my head to let anything happen to me. You and Morthram be careful as well. I know it won't be long until we'll all be back here having a slice of Mr. Ferillium's apple pie." He climbed into the carriage and closed the door. As the carriage began to move forward, Oliver waved and called out, "Give Clara a hug for me when you see her!"

"I will!" Bartholomew did his best to sound enthusiastic, but this new adventure they were on was the very definition of perilous. He remembered the words he had naively spoken on his first adventure. *'I would hardly use the word lovely to describe adventuring. Adventures can be quite perilous you know'.* How little he had known back then.

Almost a week later Bartholomew woke up to find a thought cloud hovering next to him on the bed. He hesitated only a moment before drawing it to him. His mind was filled with a bright green color. Oliver had done it. He was in the Lost Fortress, and he was safe. It was time to bring Clara home.

Chapter 23

Oliver's Tale

Oliver found the carriage ride to the Grymmorian border quite pleasant. There was no walking involved, he had brought several interesting scientific volumes to read, and he had packed a substantial lunch. The weather was delightful, and the driver pleasant but not excessively chatty. They reached the border gate in the late afternoon. Oliver thanked the driver by way of a generous tip, then picked up his two bags and marched over to the gatehouse.

"Name?"

"Oliver T. Rabbit."

"Any fruits or vegetables or insects of any kind?"

"No, sir."

"Shaper?"

"I am not."

"Purpose of visit?"

"King Oberon sent for me."

The guard looked up from his pad of paper with a startled expression. "What?"

"King Oberon sent for me."

"You're the one they're waiting for. Follow me, please, sir."

Oliver followed the guard over to a large black carriage drawn by four horses. The guard knocked on the carriage door, then opened it for Oliver.

"Please step into the carriage, sir. I will take care of your bags."

Oliver climbed into the carriage and took a seat. A distinguished looking muroidian sitting across from him smiled pleasantly. Moments later the driver shut the door and the carriage jerked forward.

"You must be Oliver T. Rabbit."

"I am indeed, sir. Formerly employed by the Excelsior Corporation as head of Research and Material Acquisitions."

"I am familiar with your work, and can tell you it is an honor to meet you. I am Grymmorian Science Master Tarami. I have a background in several disciplines, but of course nothing comparable to your levels of expertise. We were very pleased to hear you had accepted the King's offer to work with us. I hope you will find our facilities adequate. The laboratories are in a rather unique location, but as I always say, science is science wherever you find it."

"I couldn't agree with you more. I'm quite excited to begin. Are you at all familiar with the project?"

"I am, but I would rather let you see for yourself the progress we have made. If I might be candid, I have heard some intriguing rumors about you, including one that said you were designing your own shaping machine. Is this true?"

"I have given a great deal of thought to the machine and have a number of viable designs in mind, but haven't yet begun the actual fabrication of the device. The only thing I'm really lacking is a method of storing the vast amounts of necessary initial shaping energy. I am leaning towards the use of breonium crystals as the energy storage system. Ferillium crystals would be far more efficient, of course, but they are impossibly difficult to create."

Master Tarami studied Oliver carefully. "Indeed."

They chatted pleasantly about other topics for an hour or so until Master Tarami said he was tired from the long ride and thought he would take a short nap. Oliver stretched out across his seat with a good book, but was soon snoring, lulled to sleep by the rocking carriage. After the first few snores, Tarami's eyes popped open. He held out one paw and a pink cloud emerged from Oliver's ear, floating over to Tarami. Soon a stream of thought clouds was flowing from Oliver to the Grymmorian science master. When they stopped, Master Tarami sat silently for several minutes, a dark expression on his face. A thought cloud floated out of his ear, shot out the carriage window and sped off into the distance.

The carriage stopped at an inn where they had an excellent dinner, along with several different kinds of wine. Oliver tried a number of native Grymmorian dishes and found them to be both exotic and delicious. Talk turned to the project he would be working on.

"You had mentioned your laboratories are in an unusual location?"

"King Oberon decided to build the machine in a secure location. This is not a device you would want in the paws of your enemy, considering the massive shaping power involved. As I mentioned in my letter to you, we will be building a duplicate machine for Lapinor once we have a good working prototype. The labs are inside a structure we refer to as the Lost Fortress. We are uncertain of its age, but believe it to be a minimum of two or three thousand years old. We unfortunately have no idea who built it. The carvings and glyphs found throughout the Fortress are unknown to us. The Fortress was discovered by a party of the King's guards almost ten years ago. When they found it, the exterior was covered with vines and other plant growth, but the inside was pristine. We're still trying to determine how it managed to last millennia with almost no weathering or distress. It's a fascinating structure and demands a much more concentrated study than it has received. Perhaps you will be able to spend some time studying it yourself while you're there."

When dinner was over they boarded the carriage again. The driver had folded the seats down so they could sleep. Oliver pulled a blanket over him and was soon sleeping soundly, with some assistance from the two glasses of wine he had during dinner. They finally arrived at their destination just as the sun was setting the following evening.

"Welcome to the Lost Fortress, sir."

Oliver climbed down from the carriage and gave a barely concealed gasp of amazement. "Good heavens, this is the Lost Fortress? The scale of this structure is comparable to nothing I have ever seen."

The driver carried Oliver's bags across a wide bridge leading to the Fortress. At the front of the Fortress were two enormous metal doors standing nearly forty feet tall. Oliver and Master Tarami entered the Fortress through a small door at the base of the two main doors.

The sheer immensity of the interior was staggering.

"This engineering is quite unique. What kind of rock are the walls made of?"

"We're not certain. In fact, we're not even certain it is rock. It may be some sort of synthetic material. The main gates seem to be metal, but again, it's not a metal we are familiar with."

They strode along for almost a half mile until they reached a wide set of descending stairs.

"There are two levels below the main floor. The laboratory is on the first sub-level. The level below that is for storage, although the area is so vast most of it remains empty. We'll get you set up with a room, then tomorrow we can visit the laboratory and see the machine. We're all very excited to hear what you think of it."

Master Scientist Tarami led Oliver down the stairs to the first sub-level. They passed at least a dozen corridors before making a right turn, finally stopping in front of a room with a strange metallic glyph embedded in it.

"This will be your room."

"What's the symbol on the door?"

"I have no idea. I can only assume it's an ancient number or letter. Oh, work hours are uncertain at best. We have been known to work all night and sleep all day, so meals are always available in the dining hall. They'll prepare whatever you wish. I see your bags have already arrived so I will leave you to your own devices until tomorrow. I'll stop by in the morning and we can visit the lab."

"Thank you for your kind welcome, Master Tarami. You have made me feel quite at home."

"I'm glad you're here, Oliver. I clearly understand the degree of expertise you bring with you."

With a friendly wave, Master Tarami headed off down the corridor, leaving Oliver alone. Once the door was closed, Oliver took out the shaper mask bag containing the green thought. He untied it, holding the bag open until he was certain the thought had escaped. Then he unpacked his bags, put his clothes away, and retired for the evening.

At the end of the corridor Master Tarami stood watching Oliver's room. He saw the green thought float out through the door. With a grim smile of satisfaction he turned and disappeared down the hallway.

The following morning there was a knock on the door just as Oliver had finished dressing. It was Master Tarami.

"Would you like to have breakfast first, or would you rather see the lab?"

"Ha, a difficult choice indeed. My two favorite pastimes – food and science. In this case, I believe science trumps food. I would love to see your lab."

"Excellent, just follow me."

Master Scientist Tarami's lab proved to be far larger than the Excelsior Corporation laboratories, with forty lab stations and over a hundred scientists and technicians.

"This is far more extensive than I had expected. I am truly impressed with the caliber of your facilities."

"I'm glad to hear it. Would you like to look at the machine?"

"I can't wait. Lead the way."

They walked through the laboratory to a set of wide metal doors. Master Tarami stepped on a metal plate and the doors swung open. Inside was a mammoth and highly complex machine. Shaped like a gigantic donut, it stood at least fifty feet across in any direction. The ring was elevated eight feet above the ground by a spiderweb of metal framework, allowing easy access to any part of the device. As they walked beneath the ring, Oliver noticed a transparent bowl-shaped platform hanging down from the center of the machine. He suspected this was where they would place the ferillium crystal when the machine was operational. Oliver soon left Master Tarami behind, striding enthusiastically around the machine, examining it closely. There were hundreds of feet of silver tubing, miles of wiring, electronic switches and panels, any number of steam valves, and twelve monstrous electromagnets. Oliver flipped open a large panel to look at the gauges and dials, then climbed a ladder up to the ring above. He wasn't quite certain what the ring itself was made of, but suspected it was simply a more substantial version of the fabric used in shaper masks. The shaper's thoughts would travel around inside the ring at incredible velocities as they were being amplified. When he had completed his inspection, he climbed down the ladder and found Master Tarami.

"You deserve the highest accolades for what you have created here. I am also pleased to say this is remarkably similar to one of my designs. There are some sections I would modify to increase the output of shaping energy, but those would all be relatively minor adjustments. The only thing which seems to be missing is a source for the initial input of the shaping forces before they are amplified. Will you be using breonium crystals?"

"We were fortunate enough to find a large ferillium crystal. It's spherical in shape, almost a foot across."

"A foot across? Impossible. How could that be?"

"One of our geology teams found an incredibly rich ferillium deposit beside an ancient volcano in western Grymmore. The heat from the erupting lava flow must have fused tons of the raw ferillium, creating the enormous crystal. We had to carefully cut and polish it to its current spherical shape, a very touchy procedure to say the least. We almost lost several scientists before we completely understood the process."

"What a fantastic stroke of luck to find such a crystal, and what a boon for Grymmore to have a device such as this. Your country will never be wanting for food or medicines again."

"Thank you, Oliver, for all your generous comments. I would like to introduce you to our group of extremely talented scientists, but before I do that, I have one last surprise for you.

"This has been a day full of surprises. All good ones, I might add."

"Then I'm certain you'll like this one. Guards!"

Four Grymmorian guards stepped out from behind one of the massive electromagnets. They swooped over to Oliver and grabbed his arms. There was a flash of metal, a clicking sound, and Oliver's paws were manacled behind his back.

"What are you doing? Release me, sir!"

"Master Tarami rippled and blurred, reappearing as Zoran the emerald shaper.

"Did you think I wouldn't be able to read your thoughts? I've known you were a traitor since the carriage ride. There is nothing I don't know about you, including your feeble ploy with the red and green thoughts. I let you send the green thought out so your little unsuspecting shaper friends will be certain to pay us a visit. You may be assured we have an exceptionally unpleasant welcome planned for them. If you were Lapinor's master plan to put a stop to King Oberon's machine, then Lapinor is a sad excuse for a country, and the rabbits will be easy prey for Oberon.

"Guards, take him to the sub-level three cell we've prepared for him. Take everything from his pockets and take that silver ring off his paw before he can use it. Bring everything you find to me before you place him in the dungeon." Zoran turned on his heel and strode out of the room.

The guards led Oliver out of the lab. Scientists and technicians watched with frozen faces as Oliver was roughly ushered past them. There was some murmuring, but most stood silently, knowing they could be Zoran's next victim.

The four guards half walked and half dragged Oliver down the long hallways and stairs until they arrived at a massive staircase leading down to the second sub-level. After another ten minutes of walking they reached a wide corridor lined with barred cells. Each prison cell was filled with dozens of rabbits wearing shaper masks, but Oliver saw no sign of Clara. A final left turn led to a third set of descending stairs.

"Where are you taking me?"

"Big scientist rabbit like you get your own cell in sub-level three. Zoran don't want you talking to no one but your own self." The other three guards laughed. At the bottom of the stairs they turned left and headed down a short hall with a single barred cell at the end of it.

"Zoran made cell special. Nothing can break bars."

They removed his manacles and one of the guards roughly pushed Oliver into the cell. Seconds later the cell door slammed shut behind him. There was a soft clicking noise as the guard locked it.

"Have good dreams, rabbit." The guards sauntered away, leaving Oliver alone with his thoughts.

He sat down on a rough wooden bench, the only piece of furniture in the cell other than a straw mattress on the floor. There would be no escape unless someone came to rescue him. He managed a brief smile when he remembered Bartholomew coming to his rescue in the Swamp of Lost Things. Like Bartholomew, Oliver had changed a great deal since those days.

His cell was about twenty feet long and ten feet wide. The only object of interest was a metal star embedded in the wall about seven feet above the floor. The twelve pointed star was a dull silver color, about eight inches across, and looked as if it was part of the original Fortress. After an hour of sitting on the hard wooden bench, Oliver moved to the more comfortable straw mattress on the floor. He could feel his hope dwindling rapidly. He had failed in his attempt to sabotage the machine and now he was trapped in this cell with no chance of escape.

As he lay on his back staring at the ceiling, he noticed a row of symbols running along the top of the wall. He first gazed at them with idle curiosity, but his interest in them began to grow. They must be some of the ancient glyphs Zoran had mentioned. Oliver saw something oddly familiar about them. Pushing the bench next to the wall, he clambered up for a better view of the symbols. It became clear to him why they looked familiar. They bore a distinct resemblance to modern mathematical symbols. He read them carefully, making his way around the wall. If he correctly understood their meaning, the line of symbols was expressing two separate mathematical problems.

He jumped down from the bench and wrote out both problems in the thick dust on the floor. He had them both solved within a half hour. The problems were complex, but the final answers were simple. The answer to the first problem was seven, the other answer was four. Why would these problems be carved into this particular wall? Seven and four. Did they hold some cultural significance for the creatures who had inhabited the Fortress? His eyes moved to the silver star on the wall. Was there a connection between the numbers and the star? He examined the star closely from different angles, and made out the faint image of a paw on it. He pushed the star, but nothing happened. Nothing about this area of the Fortress made sense. Why would the builders put in a wide staircase leading to a dead end? He pored over the walls looking for a hidden door. Perhaps there was a secret button or latch?

The star had twelve points – could the two numbers reference two points? He stood on the bench in front of the star. He pushed the seventh point of the star, then the fourth point. Nothing happened. He put his paw in the center of the star and pushed. A section of the wall silently slid open, revealing a long hallway. Eureka.

The hallway was well lit, but with no obvious light source. The light seemed to come from everywhere, as though the walls and floors themselves had a slight glow to them. Oliver stepped through the doorway, looking back to make certain the guards weren't returning. There were two discs next to the sliding wall. One was yellow, the other pale violet. He pushed the violet disc and nothing happened. He pushed the yellow disc and the wall silently closed behind him. He had escaped, but to where?

Chapter 24

Oliver's New Library Card

Several hours later two guards sauntered in to check on Oliver. They stared blankly at the empty cell, then unlocked the cell door and walked inside, searching for him in places he could not possibly be.

"Look under bench."

"He not be under the bench. He is grown rabbit. Can't be there."

"Check under straw mattress."

"He not be there either."

"Maybe he digs tunnel in the floor and mattress is cover it."

The guard moved the mattress. There was nothing there.

"What should we do? Who we telling?"

"We tell nobody, that who we is telling. Zoran kill us if he hear rabbit escape. We keep mouth shut. If someone ask about rabbit, then we need quick disappear."

"Lock door and we go. Fortress bad. Not right."

Oliver padded quietly down the hallway and found another set of colored discs on the wall. He pushed the violet one and a section of wall slid open, revealing a large room lit with the same strange ambient light. There were racks running along the walls, filled with numerous unidentifiable objects. This must have been a storage area for whoever built the Fortress. There was one large rack containing glasslike cylinders with four narrow silver tubes running down the length of them. There was a row of five blinking yellow lights inside the glass tube. He pulled one of the cylinders off the rack and examined it. It had a dark green elliptical button about three inches long near one end of it. Oliver pressed the button. The was a soft whoosh noise and when he looked up there was a two foot wide hole in the wall that hadn't been there before. He could see through the hole into the hallway where he'd just been standing.

"Good heavens, did I do that?" He backed away from the wall and tried it again. A second hole appeared in the wall. Whatever this was, it could instantly vaporize physical matter. What kind of creatures could have created such a device? He carefully placed the vaporizing tube back in the rack and moved to another section of the room. He found larger, more complex, and probably far more powerful devices in the room but was afraid to touch them. There were also many smaller devices which vaguely resembled revolvers, but were fashioned out of glass tubing in much the same manner as the cylindrical vaporizer weapon. This must have been an armory.

He explored farther down the hallway, which

stretched out for almost a half mile and was lined with innumerable doors. Many of the rooms were filled with objects he could not identify. He had no idea whether he was looking at scientific equipment, deadly weapons, or machines to make soup, so he refrained from pushing any more buttons. One room in particular gave him quite a start. He opened the door, then wildly scrambled backwards into the hallway. The room was filled with ten foot tall silver metallic rabbits with red glass eyes. When he examined them more closely he found small panels on the back of each rabbit which he was unable to open. He had no idea what the metal rabbits were so he left them behind and moved on.

He discovered one room that had a wide gleaming shelf wrapping completely around it about five feet above the ground. Running along the shelf were many brightly colored panels containing different colored buttons and levers. There were also colorful images of tall rabbits happily eating various kinds of food, most of which was unfamiliar to him. One machine had a graphic of a rabbit eating something which resembled a cookie. The machine had three round buttons on it and a small glass door at the bottom. Oliver pushed a pale green button, and with a soft whirring noise the door flipped down and a small tray slid out. There was something like a cookie on it. Oliver picked it up. It was warm and smelled quite good, like molasses. He took a small bite, then a large bite. It was delicious. An hour later he had a tray loaded with unfamiliar but remarkably delicious food. He set the tray down on the long shelf and began to eat, looking around at the machines. The line between science and magic was fading rapidly.

As he roamed through the rooms he found many which appeared to be the sleeping chambers for whoever had lived here. All the beds had curved glass lids on them. Whoever inhabited the Fortress must have been tall, as the beds were almost twelve feet long.

Oliver finally reached the end of the corridor and stood facing a massive set of doors. He pushed a violet disc on the wall and the huge doors hissed open. The room in front of him was at least three hundred feet long and thirty or forty feet tall. As far as he could see were massive racks at least twenty feet tall filled with books. This single room contained millions upon millions of books.

"Great heavens, what is this place? I could spend the rest of my life in one small alcove of this library and not read half the books there."

He wandered down the aisles, scanning the titles as he went. Many were in languages unknown to him, but there were also many he was able to read. This was almost too much for him to absorb. He picked up a book which seemed to be about machines which were capable of flight. He opened it and began poring through the illustrations within.

"This is fantastic. This single volume contains detailed plans for any number of self-propelled flying machines. This would completely change the way rabbits–"

"Excuse me, if you wish to borrow a book, I'll need to see your identification card."

Oliver turned around faster than it seemed the laws of physics should allow. He stumbled backwards and tripped over one of the racks, falling onto his back. He was looking up at a ten foot tall silver metallic rabbit with glowing red eyes. Oliver's eyes were, as they say, as big as saucers.

"Oh, dear, I didn't mean to startle you like that. Are you all right? Would you like a glass of water?"

Oliver tried to gather his thoughts. At least the thing wasn't trying to kill him. "What... uh... who are you?"

"I am the caretaker of the Central Information Repository. I hope you didn't injure yourself, but rules are rules you know. A valid identification card must be shown to borrow a book."

"You're said you're the caretaker here?"

"For almost fifteen hundred years."

"You've been here for fifteen hundred years?"

"Approximately."

"What is this place again?"

"The is the Central Information Repository."

"Why are you here? Who borrows the books?"

"I am the custodian of this repository." One of the rabbit's eyes glowed brightly and a transparent wall of symbols appeared in front of him. He moved the symbols around with his paw. "Let's see, the last book to be borrowed was *Creating the Isle of Mandor*a, fourteen hundred and ninety-two years ago." He frowned slightly. "I see the book was never returned."

"May I ask you questions about this place?"

"Of course. My function is to answer all your questions. I contain within me the sum of all knowledge found in this repository."

"I hope this is not offensive, but are you a machine or a rabbit?"

"I am not capable of being offended. I am a machine, an artificially intelligent Model 9000 Rabbiton with the optional A7-Series 3 Repositorian

Module."

"Ahh, I see. Who built you? Where did they go? Why did they leave?"

"The Elders created me. They are an ancient race of rabbits who built this Fortress and inhabited it for over ten thousand years. Through the combined use of science and shaping they evolved at an extraordinary rate. They grew weary of this world and decided to create one more to their liking. They first built the Isle of Mandora, a single island in a world where time does not exist. Once the environment was completely functional, they began to add more land and cities. As far as I know, that is where they still are. I chose to stay behind and watch over the repository. I have been here ever since."

"Have you ever seen the world outside of this library?"

"I have seen pictures of the world in countless books and morphs."

"Morphs?"

"It is similar to what the Elders called dreams, but the experiences viewed in each particular morph always remain the same."

"I see. Could I ask a favor of you?"

"Certainly."

"I don't have an identification card, but I would dearly love to read some of these books. If I were very careful, would you allow me to sit here and read without a card?"

"That would be quite acceptable. It would please me to see someone reading in the repository again. I will also create an identity card for you. Since I contain the A7-Series 3 Repositorian Module I have that functionality. Once you have the card, you would be free to borrow up to eighteen books every two days."

"That would be kind of you, indeed." Oliver gave the Rabbiton his full name and address and the names of three references at the Excelsior Corporation.

"If you return before the end of the day tomorrow, you may pick up your card. Welcome to our Information Repository, Oliver T. Rabbit." The Rabbiton turned away and disappeared down the aisle.

Oliver found a large stuffed reading chair and sat down with a plate of semi-magical molasses cookies and a tall stack of books. He wasn't in heaven, but he could see it from here.

Chapter 25

Finding Eftar

Morthram had devised his plan to enter the Lost Fortress well before Oliver's green thought had arrived. One thing he knew for certain was that Oberon and Zoran must not suspect anyone was on their way to the Lost Fortress. If they heard rumors of shapers traveling through Grymmore, they would know who it was and what they were after. For this reason, Morthram had decided to avoid shaping altogether on his journey across Grymmore to the Lost Fortress. He knew he could easily travel on foot to the Fortress and arrive before Oberon's machine would be operational. If he planned carefully and made all the necessary preparations, no shaping would be necessary until he reached the Lost Fortress.

Morthram's master plan revolved around a rather esoteric shaping procedure. It was a technique he had never attempted, and would require Fen's assistance. Fortunately, Fen had enthusiastically agreed to help him.

On the day Oliver's green thought arrived,

Morthram and Fen retreated to one of the practice rooms off the main Guild hall. Morthram locked the door and shaped a sphere of silence around the room. As Fen watched, Morthram formshifted into a ragged looking Grymmorian. His previous disguise as a lowly servant in Oberon's castle would have been successful if not for his betrayal by Thaddeus Rabbit, so Morthram decided to use a similar form to enter the Fortress. He would become Cindar, a vagabond muroidian who was down on his luck. The first step was formshifting into Cindar, and the second step was learning to speak Grymmorian. Rather than project thoughts to Grymmorians he met along the way, Morthram wanted to actually speak fluent Grymmorian. The new shaping technique he would use required him to read the language center of Fen's brain, then duplicate it in his own brain. If it worked as planned, he would be able to speak both Grymmorian and Lapinoric.

Morthram handed Fen a book written in Grymmorian. "Read this out loud while I locate your brain's language center."

Fen began speaking in a series of squeaks, squeals, and clicking noises. Morthram sent out a pale yellow translucent sphere which enveloped Fen's head. He watched closely as different sections of the yellow sphere began to glow brightly, finally motioning for Fen to stop reading. He placed one paw on Fen's head and the other paw on his own head. Waves of shimmering light traveled from Fen's head through both of Morthram's arms and up into his own head. When it stopped, Morthram moved to a nearby chair. He lowered his head, paws covering his eyes. A dim red glow surrounded his head, then dissipated. He stood up and faced Fen.

"Can you understand what I am saying?" A series of clicks and squeals came out of his mouth.

"If I met you on the street, I would think you had spent your entire life in Grymmore."

"Excellent. It appears to have worked. Oh, before I forget, I wanted to ask you about something." Morthram reached into his coat pocket and removed the six sided silver medallion they had found in Mr. Ferillium's office.

"Bartholomew and I found this in Mr. Ferillium's vault and thought it might be important. Can you understand the writing on it? I thought it could be Grymmorian." He handed the medallion to Fen.

Fen studied it carefully. "You're right, it's Grymmorian. Take it with you. It says the bearer of the medallion is allowed entrance to King Oberon's palaces. I don't know if that includes the Lost Fortress, but it might."

"I'll take it. At the very least it says I am a trusted friend of the King. Thanks for your help, Fen. I'll be ready to leave once I shape clothing and gear suitable for a wandering unemployed muroidian."

Morthram departed in the dead of night without telling anyone. He arrived at the Grymmorian border gatehouse just as the sun was rising.

"Name?"

"Cindar." Morthram still was not used to the strange squealing noises coming out of his mouth.

"Fruits, vegetables, or insects?"

"None."

"Shaper?"

"Wish I was. I'd shape me a bag of gold, a gallon of

ale, and a rich princess."

The guard snorted.

"Occupation?"

"Unemployed carpenter."

"Try Grymssteir. I hear they're hiring."

"Thanks, I'll do that."

"Pass."

Morthram nodded to the guard and walked across the border. He headed north along a well traveled dirt road. Dozens of Grymmorians were traveling in both directions, many of them taking goods to market in wooden push carts.

The path to the Lost Fortress was relatively straightforward. Morthram would continue north on this road for four or five days, then head east through the wilderness for another two days until he reached the Fandor Mountains. The Fortress was built into the side of the range. The trip would be far easier if he could use shaping, but this way there was almost no chance of his being discovered.

He walked as many as ten hours a day. When the sun began to set he would put up his tent and crawl inside. His meals were simple, and he left no clues behind that might reveal his identity.

On the third day of his journey, a Grymmorian strolled up alongside him and began to chat.

"Where you headed?"

"Maybe Grymssteir. I'm a carpenter looking for work and I heard they might be hiring. Haven't had much luck so far though."

The Grymmorian gave him a sympathetic look. "Hmmm, too bad. Work's hard to find these days." He didn't need to say why – the outrageous taxes demanded by King Oberon had put thousands of Grymmorians out of work. "Tell you what though, I run a small mill along the Farlo River. My wife has been nagging me to repair a few things around the house, and I'm not much of a carpenter. I could pay you a little something to fix it up. I'll even throw in a few home cooked meals."

Morthram looked at the Grymmorian. Something deep inside told him to say yes.

"Sure. I'd appreciate that. The only thing worse than having work is not having it."

"You got that right, my friend. I'm Lithar, by the way."

Morthram put his paw out. "Cindar."

Several hours later they arrived at Lithar's mill. It was a modest operation, but grinding wheat for the nearby farms provided enough income for the family to get by. Lithar led Morthram into his house and introduced him to his wife. There were two young muroidians lying on the floor reading.

"These must be yours, I'm guessing. You're lucky to have a couple of healthy young pups like that."

Lithar's wife looked at her husband, her eyes welling up with tears.

"Did I say something wrong? I'm sorry if I did. I didn't mean–"

"The fault is not yours, Cindar. Our third young one, Eftar, was taken from us by a gang of local bandits to be raised as one of their own. Most of us live in fear of them. I am a miller, not a warrior, and if I had gone after him I would more than likely have lost my life, leaving my family worse off than before. We sent a rescue party several years ago for another pup who was taken, but none of them returned."

Morthram had a strong feeling that Eftar was the real reason he had been drawn here. It was part of the chain of events leading to the return of Clara and the downfall of Oberon. He had to find Eftar.

"Where did they take him?"

A spark of hope appeared in Lithar's eyes. "There's a place they call the old silver mine. I don't know if anyone ever found silver there, but that's what they call it."

"Can you draw me a map?"

Lithar disappeared into another room, returning a short while later with a roughly drawn map.

"You are only one muroid against a gang of bandits. Do you truly think you can bring Eftar home safely?"

Morthram smiled. "I will do the best I can. I have not always been a carpenter."

Lithar nodded but said nothing.

Lithar's wife prepared the evening meal for them. There was no talk of Eftar, but as they sat around the table Morthram listened to their tales of life on the river and how they had come to own the mill. It made Morthram sad to think about the blind hatred some rabbits had for Grymmorians.

Morthram shook paws with Lithar the next morning, and Lithar's wife gave Morthram a hug.

"I cannot thank you enough for what you are doing. Do be careful."

"I will do my best to bring Eftar back to you."

Morthram followed the path shown on Lithar's map and by late afternoon found himself peering through dense foliage at a dark opening in the side of a hill. It didn't look much like a silver mine, but that's what

Lithar had called it. He stayed hidden in the brush, keeping a sharp lookout for bandits. There was no activity other than one scruffy looking muroidian who exited the mine and headed south on the dirt road. Morthram decided to enter the mine, but first he had to break his own rule and do some shaping.

When he was safely concealed, Morthram shaped a battered old pickaxe and a heavy wooden bucket containing a few chunks of rich silver ore. Gathering them up, he headed into the dark mine. The tunnel was about fifteen feet tall and twenty or thirty feet wide. Something about it didn't seem right – it wasn't like other mines he had seen. He stopped several times to use his pick on the tunnel wall, knocking off dirt and rock, but found no trace of silver ore. Glowing lanterns hung down from the tunnel ceiling, casting eerie flickering shadows through the dark tunnel. He came to a set of descending stairs. Stairs in a silver mine? He was kneeling down to inspect them when he heard a voice.

"Name yourself."

"I am called Cindar. I was told about this old silver mine and thought I would explore it. I had hoped I might find silver ore the old miners had missed."

A muroidian stepped out of the shadows and looked Cindar up and down. With an undisguised threatening voice he said, "These old mines can be dangerous. Plenty of muroids have been lost in them, never to be found again."

"Mines don't scare me. I've been in plenty and I've found plenty of rich ore in the old ones. Found some already. Is this your mine?"

"It is. We laid claim to it. You found silver here?"

"I did. I have a knack for it. Not sure why, but I can always find it."

"Show me."

Morthram brought the bucket over and showed him the silver ore.

"You're right. That's rich ore. Don't belong to you though."

"I'll make a deal with you. I'll search the mine and find what I can. Then we'll split it down the middle. Half to me, half to you."

The bandit's eyes narrowed slightly. "Fair enough. I'll tell my friends you'll be coming through the mine. You won't last ten minutes without me telling them so." A dark gray thought floated out of the bandit's ear. Morthram pulled it over to him. He was filled with an intense greed and simmering rage. He heard the bandit's voice in his head. "How about this plan – we take all the silver and throw you down the shaft where the demons live."

"We have a deal then. I'll move deeper into the mine and keep looking. Where can I find you so we can split the silver? You have a camp here?"

"Four forks in the tunnel. Left, left, right, left. That's our camp." The bandit turned and disappeared around a curve.

Morthram made a point of hitting his pick loudly against the rocky wall several times while the bandit was still within earshot. Large chunks of earth and rock chipped off, revealing a smooth pale green surface beneath. What was this? He examined it carefully. It was obviously not a natural formation. He tried to scratch it with the pick but could not. Who had fashioned this tunnel?

He moved farther into the mine. Rather than turn left at the first fork, he went right. There were no lanterns, but there was a slight glow emanating from the walls. After a while his eyes became accustomed to the dim light and he could find his way without lanterns. The tunnel exited into a square cavern which had two tunnels leading out, each one in the center of a wall.

He followed one tunnel almost a half mile farther, drawing a map of his route so he wouldn't lose his way. Reaching another square cavern, he examined the walls for any hint of who the builders might have been. A slight rectangular indentation about twelve feet high and five feet wide caught his eye. He hit it with his pick, knocking some dense layers of earth off it, and kept chipping away at it until a smooth blue surface was revealed. It also revealed a glowing violet disc. He touched it to see if it moved. There was a low grinding noise and one side of the twelve foot rectangle cracked open about an inch, then stopped. It was a door. Morthram pushed with all his might but couldn't open it. After he returned Eftar to his parents he would come back and shape the door open.

He shaped another half dozen pieces of silver ore, then headed back towards the bandits' camp. He wanted to make certain Eftar was still with them. He tried to project a casual air as he strolled into the bandits' den. It was an enormous rectangular room containing four wooden shacks and ten or twelve large canvas tents. He could see several dozen bandits, some sitting by campfires drinking, some playing cards. He noticed a young muroidian carrying a pitcher of ale to a group of the bandits. He looked about the age Eftar would be.

"Why didn't you tell me you had ale here? Boy, what's your name?"

"It's Eftar, sir."

"Bring me some ale, Eftar." Eftar looked at the bandits for permission.

One of the bandits looked up at Morthram. "You the miner?"

"I am."

"You find any silver?"

"I found plenty. Just have to know where to dig. There'll be lots more in the back of the mine. That's the part they always leave. Tell you what. Give that boy a lantern and send him with me. I can dig twice as fast if he holds the light for me."

"You heard him boy. Get a lantern and go with him."

"How about that ale?"

"You'll get ale when we get silver."

"Fair enough. Don't drink it all before I get back."

Eftar took a lantern from the wall and walked over to Morthram.

"We go through there to the back of the mine, sir."

"Lead the way, boy."

Morthram followed him through at least four more square caverns. Finally, Eftar stopped and turned around. "The is the last big room. There's a deep shaft over there the bandits are all afraid of. Sometimes noises come out of it. I heard them say they cave demons live down there, but it's probably just some kind of little critters or something."

"Thanks, Eftar. I'm tired, I need to sit down for a bit."

Morthram sat down and leaned back against the

wall. Eftar did the same, setting the lantern on the ground in front of them. Morthram pointed to the lantern.

"Always liked to watch flames – the way they move back and forth like that makes me sleepy." He could see Eftar staring at the flame, his eyes beginning to droop. A blue thought cloud floated out of Morthram's ear and over to Eftar. Moments later Eftar was sound asleep. Morthram stood up and held out his paw. Eftar vanished in a small flash of yellow light, reappearing in his front yard a split second later with no memory of how he had gotten there. There was a shriek from inside the house when his mother saw him walk through the front door.

Morthram sat down next to the lantern. As he watched the flame, a smile slowly spread across his face. He had a good idea how to permanently clear the mine of bandits. He leaned back, waiting and listening for the bandits. It wasn't long before he heard the slight scrunching noise of paws on gravel and whispering voices. He would make it easy for them. He stood up and walked over to the edge of the shaft. Holding the lantern over it he could see a hundred feet or so down, but after that it was pitch black. The shaft was a perfect circle about twenty feet across, and was not a natural formation. He set down the bucket of silver ore and the lantern near the edge of the shaft.

The bandits were clumsily creeping up behind him. He waited for the push from behind. When it came, he toppled into the shaft, disappearing into the darkness. The bandits heard a terrible shriek, then seconds later a distant thud and a crashing of rocks.

"Take the silver." One of the bandits picked up the

bucket and they turned to leave. When they were halfway across the room a low raspy gurgling rose up from the shaft. The bandits looked back, terrified at what they might see. A monstrous spiky purple lizard head poked up out of the shaft. The beast clawed its way out onto the mine floor, its eyes burning red, its gaping mouth filled with rows of razor sharp yellow teeth. There was a great shrieking roar and a ball of flame shot out of its mouth towards the bandits. It was debatable who shrieked louder, the lizard or the bandits, but the bandits definitely ran faster. They were gone from the room in less than a second and every bandit was gone from the mine within fifteen minutes.

As soon as the bandits exited the room the lizard faded away. Morthram sat at the bottom of the shaft and laughed until tears ran down his face. He had transformed his physical self to a thought cloud halfway through his fall down the shaft. When he reappeared at the bottom he shaped a large sandbag speeding towards the ground, the dreadful thudding sound the bandits had heard. This was a story Morthram would tell for years to come, and each time he told the tale the bandits screamed louder and ran faster.

Chapter 26

The Birth of Edmund

It was pitch black at the bottom of the shaft, but Morthram could feel the floor was flat and smooth. He shaped a small sphere of light several feet above his head, illuminating a pale green floor made of the same material as the walls in the mine tunnel. He noticed a dim glow near the far wall. When he examined the area he found two glowing discs just like the one next to the door he had tried to open. One was yellow and one violet. He touched the violet disc and a round section of the floor silently slid open, flooding the dark shaft with light.

Morthram peered down through the opening and saw another room below, the same size and shape as the shaft. The room had four glowing discs on one side, each a different color. There was a ladder descending into the room, which Morthram quickly climbed down. The instant his foot touched the floor the circular opening above him slid closed.

There was a recessed doorway on the far side of the room, and next to the door were the now familiar glowing discs. A push on the violet disc opened the door. Morthram looked through to a tunnel that dwarfed any he had seen before. It stood at least two hundred feet tall and three hundred feet wide, flat on the bottom with a wide arching roof. Six rows of gleaming silver tracks ran off into the distance. Hovering silently above the tracks were two sparkling transparent cylinders about seventy feet long, each with four rows of seats running the length of the tube.

Morthram looked at the exterior of the cylindrical room he had just exited, realizing its function was probably the same as the elevators he'd seen in a few of the larger Lapinoric cities. It was simply a device to transport rabbits between different levels.

He walked across the platform to the glass cars. It reminded him of the train station in Penrith. The technology was completely different of course, and this station was ten times larger, but the basic concept of transporting rabbits from one point to another was the same. He looked around the station and spotted some large colorful signs with pictures of extremely tall rabbits engaged in various activities. These reminded him of the advertising posters found in any Lapinoric train station. This station must have been abandoned eons ago, but the two glass cylinder cars floating silently above the silver tracks looked brand new. He had no idea how that was possible.

He approached one of the cars, and with a whirring noise its door slid open. He instinctively jumped back. He didn't like machines that did things by themselves. When nothing more happened, he stepped into the car. The seats were enormous. He climbed onto one. Whoever rode in the cars must have been very tall, which would explain the pictures of tall rabbits on the platform. He slid down from the seat and walked to the front of the car. There was a single wide seat with a curved panel of blinking buttons in front of it. He thought about pushing one to see what would happen, but then imagined the car shooting forward at some unimaginable speed and smashing into another car.

As he turned to leave, he saw the door to a square structure in the middle of the platform slide open. Two extremely tall silver metallic rabbits emerged and looked in his direction. One of them waved to him, motioning for him to exit the car.

Morthram panicked, hitting every button he could find on the front panel. The car shot forward, pushing him back against the seat. He watched the two silver rabbits flash by, waving their arms for Morthram to stop.

About three minutes later the car began to slow down as it approached another platform. A voice from above his head startled Morthram and a protective sphere shot up around him. He quickly realized the voice was coming from a series of round gray discs lining the train car ceiling. Now he had seen everything – a talking train car. The language had a strong resemblance to Lapinoric, and was at first difficult to understand, but it didn't take him long to get used to the odd pronunciation. The car's voice was welcoming him to the new station. As the car came to a halt, Morthram crouched down so he wouldn't be seen, but was able to peer out at the platform.

The doors slid open and the voice gave permission for rabbits to exit the car. Morthram noticed some movement farther down the platform. A tall silver rabbit was sweeping the platform with a broom, but he was sweeping the same spot over and over, his motions oddly repetitive and jerky, like a broken wind-up toy. Morthram realized then the silver rabbits were machines, not living creatures. This was incredible. He thought about leaving the car to examine the sweeping rabbit, but the car doors abruptly closed and the car shot forward.

This time the trip lasted longer. The car flew past at least a half dozen stations. He saw silver rabbits on four of the platforms. At one station a group of six or eight of them were all talking to each other. If they had been covered with fur he would never have guessed they were machines. He had seen many strange things in his life as a shaper, but this was by far the most memorable.

Morthram looked out the front window when he felt the car begin to slow down. They had reached the end of the tunnel. Directly ahead was a huge wall covered with gigantic moving images of rabbits. They appeared to be engaged in some kind of unfamiliar sport, and the wall's purpose was unclear to him. Every so often groups of symbols would appear, but they were indecipherable. The car came to a halt next to the platform, the doors slid open, and the voice spoke again. He thought he heard the word 'fortress'. Morthram cautiously peered out the door, ever watchful for the silver rabbits, but he saw none. He wanted to put some distance between himself and this silent wall of moving rabbits. He kept imagining what would happen if the giant creatures jumped off the wall and began chasing him.

He exited the car, stepping quickly over to the

station wall to avoid detection. Dozens of colorful panels lined the wall, and one began speaking to him as he approached it. It became clear the machine was asking him if he was hungry. He replied he was not, but it continued speaking, describing to him various kinds of tasty foods he could purchase at a particular shop. When he turned and walked away, the panel was still talking.

He spotted a stairway about a hundred feet down the platform and made his way towards it. It took quite an effort to climb the stairs, as they were almost twice the height of stairs he was used to. By the time he reached the top, his legs were burning and he was out of breath. He wondered absently if any of the rabbits who had lived here were still alive. He had seen the silver rabbit machines but not a sign of their creators.

The stairs had led him up to another hallway which stretched out for at least a half mile. There was a row of blinking lights in the distance and he strode down the hallway towards them. Along the way he passed a great number of doors. He opened a few and peeked in, seeing nothing of great interest. They looked like offices, filled with oversized chairs and desks and many unrecognizable electrical devices, some still with glowing lights on them. When he reached the distant row of lights he recognized them for what they were – a bank of the round vertical elevator cars like the one in the silver mine. These ones looked functional, however. He walked from one to the other, looking for any clue as to where they might go.

"Have you lost your mummy?"

Morthram's insides turned to ice. He had never been so startled in his life. The voice was coming from behind him and above him. For the first time in his life he was simply too scared to move.

"No need to be frightened, little friend. I am here to help you. Do you remember where you last saw your mummy or daddy?"

Morthram finally gained control of his body and slowly turned around. A ten foot tall silver rabbit was looking down at him with a very concerned face.

"I... uh... I haven't lost my mummy. I come from a faraway land where everyone is the same size I am. I am lost though." Morthram tried his best to look helpless.

"Ah, I see. I would be happy to assist you. Where are you trying to go?"

"I may have gotten off at the wrong platform. What is this place called?"

"This is the Fortress of Elders. It has not been a true Fortress for over five thousand years of course, but it still bears the original name."

"That's it! I have been trying to reach the Fortress. What an incredible stroke of luck. Can you tell me where these elevator cars go?"

"These are gravitators. Unfortunately, only two of them are functional at this time, and I'm rather concerned over their general state of disrepair. I reported the malfunctions at least five hundred and eleven years ago, but the A4 Rabbitons still have not arrived to make the necessary repairs. I would have mentioned it to one of the Elders, but none have ridden the gravitators for well over fourteen hundred years. I'm afraid I have no idea where they are."

"The Elders are the rabbits who live here?"

"Yes, of course."

"You haven't seen one in over fourteen hundred years?"

"I have not, but I expect they shall return presently, so I continue on with my duties as an R9 Informational Rabbiton, giving needed assistance to visitors and citizens alike. To answer your question, this gravitator goes to the Central Information Repository, and that one to the main entrance hall of the Fortress."

Morthram thought quickly. The repository sounded like a safer place to go. There probably wouldn't be many Grymmorians there, if any. "The repository is where I had planned to meet my friend. That will be perfect."

"Very good, sir. I wish you a pleasant day and do enjoy your visit to the Fortress of Elders." He reached out and pushed a disc next to the gravitator. The door slid open and the Rabbiton motioned for Morthram to enter. Once Morthram was inside, the Rabbiton touched a second disc and the door closed. The car rose up the shaft for several seconds then came to a gentle stop. The door opened noiselessly and Morthram stepped out to find himself in the largest library he had ever seen. This underground city was truly a world of wonders. He looked down the length of the room and saw a silver Rabbiton talking to someone sitting in an oversized stuffed chair. Morthram quickly stepped behind a towering row of book shelves, then quietly padded down the aisle until he could hear their conversation.

"These are delightful. Do you happen to know how the filling is prepared?"

Morthram laughed out loud, recognizing the voice. He shifted back to his true form and stepped out from behind the book racks.

"Oliver T. Rabbit, I presume?"

"Ah, Morthram. Have you defeated Oberon and freed Clara?"

Like Bartholomew, Morthram sometimes found Oliver's thought process to be more than baffling. "Not yet, I'm afraid. I just arrived here after a long and eventful trip."

The Rabbiton spoke up. "Would you care for something to eat? Our food synthesizers are fully functional and capable of preparing whatever you might like. Following Oliver's instructions, I have synthesized this tray of éclairs which he has told me are to his liking."

"A large salad would be wonderful, with fresh carrots."

"I believe I know just what you are referring to. I will return shortly with your salad."

Morthram turned to Oliver. "Have you heard anything from Bartholomew? I have no idea when or where he had planned to arrive."

"I haven't seen him. Zoran disguised himself as a scientist and discovered my plan to sabotage the machine. He put me in a cell, but I escaped through an ancient hidden doorway, and eventually found my way here. I did discover some rather ghastly weapons capable of vaporizing matter, but I had no idea what to do with them."

"There is no end to the miracles found in this Fortress. Guild law prevents me from using such weapons against living creatures, but we could certainly use one to vaporize Oberon's machine. He probably has protective spheres surrounding it to deter shaping attacks, but it might not be able to stop one of those guns. We'll bring one or two with us."

"I saw no defensive spheres around the machine when I was there, but perhaps he will shape them once the machine is operational."

The Rabbiton returned shortly with a bowl of salad large enough to feed twenty rabbits. "Being unfamiliar with your eating habits, I was not certain how large to make the salad. I hope this will suffice."

"Yes, most certainly, that will do nicely. Thank you..." Morthram stopped. "I'm afraid I don't know your name. What are you called?"

"Called?"

"Yes, your name. What name should I call you?"

"I don't have a name, sir. I am a Model 9000 Rabbiton with the optional A7-Series 3 Repositorian Module."

"Oh my, I can't call you that every time I see you. Why don't you choose a short name and that's what we will call you?"

The Rabbiton looked surprised but also extremely pleased.

"Oh my, a name. I admit I have thought about this on occasion, but..."

Morthram thought the Rabbiton might burst into tears. How curious.

"I have read every book in this repository many times, and there are some volumes which gave me uniquely indescribable thoughts. I have wondered if these thoughts might be what the Elders referred to as feelings. One of my favorite books chronicles the life of a famous Elder explorer name Edmund. He traveled through this world and many others, returning with untold treasures and amazing stories from wondrous places. I have a faint memory of meeting Edmund the Elder soon after my creation, but that was a rather confusing time for me and my memories are quite vague. I would like to be called Edmund."

"Edmund it is then. Edmund, I thank you for the delicious salad you brought to me."

Edmund stood staring at Morthram, his red eyes pulsing strangely. He turned away for a moment, then looked back again. "Please excuse me, I was experiencing a small sensory malfunction, but I am fine now. You are quite welcome for the salad. If there is anything else you need, don't hesitate to ask for Edmund."

Chapter 27

The Fly

Ravens were a common sight along the Fandor Mountains, so no one paid any attention to the one circling high above the Lost Fortress. It swooped and glided, as ravens do, eventually finding itself several hundred feet over the massive structure. The raven pulled in its wings and dove down towards the Fortress keep. When it was about fifty feet away from the outer walls it exploded in a ball of fire. The raven had hit an invisible protective dome surrounding the Fortress.

"Drat. I was afraid of that." Bartholomew peered out from behind a boulder almost a half mile away. He had shaped an illusory raven to test for any defensive spheres Zoran might have in place. His plans to formshift into a raven and enter the Fortress from above had literally gone up in flames. Next, he shaped a large blue thought cloud and sent it sailing towards the invisible dome. When it hit the protective wall, the cloud simply vanished. "Now I know I can't blink myself into the Fortress. If I try to pass through the barrier as a thought cloud, I will also meet an untimely end. I must find another way to enter the Fortress."

Later that day, a large black carriage pulled by four white horses came to a halt at the end of the stone bridge leading to the Fortress gatehouse. A Fortress door opened and a Grymmorian guard emerged. He crossed the bridge, stopping at a glass pedestal. Removing a translucent orange sphere from his pocket, he placed it gently into a concave indentation on the top of the pedestal. He stooped down and picked up a small pebble, then tossed it out in front of him. When nothing happened, he stepped off the drawbridge and walked to the carriage. He was quite familiar with this particular carriage and with its passenger, but only this morning Zoran had warned the guards under penalty of death to make absolutely certain anyone who entered the Fortress was who they said they were. He circled the carriage slowly, poking and prodding, looking for anything suspicious. Finding nothing amiss, he spoke first with the driver, then with the passenger. Both showed him papers, and the passenger held up a six sided silver medallion for him to see. The guard asked the passenger a number of questions which he successfully answered. Finally the guard motioned for the carriage to cross the bridge. One of the massive Fortress doors opened with a low groaning noise and the carriage rolled in through the gate. The guard put the orange sphere back in his pocket, backing carefully away from the invisible dome. He entered the Fortress and the doors closed behind him. Bartholomew had made it safely inside the Fortress.

The driver climbed down from the carriage and opened the door for the passenger, one of Oberon's most senior advisors. The passenger stepped down and walked off with the guard. The driver went to the back of the carriage and opened its leather trunk, removing four feedbags for the horses. He then walked to the front of the carriage and strapped a bag on each horse, all the while swatting at the buzzing flies which seemed to be a permanent fixture around the horses. One of the flies shot out in a wide arc and flew off after Oberon's senior advisor.

At first it was confusing to be a fly, with six legs and a pair of wings, but Bartholomew was finally getting used to it. He'd practiced flying until he felt comfortable in his ability to mimic the insect's behavior, and could buzz around easily in all directions. He didn't have to think much about moving his wings, as most of it was quite instinctive.

He buzzed along near the ceiling, far above the guard and Oberon's advisor as they walked together down the long hallway. After making their way down to the first sub-level corridor, the guard opened a door, motioning for the advisor to enter.

"King Oberon and Zoran will be with you shortly, sir."

The advisor's only response was a grunt. Bartholomew darted into the room before the guard closed the door. Once inside, he found a safe hiding spot on top of a bookshelf where he sat, waiting for the meeting to begin. He may have struck pay dirt. If Oberon and Zoran were going to be here this could be a very informative meeting. He was not disappointed.

Zoran was next to enter the room, followed shortly by King Oberon. Oberon turned to the guard. "We are not to be disturbed under any circumstances."

"Yes, Your Highness." The guard nodded, closing

the door behind him.

Zoran held out his paw and a blue beam shot out, enveloping the advisor with a pale blue cloud. The advisor waited patiently until the blue cloud had faded away.

"Yes, Zoran, it's really me. I am not a formshifting rabbit who's come here to pinch your nose."

"Lucky for you you're not one." Zoran and the advisor were not on the best of terms.

If flies had eyebrows, Bartholomew would have raised them in surprise. Zoran had a method of detecting formshifters. He hoped Morthram hadn't tried to enter the Fortress as a Grymmorian.

The three Grymmorians took seats at a long ornate wooden table. Oberon sat at the head of the table, looking darkly at his advisor. "What have you learned about the ferillium mine?"

"I'm afraid nothing very helpful, Your Highness. It was definitely the work of the Shapers Guild. No one was harmed, a sure sign the Guild was behind it. The tunnel and the mine were shaped full of a solid granite which is highly resistant to drilling or shaping. The mine will never open again. Mr. Ferillium and the innkeeper have vanished, and no one seems to know where they went. The good news is we already had enough ferillium to create the crystal, and it should be ready to place in the device within a day or two. It has been more difficult than we expected to carve the necessary spherical shape due to its absorption properties. We almost lost several of our scientists in the process."

Oberon nodded. "We were going to shut the mine down anyway in a few months, so they simply saved us the trouble of disposing of several thousand rabbits. I'd still like to know how the Guild learned of the mine, and why they felt it was worth the risk to close it. They have no idea what we're using the ferillium for."

"They probably learned about it from the four prisoners who escaped. As to why they undertook such a venture, I suppose they simply didn't like the idea of us using rabbits as slave labor. A lot of good it did them. They'll all be slaves soon enough. What's more worrisome is that one of the escaped prisoners was a Grymmorian."

"Who was it? Did we put him there?"

"No one seems to know, and all the records were lost when the mine was destroyed."

"Hmm. I'm probably worrying more than I need to. It will all be over in a week anyway. Zoran, has anyone tried to enter the Fortress?"

"No, Your Highness. We have been on high alert but there have been no suspicious events, other than Oliver T. Rabbit's capture. He's locked in a cell, and his two friends, Morthram Rabbit and Bartholomew Rabbit, never showed up. Hopefully they were both killed trying to get past our ring of defenses."

"When do we move the shapers?"

"Everything is going according to schedule. In a few days the crystal will be placed in the machine. The time suspended shapers will be wakened and moved into the room with the device. They'll all be wearing shaper masks, of course. All the other shapers will follow shortly after. Once they're in position, we'll take their masks off. They'll be in for a rather unpleasant surprise I'm afraid." Oberon gave a snort.

Zoran continued. "It will take a day or two for the

ferillium crystal to adequately charge. Once it's ready, you can enter the control room and put on the shaper helmet. Flip the red lever I showed you and send out your thought. The power of three hundred shapers will drive your thought into the machine, where it will be magnified over a thousand times before being sent out into the world. In a fraction of a second it will be over Lapinor, spreading out like some monstrous black storm cloud. Life as the rabbits know it will come to an abrupt and very unhappy end. Within an hour every memory of every rabbit will be gone and replaced with the thought you send. Their loved ones will become strangers to them, and the only thing they will know is they are, and have always been, loyal and willing slaves of the Grymmorian empire. Lapinor will be ours for the taking."

King Oberon clapped his paws together gleefully. "That day can't come soon enough."

Bartholomew was in shock. "They're going to turn the rabbits into mindless slaves? Fen had been right – the fate of all Lapinor hung in the balance. Oberon must be stopped, even if it means sacrificing my life."

The meeting ended and the three Grymmorians exited the room. Bartholomew remained on the bookshelf, desperately trying to think of some way to destroy the machine. He had to find Oliver and free him if he could. Maybe he'd already sabotaged the machine before he was captured. Bartholomew decided to fly through the science laboratories to see if he could learn where Oliver was being held.

He buzzed off the bookcase and circled the room looking for an exit. He spotted a narrow gap beneath the door, landed next to it and scurried out into the hallway. As he flashed down the wide corridor he kept his eyes open for anyone resembling a scientist. He spotted three Grymmorians wearing white lab coats, standing around talking near an open doorway. When he flew past he saw the room was filled with rabbits and muroids wearing similar garb. He swung around and shot back to the room, circling it several times before landing on a ceiling lamp. He was surprised by how well a fly could hear. Even a low whisper from across the room was quite audible to him. He was rewarded after a tedious half hour of listening when he picked out the word 'Oliver' from a conversation. He buzzed over to the whispering scientists, landing upside down on the ceiling.

"Oliver? Oliver T. Rabbit a spy? That seems highly unlikely. He's not that kind of rabbit, from everything I've heard. He's not concerned with politics, only science."

"Zoran must have caught him doing something."

"What do you think they did to him?"

"I don't know exactly, but Zoran told the guards to take him to the sub-level three dungeon. I didn't even know they had cells down there. We shouldn't be talking about this. Next thing you know we'll be locked up with all the shapers. Or worse."

Bartholomew flipped over and buzzed out of the room. Oliver was in sub-level three. This was sub-level one, so he had to go down two more levels. He flew up and down the corridors until he found a set of descending stairs, buzzing down to sub-level two. Cruising through the hallways he found himself passing cells filled with dozens and dozens of shapers wearing masks. "This has to be where they're holding Clara."

He explored some of the larger cells, flitting through them quickly to avoid being swatted. When he zipped into the fourth cell his heart almost stopped. He saw Clara. She was sitting in the corner talking with another shaper. She was safe.

More than anything in the world he wanted to transform back to his own form and blink her out of the Fortress, but he knew this was not the time. It wouldn't be safe now, not with all the traps Zoran had in place. Any rash attempt to rescue Clara would end very badly, probably with both of them being killed by a trap or by Zoran. Besides, this was bigger than just him and Clara. He had to stop Oberon from enslaving all of Lapinor. He sped out of the cell and down the corridor.

After searching a dozen more hallways he found the final set of stairs and streaked down them to a narrow dead end corridor with a single prison cell at the end. Oliver was nowhere to be seen. He buzzed past the bars into the cell. This is where Oliver was supposed to be, but he was obviously gone. He searched for clues, quickly recognizing Oliver's writing in the thick dust on the floor. He had been here, but where did he go? Bartholomew flew up to the ceiling and studied the symbols on the wall. He had no idea what they meant, but they were the same symbols Oliver had written on the cell floor.

He flew across the back wall and felt a breeze cross his path. Landing on the wall, he walked around carefully until he found the source of the breeze. There was an almost imperceptible crack in the wall letting air through from the other side. He buzzed back to view it from a distance and could now see it clearly. There were two vertical cracks in the wall. Could it be a hidden door? The word “door” was echoing in his thoughts when the huge slab of stone slid silently down, revealing a hallway beyond. Standing in the doorway were Oliver and Morthram.

Chapter 28

The Falling Ring

Bartholomew almost crashed into the wall. He instantly shifted back to his true form. Oliver and Morthram instinctively jumped back when Bartholomew appeared, a sphere of protection popping up around them.

Bartholomew grinned. "Anyone know where you can get a good éclair around here?"

Morthram reached out and grabbed him, dragging him into the hallway and slapping the yellow disc. The secret wall slid down again.

"This is fantastic! You both made it here and you're both safe. Oliver, I was so worried about you. I heard the scientists say Zoran had accused you of being a traitor?"

"He did. He formshifted into a scientist and read my thoughts on the carriage ride here. He waited until I'd sent the green thought out and until I'd given my stamp of approval on their machine. Then he threw me into that cell. Fortunately, I discovered the secret doorway."

"Well, thank goodness you're safe. I have news. I

found out what Oberon's plan is, and it's bad. He is going to send out an amplified thought cloud which will wipe clean the memories of every rabbit alive and turn them into his willing slaves. Oberon is creating an empire, and he plans for Lapinor to be his first conquest. We have two days to figure out a way to stop him."

"Good heavens, when I was in the lab I heard no mention of anything like that."

"I think the only ones who know his real plan are his top advisor and Zoran.

Morthram spoke up. "We need to revise our own plans now that Bartholomew is here. Let's go back to the library and discuss this."

Bartholomew noticed Morthram's vaporizing gun. "What's that thing?"

"Oliver found them in an ancient armory. It's a weapon that vaporizes matter. The Elders left them behind in the Fortress."

"Who are the Elders?"

"I'll tell you on the way back." Morthram added with a grin, "I can't wait for you to meet my old friend Edmund. And when I say old, I mean *old*."

Half an hour later they were in the Central Information Repository, seated in oversized reading chairs. Edmund had brought them a tray of freshly fabricated molasses cookies and a pitcher of lemonade.

"Would anyone care for more cookies?"

"We're fine, Edmund, thank you for asking though."

Edmund stood by as the three rabbits began devising their new strategy to destroy the shaping machine and rescue Clara. Every time Zoran's name came up they found themselves at an impasse.

Morthram put his paw on his forehead. "All right, let's begin again. We can send out the same spheres as we did in the ferillium mine to put the guards into a deep sleep, but those spheres will have no effect on Zoran. He would easily anticipate such an attack and counteract it, more than likely with deadly results. His skills as a shaper are far beyond ours, and he has no qualms about taking lives."

"Maybe there's some way we can outwit him, although nothing comes to mind right now. I watched him use a shaping skill which reveals formshifters, so we can't trick him that way."

Edmund cleared his throat several times. When they looked up he said, "I must say this is all rather thrilling. It's similar to some of the books I have read, but instead of reading words on a page, I am watching the event unfold right in front of me. I quite like it. Would it be possible for me to accompany you when you attack Zoran? I would be no bother."

They looked at each other, then Bartholomew spoke. "Edmund, we appreciate your offer, but it's going to be very dangerous. We're going up against the most powerful shaper in the world."

"I am quite indestructible, I assure you. When the Elders created the Rabbiton 9000 series they made us impervious to any form of attack."

"You're unaffected by shaping?"

"Quite so."

"May I try to blink you across the room?"

"If you wish, but you will not be able to."

Morthram held out his paw. There was brilliant flash of light, then, nothing. Edmund was still standing there.

"This is astonishing. Can you make us impervious to

shaping?"

"I don't believe so. My resistance to attack comes from the inherent nature of the silver metallic substance I am composed of."

Oliver asked, "Do you have any weapons available to you?"

"I do not. The Elders did create Series 6 Warrior Rabbitons, but you would not like it even the tiniest bit if they were to make an appearance." He laughed nervously.

Morthram broke in, "We can't use Rabbitons as weapons to destroy Zoran. It's against the Guild code."

Bartholomew spoke up. "I've had a partial plan rattling around in my head, but couldn't quite finalize it until now. Edmund, rather than just observe, would you like to play an actual part in our plan?"

"I would be more than happy to. I've never done anything like that before."

"Are there other Rabbitons who could help us?"

"There are some in a storage room near the armory. They are older Model 8000 Series 4 Maintenance Rabbitons, but they are also indestructible."

"We only need two. Can I put you in charge of the other Rabbitons?"

"Of course. I'll go reactivate two of them now and return shortly." He strode off to the armory.

"What's your plan?"

"I can't tell you. I don't want Zoran reading anyone's thoughts. I will tell you that my plan lies on the very edge of the Guild's ethical guidelines."

Morthram looked at Bartholomew. "They are called guidelines for a reason. If you feel in your heart this is something which must be done, then you have the

Guild's blessing."

Edmund returned an hour later with the two maintenance Rabbitons. Bartholomew took Edmund and the two new Rabbitons into a private reading room and discussed his plan with them.

The following morning they all assembled by the secret sliding door leading to Oliver's old cell.

"Morthram, once we're in the hallway you and I will send out several thousand sleeping spheres to take care of the guards. Hopefully one will land on Oberon, but our real battle will be with Zoran. He'll be able to repel the spheres and we'll have no choice but to face him head on. Oliver, you have the vaporizing gun. When the time comes, use it to destroy the machine, but it's also vital that you destroy the ferillium crystal. The room will be filled with hundreds of shapers, so it goes without saying, aim carefully."

"I know exactly where the crystal is located."

"Edmund, do you remember what the Rabbitons are supposed to do?"

"I do."

"Time to go then."

Bartholomew touched the violet disk and the wall slid down. The entered the cell and Morthram flicked his paw, turning the barred door to dust. They stepped into the hallway.

"Ready?"

Morthram and Bartholomew linked paws and concentrated deeply. Immensely brilliant lights appeared and thousands of small red spheres began streaming down the hallway. Each sphere would find a Grymmorian guard and put him into a deep sleep lasting over a week. They waited several minutes for the spheres to do their work.

Bartholomew motioned Edmund to move forward. "Edmund, you and your two friends walk in front of us. You will block some of Zoran's attacks, but more importantly, you'll conceal my actions from him. The Rabbitons stepped forward, and the three rabbits took their places behind them. They walked up the first set of stairs to the second sub-level. The spheres had done their job, and there were guards asleep all along the corridor. They reached the stairs leading up to sub-level one, cautiously making their way to the main corridor.

With a brilliant flash of light, Zoran blinked into view about fifty feet in front of them.

"Ah, they have finally arrived. The three little rabbits who have come to destroy me. This is the best you could do? Three ridiculously tall silver rabbit illusions? Did you think they would scare me and I would run away like a little bunny? I expected more from you, Morthram. I believe I shall destroy your two friends first, and rather painfully at that. I shall cherish the look on your face as you watch them depart this world."

Bartholomew called out to Zoran. "These are not illusions. They are Series 9000 Rabbitons created by the Elders before they fled the Fortress. Their power is unrivaled by any creature on earth. They are armed with potent and deadly energy beams which vaporize all matter, and they are impervious to shaping. At my command you will cease to exist, Zoran."

"What a sad little liar you are. Your pitiful fairy tale has not impressed me in the least." A blindingly brilliant beam of green light shot out from Zoran's paw, sizzled down the corridor and hit Edmund square on the chest. A moment later the smirk on Zoran's face vanished. Edmund had not been affected at all by Zoran's deadly blast of light.

Edmund called out to the other Rabbitons, "Prepare vaporizing energy beams!"

The look of disbelief on Zoran's face turned to one of absolute fear. He stared at Edmund, his eyes wide. "What *are* you?"

Edmund's red eyes glowed fiercely.

"I AM EDMUND, AND I AM HERE TO DESTROY YOU!" The three Rabbitons raised their right arms in unison, each pointing a single finger at Zoran. The tips of their long silver fingers glowed with an eerie purple pulsing light.

Bartholomew flicked his paw, a gesture carefully hidden from Zoran.

Edmund called out loudly, "Fire energy beams!"

Zoran blinked out and vanished.

Morthram cried out, "He's blinked! Keep your eyes out for him!"

Bartholomew held up his paw. "He won't be coming back."

"What do you mean he won't be coming back? Where did he go?"

There was small clinking noise near where Zoran had been standing. A small, shiny object had fallen from the air and rolled across the floor.

"What is that?"

"Go look."

Morthram ran towards it, his eyes still darting around for any sign of Zoran. He reached the object and stopped, then turned and looked at Bartholomew. "What did you do?" He reached down for the object, then held it up for them to see. “It’s the Emerald Ring.”

Morthram brought the ring back to Bartholomew. “What happened here?”

“It was something you taught me. I surrounded Zoran with a time shield – the same one ancient shapers used as a defense against arrows.”

A light came on in Morthram’s eyes. “When he blinked out his thought cloud hit your time shield and slowed him down. It takes almost a full minute to pass through the shield. He was in cloud form too long and couldn’t convert back to his physical form. He really is gone.”

“Technically, he’s alive, just not in this world.”

“Amazing. Well done, Bartholomew.” He handed the emerald ring to Bartholomew. “This is yours now.”

“No, this ring should never be worn again. Keep it in the Guild vault.” Bartholomew put his paw on Edmund’s arm. “You were amazing, Edmund. You are welcome to join us on our adventures anytime you wish.”

“That sounds quite exciting,” said Edmund, looking very pleased.

Morthram interrupted them. “It’s time to shut down Oberon’s infernal machine.”

Chapter 29

The Sacrifice of Bartholomew Rabbit

Oliver led the way to the lab. The guards were no longer a threat and neither was Zoran. When they entered, they saw the Grymmorian scientists and technicians lying on the floor in deep slumber.

Morthram shrugged. “I sent spheres in here, too. I thought we should err on the side of caution.”

They hurried through the lab and opened the doors to the shaping machine room. Bartholomew gasped. Hundreds of shapers lay on the floor barely breathing. The ferillium crystal was radiating and pulsing with a brilliant living orange fire, light and shadow dancing wildly about the room. The crystal was absorbing all the shaping power and energy of the shapers, leaving them nearly lifeless.

“None of them have masks on, so why didn’t they destroy the machine?” Bartholomew held out a paw and shot a flaming red bolt of light at the infernal machine. The blazing beam of light twisted and veered over to the crystal and was sucked into it, causing the ferillium to flare and glow brilliantly. He turned to Oliver. "Destroy the crystal with the vaporizer gun!"

Oliver pressed the green button on the glass weapon, firing directly at the crystal. The ferillium crystal absorbed the gun's energy and flared brightly.

Bartholomew felt himself weakening. The crystal was draining his life force.

He heard someone whisper his name. It was Clara. She was sitting up against a wall, using all the strength she had left to stay conscious. He ran to her and took her paw. "Clara, it's me."

"Bartholomew, I'm so sorry I asked you to come here. You can't stay. It will be all right. We will find each other as we always do." She squeezed his paw gently.

"No! I won't let this happen. I won't!"

He heard a voice in his head.

"Clara's thought."

Bartholomew looked desperately at Clara. "Hold on." He staggered towards the ferillium crystal, his legs barely able to carry him. When he touched the crystal it felt as if a huge paw had reached inside his chest and was tearing out the very core of his being. He watched in horror as the life force streamed out of him into the crystal. It would be only moments until he fell. He wrapped one arm around the crystal and picked it up.

Morthram cried out, "What are you doing? The crystal will kill you! We have to leave. I can still save Clara." Oliver was slumped down on the floor.

Bartholomew looked back at Clara and time stopped. They spoke silently, just as they had in their dreams.

"Don't do it, Bartholomew, not for me. Save

yourself."

"I have no choice. I have loved you always. I can't let you go. I can't."

Clara's head slowly fell forward.

Bartholomew slid his paw inside the shaper mask containing Clara's thought. He rippled for a moment and was gone.

Chapter 30

Bruno Rabbit

"Ah, there it is. This really is an amazing crystal. I've never seen one this big. The Elders will be pleased. So, all's well that ends well, right?"

Bartholomew was barely conscious. He cracked his eyes open at the sound of the vaguely familiar voice. He tried to focus but couldn't, and closed his eyes again.

"Give it a little time and you'll feel better. Ha! Give it a little time? We're on the Isle of Mandora? Nothing funnier than a time joke on Mandora."

Who *was* this? Bartholomew was beginning to feel a little stronger, as though his life force was returning. This time he managed to open his eyes and focus them. He was looking at a tall rabbit wearing a long green cloak with a hood pulled over his head.

"Who are you? I know your voice from somewhere."

"Indeed you do. I believe you know me as the Great Tree."

"You're the Great Tree?"

"Well, that's the name I gave the Tree of Eyes. It

suited their needs more than my real name, Bruno Rabbit."

"What are you doing here? Why hasn't the crystal killed me?"

"Ah, yes. I suppose you would be curious about that. All part of the Elders' plan, of course. The ferillium crystal does not absorb energy in a timeless environment. The moment you chose to sacrifice your life was the moment you saved it. Rather funny when you think about it."

Bartholomew stared blankly at Bruno Rabbit. "Funny?"

"Mmm...perhaps funny was not the most appropriate word. I suppose ironic would have been a better choice."

"Is Clara..."

"She's fine. When you took the crystal their power began to replenish itself, just as yours is doing now. I have told Clara you are fine, so no need to worry about that."

"You said it was part of the Elders' plan, but they're gone, so how could–"

"They are most certainly not gone, my friend. They still live in cities they created out there in the shimmering sea. Cities your eyes cannot yet see. When you're feeling stronger I'll show them to you. One of the Elders needed a large ferillium crystal for a project he's working on. He was the one who started the chain of events which would bring this crystal to the Isle of Mandora. That was almost one hundred of your years ago."

"He waited one hundred years for the crystal?"

"Oh, good heavens no. That would be silly. Time is

quite different in the cities of the Elders. For each day there, almost one hundred years passes in your world. When the Elder realized he needed a large ferillium crystal, he started the chain of events you have recently become so fascinated with. For him, the crystal arrived the next day."

It was almost too much for Bartholomew to process. "How do you know the Elders?"

Bruno was staring out across the sea. "They came to me. With all due modesty, I am the most powerful shaper in this world, but I have kept to myself most of my life. I learned a long time ago that rabbits fear the unknown, and fear anyone who is too different. I moved to the mountains and was living a solitary life when the Elders contacted me. They asked me to come and live with them in the City of Mandora. We have a surprising number of things in common, not to mention all the wondrous knowledge they will share with me. You don't know it, but you walked past my home once. Or more accurately, you went flying past in a wildly out of control duplonium wagon."

"Pterosaur Valley. You were the one who shot out the blue beam and saved us from the pterosaurs!"

"Guilty as charged."

"You shaped the pterosaurs? They were only illusions?"

Bruno hesitated, carefully phrasing his answer.

"You are the only one who can know this. Well, other than Clara. The pterosaurs are not illusions. They are real living creatures, no different from you or me. I created them."

Bartholomew looked at Bruno in disbelief. "You created life?"

Bruno laughed. "In the same way your parents did." He laughed again. "Now that I've said it out loud, I realize that's a rather embarrassing analogy. I didn't create life, but I did place a small amount of my own life force into another physical body. In this case I transferred some of my life force into the form of a pterosaur which I had shaped. It's like lighting one candle with another that is already lit. No creature in our universe can create life, and yet every day billions of new lives are formed."

Bartholomew stood up. He was feeling much better now, almost normal.

"What about the Tree of Eyes?"

"My creation also. There was a time in my life when I was filled with a terrible loneliness. Until I met the Elders I had no one to talk to about the things which were important to me, the very definition of loneliness. I wanted to create a creature which would never experience that feeling. The Tree of Eyes will never know loneliness. It has someone to talk to every moment of every day."

"I mean no disrespect, but why did you create the Tree of Eyes to be so... oh, I don't exactly know how to put it..."

"Irritating and infuriating?"

"Yes, something like that."

"How about 'universally disliked by the few rabbits who have met it'?"

"How did you know about that?"

"I'm afraid there never was a Dr. Mazlow. His journal was a little shaping project of my own to lead you to the Tree of Eyes. To answer your question, the Tree of Eyes will live to be many thousands of years old. It is very young now, and has the irritating sense of humor of a five year old bunny and the shaping skills of a ruby ring. Twelve hundred years from now its wisdom will prevent the annihilation of your planet."

"What about when I heard the word *Clara* in the night?"

"Me again. Many of the clues you found were from me, many from the Elders. The Golden Sword was their idea, along with your unusual loss of hope in the swamp. There were far greater forces at work here also, part of the Infinite Chain, but they are well beyond your current level of understanding."

"Suppose I had just walked out of the shaping machine room? Suppose I had decided not to sacrifice myself?"

"If you know enough of the variables, the correct outcome can be predicted. The Elders are seldom wrong, but they do make mistakes. The treatment of the rabbits in the Ferillium mine was not part of their plan. It was supposed to be a well run commercial enterprise. The Elders are truly sorry for that. It never should have happened."

Bartholomew nodded. "It wasn't really their fault. It was the fault of creatures filled with greed and a lust for power – creatures like King Oberon, Mr. Ferillium and the brutal Grymmorian guards."

"You're right, of course, but that doesn't make it any less painful. The Elders have moved beyond behavior like that. It's why they chose to leave your world and create their own, and why I am leaving. I have outgrown the lessons to be learned in your world. I won't be coming back, and I will have no reason to. After one day in the City of Mandora, one hundred years will have passed in your world. Everyone I know will be gone."

"You're leaving now?"

"I will send you back to the Fortress of Elders before I go. I imagine Clara is quite eager to see you. She is more like you than you know. I would say more, but I will let Clara tell you the rest. There is something else I need to tell you before I go."

Bruno pulled a gold ring off his paw and held it out for Bartholomew to see. "Do you like it?" It was a Guild ring with the image of an eye on it, but there was no stone in the center of the eye.

"You lost the stone?"

Bruno seemed to be quite tickled by Bartholomew's question. He laughed loudly. "Yes, I did, in a manner of speaking." Bartholomew didn't quite understand the humor but laughed politely.

"Morthram is a wonderful rabbit and a masterful shaper. The world is a far better place with him in it, but there is much he does not know. That is to be expected. There are many things even the Elders do not know. Morthram doesn't know this ring exists. There are not ten rings, there are eleven. You are looking at the Eleventh Ring."

Bartholomew was mesmerized. The ring radiated a power he was not familiar with. "Eleven rings. But... where did this come from?"

"It is old. Bartholomew, the universe is old beyond our comprehension. Many civilizations and species have come and gone before us. We are not the first to be here, and others will follow us long after we are gone. This ring was ancient when the Elders found it. There is only one in any world, and it is worn by the most powerful shaper in that world. It is handed down from shaper to shaper."

Bartholomew nodded slowly. "It's an honor to see it, and a great honor to meet you."

"Yes, yes, now hold out your paw."

Bartholomew looked at Bruno curiously but extended his arm. His ruby ring vanished in a blink of light. Bruno slid the Eleventh Ring onto Bartholomew's paw. "All hail the Eleventh Ring."

Bartholomew was speechless.

Bruno continued, "You still have much to learn, but the day will come when you will be the most powerful shaper on Earth. The Eleventh Ring is more than just a symbol of power. It gives the wearer a set of unique shaping skills. One of them allows the transference of life force into another physical form, as I did with the Tree of Eyes and the pterosaurs. You must discover on your own what the other skills are. No one will know you wear the Eleventh Ring. They will see what they expect to see. When Morthram looks at your paw he will see a ruby Guild ring."

"All I can do is thank you."

"You can do far more than that. You can live the best life you can." Bruno grinned and began twiddling his thumbs and whistling, as though he were waiting for something. "Notice anything different?"

Bartholomew looked confused. "What am I supposed to – whaaahhh!" He almost fell over backwards. Standing a mile or two past the island was an immense translucent city with hundreds of buildings, some close to a mile tall. "Where did that come from??"

"Ah, you have seen it then. You may thank the

Eleventh Ring for that. You are looking at the City of Mandora, the first city built by the Elders, and my new home. Now, are you ready to go back and see Clara?"

"I am."

"Oh, one very last thing. My home in Pterosaur Valley is yours now. It's quite large and I think you will like it, although you may have a little trouble finding it. As long as you're wearing the Eleventh Ring the pterosaurs will be as docile as little bunnies, so no more wild rides in duplonium wagons." Bruno grinned and flicked his paw.

Bartholomew was standing next to King Oberon's shaping machine.

Chapter 31

King Fendaron

There were at least a hundred shapers milling around the infernal machine, but it took Bartholomew only a moment to spot Clara. She was standing on the other side of the room holding Oliver's paw and talking to Edmund. Bartholomew grinned like a ten year old bunny and crept over towards her, taking care not to be seen. Sneaking up behind her, he motioned for Oliver and Edmund not to give him away. He was just about to say, "Boo!" when she turned around and looked at him, shaking her head. "Did you really think I wouldn't know you were there?"

Bartholomew was unexpectedly flooded with a sea of emotions he had kept buried inside him since he was a bunny. He had no words. He put his arms around Clara and held her close to him. When Oliver finally spoke, Bartholomew had no idea how much time had passed.

"I believe you may be making Edmund slightly uncomfortable."

"To the contrary, I am not uncomfortable in the

least. I am curious, however, what it is they are doing. Is it a social convention of some kind? Would it be appropriate for me to put my arms around Clara also?"

Oliver rolled his eyes, then laughed. "Rabbitons." He patted Edmund on the arm. "It's called hugging. You have a lot to learn about rabbits, my tall silver friend."

"Indeed I do. That is why I have decided to accompany you on your next adventure. As a scientist, you will be able to teach me all I need to know about your cultural conventions."

"I could not ask for a better traveling companion, Edmund. When you are ready, our first adventure will be a journey to the utterly unique and universally disliked Tree of Eyes. You will not find a single mention of him in all your books, and you will be the first Rabbiton to set eyes on this astonishing creature."

"I will be the first Rabbiton adventurer. Do you think I could wear some type of adventurer's hat? I've always wanted to wear a hat."

Bartholomew interrupted. "Would someone please tell me what happened after I left?"

Oliver jumped right in. "It was fantastic. Once the crystal was gone, the shapers' powers quickly returned. Within half an hour everyone was at full power again, and sent all the sleeping guards back to cells in Malgraven Castle. We found Oberon hiding in the shaper machine control room. He was powerless without his guards, but he still threatened all of us, describing in rather graphic detail the grisly fates in store for each of us. Finally, Morthram put a sphere of silence around Oberon's head so we wouldn't have to listen to his raving. He's resting quietly now in a cell on sub-level two, along with several of his advisors."

Morthram's voice boomed out from across the room. "Bartholomew!" He strode quickly through the crowd and threw his arms around Bartholomew. "Clara told me what happened with the crystal and that you were safe. How lucky we were the ferillium crystal didn't absorb energy on the Isle of Mandora."

"Lucky indeed." Bartholomew made no mention of Bruno.

"And I see you've found Clara. It is an honor to stand before the two greatest shapers in all of Lapinor."

Clara laughed. "It's amazing how many shapers are here. Some of them have been frozen in time for well over twenty years. It's going to take a while for them to become reacquainted with the world again. The Guild will no doubt be gaining many new members."

Morthram clapped his paw to his forehead. "I almost forgot to tell you. I have received a message from Fen. The general council has removed King Oberon from power and there is a new King. Long live King Fendaron!"

"Who is King Fendaron?"

"None other than Fen himself, sole heir to the throne of Grymmore. Your vision about him was correct, Bartholomew. He will make an excellent King. He has already proclaimed shaping is both allowed and encouraged in Grymmore. He asked me to move to Malgraven Castle and be their first Guild Master. I think I'm going to do it. It will be a wonderful opportunity to teach the craft to new shapers. And being a rabbit, I am hoping my presence there will help diminish some of their fear of us. Of course, my absence will mean we'll need a new Guild Master in

Penrith. Does anyone know of a rabbit who wears a ruby ring and might be interested in such a position?" He looked pointedly at Bartholomew, but it was Clara who stepped forward.

"I would like that position. I spent most of my childhood being frightened and confused by my shaping abilities. I would like to help young shapers so they won't have to suffer through a similar experience."

"The job is yours. I don't believe there is another shaper in Lapinor who is better suited for it."

Bartholomew put his arms around Clara again. "Congratulations."

Edmund whispered loudly to Oliver, "Why does he keep hugging her? Are you quite certain I should not be hugging someone?"

Clara laughed, breaking away from Bartholomew. "I would love a hug from you, Edmund."

Edmund smiled proudly and bent way down, putting his long arms gently around Clara. When he stood up again he announced, "That was my first hug." Oliver clapped and gave the thumbs up sign to Edmund.

By the end of the next day the Fortress was nearly empty. Most of the shapers had left and King Oberon had taken up residence in the Malgraven Castle dungeons. Bartholomew had sent a message to Parfello letting him know everyone was safe and he had found Clara.

Chapter 32

Edmund's New Job

The next morning found Bartholomew and Morthram talking to Edmund in the main hall of the Fortress.

"Edmund, when I rode through the subterranean train stations on my way here I saw quite a number of Rabbitons still actively performing their duties. Do you know how many Rabbitons are still functional?"

"I will check for you." A transparent screen appeared in front of him. He flipped this way and that through dozens of pages until he found what he was looking for. "It appears there are seventy-nine active Rabbitons and fourteen thousand six hundred and twenty-one inactive Rabbitons."

"What does inactive mean?"

"They are currently in storage waiting to be activated. There are many different models with a wide variety of functions."

Morthram turned to Bartholomew. "There are far more than we had expected. This should work."

"Edmund, I have something to ask you."

"Of course, Bartholomew."

"I have had a request from the new King of Grymmore which concerns you. If you would like, he will appoint you as Master of Rabbitons to the Fortress of Elders. You would be in charge of all the Rabbitons, being responsible for their welfare and reactivation. King Fendaron would like the Fortress to be as it was when the Elders lived here. That would mean the reconstruction of all the underground tunnels and trains and whatever else you deem necessary. The Fortress and surrounding areas will be inhabited by Rabbitons. What do you think?"

"I would be honored. I remember precisely what the Fortress was like then. I will begin tomorrow. Hmm, I think all the Rabbitons should choose their own names. Yes, I like that idea. They could also choose which programming module they would prefer. I will talk to you tomorrow. I am quite busy now with my duties as Master of Rabbitons." He turned and walked away, but not before giving Bartholomew a hug.

* * *

Bartholomew and Clara were sitting on a parapet looking out across the Fortress of Elders. The warm summer sun was sinking down towards the horizon.

"Bruno said we were more alike than I knew. What did he mean by that?"

Clara took his paw in hers. "What he meant was that you and I have the same inner voice. That is why we have the connection we do. An outer self may only have one inner self, but an inner self often has more than one outer self. The Cavern of Silence you talk to is the same inner self I talk to."

"That's rather confusing."

"It doesn't need to be. Perhaps if you hug me it will become less confusing."

"Hmmm. I think it's working. Will you marry me?"

"We've been married many times before and that worked out quite well, so my answer is yes."

"We've been married many times before?"

"We have, but that's a story for another day."

CPSIA information can be obtained
at www.ICGtesting.com
Printed in the USA
LVHW081557250119
605132LV00018BA/442/P